PART ONE

A GOOD BOY

'And the day came when the risk to remain tight in a bud
was more painful than the risk it took to blossom.'
Anais Nin

Chapter One

David Alexander stood in the orange glow of the street light and stared at the door entry panel to the property before him. It was a three-storey Regency house bounded by metal railings. The solid front door of the house was framed by two pillars and approached by wide stone steps. This elegant dwelling was in a quiet and graceful part of Brighton, the vibrant seaside city on the south coast of England that had been David's home for most of his 35 years. It was a warm night and the air was mild, just a slight salty breeze that had blown in off the Channel.

David felt a knot in his stomach and an ache in his groin and a confusion of emotions in his mind. What on earth was he doing here at Isabella Stern's address at this time of night? What was he doing here at all for that matter? He barely knew the woman, for God's sake, although he knew enough to be aware that she was married. That in itself ought to have deterred him from coming here but it hadn't. He knew that she was heavily into kinky sex too. That should have deterred him as well, shouldn't it? *Shouldn't it?*

David felt dog tired all of a sudden, drained of all strength, and sick of himself for being so weak-willed as to have come here in the first place. He felt frightened too, couldn't stop himself from trembling. But it wasn't too late. All he needed to do was to go back to his car and drive home, nothing could be simpler. He was sorely tempted to do that too, went so far as to feel in his jacket pocket for his car keys. But he didn't pull them out. Instead his fingers came out of his pocket as if of their own accord and punched at the entry panel. And that was when the die was cast; that was when David's fate was irreversibly sealed.

What if? he used to say to himself afterwards. What if he had known then by means of some strange quirk of chronology what was going to happen to him? What would he have done? Turned around and got in the car and gone home again? Because if ever there had been a point at which he could have changed things it had been when he'd been gazing at that entrance panel, trying to decide whether to go home or to press to request entry. But "What ifs" didn't help at all, they were irrelevant. The fact is that he did what he did and from that point on he was lost.

The next few moments passed as if in a dream and suddenly David found himself in a big, high-ceilinged living room filled with pristine antiques, rare china and fine oil paintings. The room was very imposing but then so too was the imperious raven-haired beauty in high stiletto-heeled boots and a skin-tight cat suit who had let David into the property and before whom he was now standing.

That exquisite black leather outfit accentuated Isabella Stern's shapely form exceptionally well, moulding itself beautifully to her perfect curves. Indeed everything about Isabella was perfectly formed. She was truly stunning to behold and conveyed such a powerful image of dark desirability and dominance that it made David's blood race through his veins. Her lustrous shoulder length hair was jet-black. Her large shining eyes had a strikingly Asiatic cast and, just as strikingly, were as black as coal. She had luminescent white skin by contrast, high cheekbones and a wide, sensuous mouth. Her sleek, exquisitely shaped body moved with a feline insolence, cat-like indeed in the tight leather cat suit that clung to it like a second skin.

She had an extraordinary presence too, a regal bearing, a poise and elegance that immediately commanded respect. The expression she was wearing on her face right then was cold and cruel, though. In fact she looked incredibly cruel. In truth, Isabella looked at that instant essentially what she was: a predatory bitch-goddess, an extraordinarily sadistic femme fatale. David couldn't possibly have known the amazing depths of Isabella's sadism and depravity, not then. But he did know that she scared him to death … and excited him immensely. A sudden shiver of fear ran through him and connected to his cock, giving him an erection that pressed with painful urgency against the crotch of his black jeans.

Isabella hadn't said anything when she'd let David in, had just led him through to her luxurious living room. She remained silent now. As for David, he *couldn't* say anything, couldn't stop shaking either. He knew instinctively and without doubt that what was about to happen to him was going to change his life for ever, that he was going to emerge from this encounter a different man.

Isabella stared at David, her heavy-lidded eyes hypnotic, her lips so sensuous that he yearned to kiss them but, of course, he didn't dare do any such thing. His heart was beating fast and he felt barely able to breathe. The silence in the room became deafening but still she didn't say a word, nor did he.

Then Isabella did finally speak. 'Strip naked for me,' she commanded, staring into his blue eyes. David immediately obeyed, taking off all his clothing in double-quick time. He tried to control his shaking, but couldn't. He tried to control his sexual excitement too, but couldn't do that either. His cock was rigidly erect now and pulsing constantly. Isabella gave him a slow up-and-down look, her sinful black eyes moving hotly over his body as he waited, waited for her first touch. But she was in no hurry. Her eyes lingered on his skin, disturbing and exciting him more and more. She strode round him in a slow circle, seeming to examine every detail of his fine, toned body, until she'd completed her circle and was standing in front of him again.

Still Isabella didn't touch David, though, simply kept looking at him. But what a look! Her shining eyes were as intense as search lights, and David was now irrevocably caught in their beam as she gazed directly into his eyes. Nobody had ever looked at him like that before. He could feel Isabella's eyes boring into him, tormenting him with desire. His body cried out for her touch, couldn't stop shaking. But still she kept staring and staring into his eyes. And that piercing, hypnotic stare had the strangest effect on David. It made him feel as if

3

he was starting to be transformed right there and then into another person, not himself.

When David thought back, he was sure that it was at this point in his visit that Isabella had begun to hypnotize him or brainwash him or whatever the hell it was she'd gone on to do. He remembered that she had only been gazing at him in that amazingly intense way for a short while before he got the weird sensation that he was beginning to be transformed. Then something happened to the focussing mechanism of his own eyes. Everything blurred and disappeared for what seemed like only a moment. But when his vision reasserted itself and David readjusted his eyes to the reality of the world, that world seemed to have shifted on its axis and he was no longer the man he'd once been but was someone else instead.

At last Isabella averted her hypnotic gaze from David's eyes. He took the opportunity to glance down, to reassure himself that he was still there, to check whether she had exchanged him in some way for somebody else. It was the same body he'd arrived in. But that didn't help somehow because he felt different inside his own skin.

Isabella reached out her hand in the direction of David, or the person who resembled him as closely as if he was his identical twin. She moved her fingers lightly and with agonising slowness over his mop of dark hair and down the cheeks of his finely sculpted face to the smooth, muscular contours of his arms and his chest. David could feel his heart pounding against his ribcage. He could hear his breathing coming faster as Isabella moved her hand tantalisingly further south before taking hold of his erection and squeezing it. That touch was like an electric jolt; it made him gasp, nearly climax.

Isabella slapped his cock away from her dismissively. 'Kneel before me,' she demanded, her voice as hard as a hammer hitting a nail, and down on to his knees David went without even thinking. He felt faint with excitement as he waited for her next move; he was still shaking. His heart was racing. His breathing had become even more laboured. Isabella moved behind David again so he couldn't see her. Then he couldn't see anything as he felt the soft leather blindfold cover

4

his eyes and felt Isabella buckle it into place behind his head. Then nothing. He could see nothing, could hear nothing but the uneven rhythm of his own breathing. David didn't know where Isabella was now. He didn't know where he was really, felt as if he'd been transported to some strange erotic limbo land.

But David knew where he had been less than an hour ago when he'd got Isabella's call. He had been in his house and fresh out of the shower. He'd picked up the phone on the second ring and held it to his ear. 'Are you on your own?' she'd said and he had replied that he was, asking what he could do for her.

'Get yourself over to my place now,' had been Isabella's reply. Then the line had gone dead.

And here he was at her place, naked and blindfolded and on his knees, shaking like a leaf, breathing heavily ... and more sexually aroused than he'd ever been in his entire life.

David was shaking more than ever now, could feel spasms of desire shuddering through his body. His breathing was short and shallow, coming in ragged bursts from his chest. His cock was steely-hard and throbbing fit to burst.

Isabella! How he wished he could see her, hear her voice, feel her touch on his skin, this woman he barely knew but to whom, in some inexplicable way, he now felt he belonged.

Time stretched like infinity and all remained complete silence from Isabella, not a word from her, not a sound. Isabella didn't speak to David, didn't touch him, didn't seem to even move or breathe; it was eerie.

Then he heard her moving behind him and everything in him stopped: his heart, his breathing, his thinking even – that is, until he felt her fingers on the back of his neck. Then David's imagination suddenly went into complete overdrive. What in hell's name was Isabella going to do next? Trail her fingers down his back before – what? – hand-spanking him? Or would she take a belt to him instead, or a whip or a paddle? Would she beat him really hard, beat him black and blue? *Ohmigod!*

But Isabella did none of these things. Instead she brought her fingers up from David's neck to the back of his head and unbuckled his blindfold. 'Get dressed and go home now,' she said, her voice icy cold. 'When I want to see you again, I'll call you. Don't ever call me.'

And that was that. It was over.

In what seemed like no more than the blink of an eye David found himself back on the street, walking like an automaton towards his car in the sulphur glow of the street lights. Isabella Stern had done nothing to him, *nothing*. Yet already he'd started waiting for her next call, knowing that he would be unable to put her out of his mind for even a moment until he heard from her again.

David felt that he belonged to Isabella now. She could do anything she wanted to him. He would obey all her instructions, follow her anywhere, submit to any of her demands, no matter how extreme they might be, no matter how sadistic. But this was all complete madness, wasn't it; madness heaped upon madness. Where were these demented thoughts coming from? David simply had no idea. Isabella had done nothing to him. She had hardly touched him – physically, that is; but mentally, oh dear, that was a very different matter.

David didn't understand the dramatic, the profound, the sinisterly bewitching effect Isabella had had on him, didn't understand it at all. It terrified and aroused him in equal measure; he was still rock-hard when he climbed into his car. Isabella Stern was some sort of demonic force he was powerless to resist, was that it? Or had she hypnotized him in some way, put him under her dark spell? Or was it a perverse combination of the two? It was all thoroughly irrational, this distorted, demented way of thinking, utter lunacy. But if anyone had tried to tell David that, he wouldn't have taken any notice.

There was no logical explanation for why he should feel the way he did but David knew – just knew – that he belonged to Isabella now, belonged to her completely. It wasn't a rational thing at all. It was a visceral thing; he felt it in his gut, felt it to the very depth of his being. He felt it more deeply than he'd ever felt anything before. He yearned – no *ached* – to see her again.

Chapter Two

David waited and waited for Isabella to call him again, and waited and waited some more. He didn't work these days – was in the privileged position of not needing to – so he had all the time in the world to spend waiting. Every day that passed was an intense erotic torment for him. He waited by the phone when he was at home, and kept his cell phone with him all the time he wasn't. He shivered with sexual anticipation each time either phone rang. But whenever it happened it was never her.

David thought of nothing, nobody but Isabella. He thought about her dark and dominating allure, her perverse sexuality. He thought about her flawless beauty: her glossy black hair, her arrestingly beautiful face, her perfect alabaster skin, her full lips, her hypnotic eyes that were the colour of black ice and just as hard. He thought about the electric touch of her hands on his skin, the commanding tone of her voice. He played over and over in his head like an endless tape loop the few words she'd actually ever spoken to him.

Why did he yearn for Isabella so much? Why did he ache for her the way he did? What was the secret of the hold she had over him? How had she been able to bewitch him so totally? Isabella's face and body and voice were unsettling enough to David, but what had really got under his skin was her cold-hearted impulse towards domination and – he was sure of it – great cruelty. It had touched a raw nerve of submissiveness in him that had previously lain buried well beneath the surface, sublimated by the very conventional way of life he'd led before meeting her. But it was more than submissiveness. David now recognised his innate sexual masochism too, something of which he'd previously been entirely unaware at any conscious

7

level. With each passing day, his yearning for Isabella grew stronger and so did his yearning for her to dominate and discipline him.

Every morning, David's first thought as he awoke was that maybe this would be the day Isabella would call him. But she didn't call. Perhaps she'd forgotten him, he wondered, or had decided to turn her attentions to someone else, or perhaps even return her attentions exclusively to her husband. Such ideas were too unbearable to contemplate.

Maybe Isabella had thought about it and decided that he wasn't worth bothering with, that he wasn't worthy of her. That would be understandable; he knew he wasn't worthy of her. But he was willing to give his all to her, pay homage to her, devote himself to her pleasure. She could do what she wanted with him. She could treat him as sadistically as she liked, beat the fuck out of him. He could take it, *wanted* to take it. He would do anything she ordered him to do, no matter how humiliating it was for him, no matter how painful, how perverted.

David thought about Isabella all the time and it was driving him crazy – literally. He realised that he was now in the iron grip of some powerful form of erotic dementia. And, strange though it may seem, that didn't concern him, not at all. He wanted to be in its grip. David couldn't do without Isabella. He waited in a permanently sexed-up state of anticipation for her to call him, prayed for her to send for him.

Whenever David thought about Isabella it made his cock hard and he masturbated. He thought about her constantly and his cock was constantly hard. He took to going nude and tumescent around his house, which had thick net curtains at all the windows – David was a man who greatly valued his privacy. Naked and stiffly erect, he masturbated constantly, thinking about Isabella all the time. He would fantasise about her and masturbate for hours at a time, edging all the while – holding back his climax – and when he finally allowed it to come, it would be overpowering, the shuddering spasms seeming to go on for ever. And then before long he'd start thinking and fantasising about Isabella all over again, and get hard again, and masturbate again for ages and ages, and eventually climax again, and the climax would be overwhelming. And so it went on. David was racked with desire for Isabella, consumed by his desire to see her. Every day his burning desire to see her grew stronger.

Isabella had to phone, she just had to. After all, David couldn't prove to her what he was capable of if she didn't at least give him a chance. He couldn't show her how submissive he could be, how degraded, how much pain he could take. He couldn't prove to her that he was willing to give himself to her totally, unreservedly.

David was unable to sleep without thinking about Isabella, was unable to sleep because of thinking about her. He couldn't get through a single hour of the day without thinking about her constantly, masturbating constantly – stroking, stroking, always stroking. David thought about Isabella all the time as he stroked his cock, imagining S&M scenarios where he was completely at her mercy. He thought about prostrating himself naked before her. He thought about being trussed up tightly by her, his limbs immobilized. He imagined being beaten most cruelly by her as he struggled futilely against the tight ropes with which she'd bound him, gasping into the ball gag with which she'd gagged him.

David imagined Isabella bringing her flogger down harshly on his backside over and over again, every one of her lashes intensely sharp and stinging. He imagined the series of angry red welts that would appear on his naked flesh as a result of the harsh beating she was inflicting on him, imagined the muffled cries he would emit from beneath his ball gag as the beating went relentlessly on. He imagined Isabella flogging him with amazing savagery now, beating him so harshly that agonizing pain began coursing through him.

As David imagined the agony Isabella was inflicting on him with her whip, he wallowed in his imaginings, luxuriated in them, got more and more turned on by them. And the more turned on he became, the more he masturbated – although he was always careful to hold his climax in check. Eventually however the sensation became so intense that he knew he wouldn't be able to hold out very much longer, that he was ever closer to climaxing, and he began to surrender to the feeling.

The closer David got to climaxing, his hand moving rhythmically over his pulsing erection, the more intensely he fantasised about the incredible torment to which Isabella was subjecting him. In his mind, she was showing him no mercy whatsoever as she sexually tortured him, making him writhe and squirm helplessly within his tight rope bondage in intense pain as the ferocious lashes from her whip carried on landing across his rear.

In his mind, Isabella continued beating David without mercy, causing him to breathe heavily with the pain that he fantasised was searing through his body. And as he drew breath after shuddering breath in reaction to this imagined torture, he felt himself on the very brink of climaxing. The waves were spreading, filling him with wild pleasure. He was shaking, palpitating; his heart was thumping.

And then David was past the point of no return. He felt his cock swell and throb within his fist as he reached his peak. He tensed his body in his imaginary rope bonds, gasped into his imaginary ball gag and then gave himself to the surging sensations that had taken over his body. David stroked his aching erection to a gushing climax, ejaculating rope after rope of creamy come as the torture being inflicted on his body by Isabella continued unabated … inside his mind.

Masturbatory fantasies such as these – *constant* masturbatory fantasies such as these – about Isabella and the sadistic things he'd like her to do to him were all very well. But when would he actually see her in person again? He already knew he couldn't do without Isabella. But she could obviously do perfectly well without him. Because she didn't call. She'd abandoned him, it seemed, after giving him a tantalising glimpse of her dark and deviant world. David wanted so much to be part of Isabella's world, wanted to let her take him into the very darkest parts of that world, parts more utterly depraved and sexually perverted than he'd ever dreamed could be possible.

Time passed – weeks – and the torment of not hearing from Isabella did not ease. It got much worse. How could he have let this happen to him, he wondered desperately. Why couldn't he just forget all about Isabella, forget the seductive lure of pain and submission that she held out for him? But he couldn't forget about her. She had become his complete obsession, consuming all his thoughts and leaving no room for anything else.

David didn't know who he was any more, felt he no longer really existed. Except he did exist because he belonged to Isabella. But that was the only sense in which he existed. Never in the past could he have foreseen that he would end up in a situation like this, ready to submit himself totally to a woman he hardly knew, who treated him in such a cruelly indifferent and cavalier manner – ready to submit totally to her *because* she treated him that way. Isabella had done all this to him. He felt as if she'd pulled some invisible lever causing him to plunge through the false floor of his "normal" world and drop into the wholly different reality of her dark world, the place he'd wanted to be all along without ever before realising it.

The old David Alexander had been a footloose and fancy-free bachelor. That's how he'd liked to think of himself anyway. He was very good-looking and dead sexy; he'd been told that enough times by former lovers, of whom there had certainly been no shortage. They never used to boss him around either, those legions of young women. David had always been the one that made all the running, who'd loved them and then left them when he wanted to, tossing them away as casually as sweet wrappers. Then Isabella had come into his life and changed it beyond recognition, changed *him* beyond recognition. And now he had to endure the emptiness of not seeing her, the pain of her sheer indifference, his insatiable aching desire for her.

David's cell phone rang.

It must be her.

It had to be her.

It wasn't her.

Why didn't Isabella call? She had to call soon. David was

11

desperate for her to call. But she didn't. Why had she deserted him like this? He didn't understand. It didn't make sense. None of it made sense.

Why couldn't he go back to living his life as it had been before he'd met Isabella? Why? Because in some devilish way she'd turned him into another person, that's why, a person who only existed for her cruel pleasure. If she'd only call he'd come running instantly. He was ready for anything she wanted to make him do, no matter how depraved it might be, no matter how painful for him. As long as it gave her pleasure, that was all that mattered. Isabella could do what she wished to him, order him about to her heart's content, bring him to his knees again, make him crawl naked to her. She could mistreat him horribly if she wanted to, beat him as hard as she liked, beat him so hard that he *bled;* she could make him her *thing*.

David's heart ached for Isabella; his cock ached for her; he continued to have an almost permanent hard-on. He got hard whenever he thought about her and he was always thinking about her and masturbating.

Perhaps it would have been different if he'd had to go to work, had to concentrate on earning a living. But he'd sold his business for a small fortune and was now a man of leisure. And just look at the way he was spending all that leisure time: obsessing and masturbating, a compulsive onanist with a raging libido and a one-track mind filled with masochistic fantasies about Isabella Stern and how excessively she might ill-treat him.

The hours and days and weeks became ever more unbearable. Isabella continued not to call David and he had to be content with … nothing, nothing that is but the pain of her absence. All he could think about was her. David felt so incredibly alone, he felt so incredibly horny. He carried on masturbating compulsively, thinking only of Isabella.

He couldn't stop thinking about the first time they'd met: that dinner party at the home of his best friend Matthew. At the end of the evening Isabella had handed David a card on which was printed her name, phone details, email address and the address of her Brighton property – she and her husband had at least one other splendid home, he knew – and he'd reciprocated, giving her his card. Isabella had then said, 'Wait for my call.' David had familiarised himself with her address, and he'd waited to hear from her. A fortnight later, he'd received that curt instruction when he'd answered his phone and confirmed to her that he was on his own, 'Get yourself over to my place now,' she'd said, her voice hard and meant to be obeyed. He'd gone immediately.

Weeks after that, hell, one whole fucking month after that – at last – David received another curt message when he answered the phone and confirmed that, as before, he was on his own. 'A courier will deliver an envelope and a package to you in about ten minutes.' That was what Isabella Stern had to say to David. Then the line went dead and his heart stopped beating.

Chapter Three

Ten minutes later the doorbell rang and David, who had been naked when he'd received Isabella's call but who now had some clothes on, went into the entrance hall and answered it. He opened the front door to the courier and took the envelope and the package he handed to him. Thanking the courier, David closed the door and returned to the living room. There were several throw rugs on the parquet floor, a black leather couch, and black-lacquered furniture. David sat down on the couch and opened the envelope with trembling fingers. He read its typed contents, his hands continuing to shake.

I want you to do the following, the note from Isabella read. *Strip naked, and then open the package in which you will find a black leather blindfold and an enema kit. Take the enema kit up to your bathroom and clean yourself thoroughly with it. When you have done that, return downstairs and put your front door on the latch. Then go back to your living room and blindfold yourself with the leather blindfold. After that get on to your hands and knees on the floor and wait for my arrival. Finally, let me emphasise one thing: You are not to utter a single word throughout the entirety of my visit.*

David sat where he was, the hand holding the letter still trembling, his heart hammering in his chest, and he tried hard to pull himself together. He realised that he needed to get a move on because he didn't know when Isabella would arrive. He must be ready for her when she got there, it was essential. She would not be at all happy if she turned up to discover that he was not yet prepared for her. David got up from the couch and hastily stripped off the clothes that he'd just as hastily put on beforehand when he'd needed to be able to answer the door to the courier.

He sat down again, opened the package, and took out the blindfold and the enema kit. Leaving the blindfold on the couch, David took the enema kit with him up to the bathroom. He got on with doing what he'd been told to do next, well aware of the implications of what he was doing. David realised that it was almost certain that he was going to be sodomized by Isabella, whether he wanted it or not. He wanted it all right, he had to admit. He wanted it an awful lot. But it frightened him too.

David padded back downstairs nervously, put the front door on the latch, returned to the living room and put on the blindfold. He got on to his hands and knees on the floor, his splayed backside facing in the direction of the door. It would be the first thing Isabella would see when she walked into the room. David was completely naked and yet felt more than naked. It was as if he had shed his skin and exposed raw nerve endings, charging his desire even further. David was ready for Isabella, his body tingling with anticipation, his veiny shaft as hard as a rock. He knew she would come because she'd said she would. But when would she come?

Kneeling on all fours, David thought once again about the power Isabella Stern had over him. He would do anything – *anything* – she commanded of him without a second thought and it seemed that she was only too aware of that. But how had she known that she'd have such an overpowering effect on him? She'd hypnotized him in some way when he'd visited her house a month ago, that was his theory in any event. But he'd read somewhere that a person couldn't be hypnotized to do things that went against his fundamental character. So, how had she recognised his fundamental character when she'd first met him, recognised exactly what kind of man he was beneath his civilised veneer? How had she been able to do that when he'd had no inkling of it himself until she'd entered his life?

David would follow Isabella to the ends of the earth, and she knew it. But how did she know it? How had she known that he'd wait for her to call when she first told him to? How did she know he'd wait for her like this: stark naked and blindfolded and on his hands and knees, his anal hole pink and clean and open and ready for her, his cock fiercely erect. How had she known with such certainly that he'd wait these last four weeks for her to call? All this interminable waiting, David didn't think he could stand much more of it. He didn't have to.

David heard his front door open with a creak and close with a bang. He heard footsteps, the click-clicking of high heels on the parquet floor of the entrance hall. He heard the living room door open and close, more footsteps on parquet flooring, and then muffled steps on one of the rugs. He could feel his heart beating more quickly. David reckoned that Isabella was right behind him now. But he couldn't be entirely sure she was because he couldn't see her due to the blindfold he was wearing, which cut out even the tiniest sliver of light. All he could see was black – pitch black that was made of tar. David assumed that Isabella was looking at him; she must be doing that surely. Did she like what she saw? Did she like the look of his well shaped, muscular backside, his pulsating anus, his throbbing rock-hard erection? She couldn't keep looking at him for ever. When would she make her move? The erotic anticipation David felt was acute. His breathing became ever more ragged the more intensely excited he became. He was shaking uncontrollably with a heady mixture of fear and desire and anticipation.

David felt the cold sensation of lubricant being squeezed into his anus. He realised that the time had arrived: Isabella was going to sodomize him now. Open mouthed and panting, David awaited the inevitable with a huge sense of sexual anticipation. He arched his back and spread his thighs a little further in readiness. Then he felt something being pushed against the opening of his anus, felt that same something being forced painfully through his reluctant sphincter, felt it being plunged right into the depths of his anal hole. It was a strap-on dildo, David was certain of it. And a big one too because it hurt like hell as Isabella, the palms of her hands on his hips, forced it deep into him; it felt as if he was being torn apart.

Isabella withdrew the dildo, plunged it into David again, then withdrew, then paused before plunging in once more. She then began a slow regular thrusting motion that caused the big rubber shaft to slide in and out of his anus. Isabella pushed the dildo in and out of his hole, impaling him again and again as she started to build up momentum. Finally she began to really fuck David in the arse in earnest, ploughing into him hard, and it felt wonderful, ecstatic; extreme pain had turned to extreme pleasure. His anal muscles squeezed and released deliciously around the large intruder she was pounding into him so expertly. He threw back his head and groaned with pleasure at each stroke, which made Isabella sodomize him faster and then faster still, grinding her hips over and over again as he bucked beneath her.

Then David felt the electric sensation of Isabella's right hand move from his hip to grasp his hard cock and the short brisk strokes of that same hand as she went on to masturbate him. And all the while she kept on buggering him, not pausing for a moment. Her rhythm was fast and strong, each thrust going deeper into his anus, filling him, penetrating him, exciting him beyond belief. As David felt Isabella grind into him so powerfully, masturbate him so skilfully, it made him feel helpless in a way he had never known before. Her thrusts and strokes became frenzied and his mind darkened as she rammed into him like a jack-hammer and masturbated him ever more furiously. David felt overcome with excitement, propelled into a heedless loss of control.

And that was when it happened. A shock ran through him and David started to shudder and shake as exquisite oscillations began pulsing through his body. Oh God, he thought. He reached the point of no return and climaxed deliriously. Spasms of erotic delight shook his frame and he had to force his mouth tight shut to prevent himself from crying out loudly when he started to ejaculate. The orgasm he experienced was incredible, overwhelming, the ecstatic convulsions went on and on.

Then the convulsions did finally stop. At last it was over, David was thoroughly spent. His mind was calm and blank for a while. He tried to hold on to the still silence for as long as he could, tried to hold on to Isabella for as long as he could too.

Then he felt her slip her hand away from his shaft and ease the big strap-on dildo out of his anus. 'Remove the blindfold after a slow count to one hundred,' she ordered.

And when he did, she was gone. It was like she'd never been there at all, like he'd dreamed the whole thing. David soon became anxious, felt bereft. Isabella had come to him and now she was gone. He felt so lost, so alone. He needed her words, her orders, her presence. He went back to waiting … and wanking. There was nothing else he felt he could do.

Chapter Four

More days went by; more weeks: four weeks, five weeks. There was no word from Isabella. Once again David was left waiting desperately, interminably, for her to call. He had to see her, simply had to. She'd left it even longer this time. How could she? Didn't she want to see him? The waiting was so damned hard. And so was his cock an awful lot of the time. He continued masturbating compulsively, thinking only of her. Why was he letting Isabella do this to him, he asked himself, and who had he become that he would let her? Then – oh, happy day – the phone rang and it was Isabella. David felt almost too choked to get any words out. 'Hello?' he managed to croak. He held the phone close to his face, breathing deeply.

'Go straight away to the Grand Hotel and collect the key to room 45 from reception,' Isabella instructed. 'Then go to the room and let yourself in.' The line went dead after that; she'd rung off.

David didn't delay. He set off immediately for Brighton's most famous hotel without giving the matter a second thought, simply pleased beyond words that he'd finally heard from Isabella.

By the time David had arrived at the Grand, however, his nerves had begun to get the better of him. There were butterflies in his stomach and he was feeling faint. He went up to the receptionist and in a voice that sounded a lot surer than the one in his head, asked for the key to room 45. She handed it to him with a brief smile.

David walked toward the lift area, his steps deceptively confident given that his legs felt like jelly. Emerging from the lift, he walked down a long, carpeted corridor until he got to room 45. His hands were shaking as he unlocked and pushed open the door to the room. Would Isabella be there, waiting for him? God, he hoped so. It had been such a long time since he'd seen her last – except of course he hadn't actually seen her on that last occasion, he reminded himself, because he'd been blindfolded the whole time.

But Isabella wasn't there, waiting for him. The room was in complete darkness, the heavy curtains closed tight. David found the light switch and flicked at it. The wall lamps came on, bathing the room in a soft radiance. David's eyes were drawn to the double bed on which sat a shiny black box. It was rectangular in shape and about the size of a shoe-box, and to one side of it was a folded piece of paper.

David crossed the room, his footsteps silent on the thick wall-to-wall carpeting, and sat down on the bed. He then picked up and unfolded the piece of paper. It contained another typed instruction from Isabella. Jesus, what did she want him to do this time? David closed his eyes momentarily, trying to compose himself, and then opened them and read what Isabella had to say.

I want you to do the following, David, her note read. *Open the box on the bed. In that box you will find a ball gag, a blindfold, and a set of metal handcuffs. Strip naked, and then gag yourself with the ball gag. After that, put your left wrist into one of the handcuffs and snap it locked. Then put on the blindfold, lie flat on your stomach on the bed, put both hands behind your back, put your right hand into the other handcuff and snap it locked. Once you've done all that do nothing else. Simply lie there and await my arrival.*

David read Isabella's note twice, steeping himself in the words. He began to feel feverish, hot and cold at the same time. He sat stock still for a short while, trying not to hyperventilate any more than he already was. He reflected in alarm on what it was that Isabella wanted him to do in this plush hotel room. She didn't want him to see her as such, wanted him blindfolded again. Well, so be it; that wasn't a problem, nor was the fact that she wanted him gagged as well this time – she'd put what you might call a gagging order on him the last time, which amounted to pretty much the same thing.

What was a problem, however, was that she was seriously expecting him to put himself – lock himself – into bondage so complete that it would render him entirely at her mercy. Because, make no mistake, once he had snap-locked those handcuffs behind his back he'd have put himself into a position he was helpless to alter. Isabella would be able to do anything to him she wanted when she arrived. Anything.

How had he let himself get into such a terrifying situation? Such a potentially terrifying situation anyway; he hadn't actually done the reckless deed yet. And it would be utter recklessness on his part, sheer insanity, to comply with Isabella's instruction this time. He knew what he was going to do now, what he had to do.

And what was that? David was going to do precisely what had been demanded of him in that note he'd received from … from whom? From a woman he barely knew, but who he felt in some strange way – through some kind of hypnotism or witchcraft or whatever the fuck it was – owned him body and soul.

David picked up the shiny black box, lifted its lid and slid out its contents onto the bed. He stood up then and got out of his clothes. He felt very frightened but also intensely excited, his cock steely hard and throbbing, as he proceeded to do precisely what Isabella had told him she wanted him to do.

David could see nothing because of his blindfold and could hear nothing but the beating of his heart and the sound of his breathing, made ragged because of his ball gag. His wrists were locked behind his back by metal handcuffs that dug into his skin. David wondered how long exactly he had been lying here waiting for Isabella to arrive. It seemed like an eternity.

Where was she now: outside the hotel? Outside the lift area? Outside the room? What was she going to do to him when she finally arrived? – *If* she arrived. What did he mean, if? Of course she'd come, he told himself firmly. Of course she would. Why wasn't she here then? Why? She couldn't just leave him like this. Could she? *Could she?* David felt a hand clutch at his heart and a sick feeling fluttered in the pit of his stomach. He began to panic, his thoughts rampaging without control through his brain. What a fool he'd been, what an idiot!

It was then that he heard the door to the room open and close. But that was all he heard. David knew that Isabella had arrived. He assumed it was Isabella who'd walked through that door anyway; it had to be her. But she didn't announce her presence. She didn't say a word, didn't make a sound. He didn't hear her moving. He didn't know where she was. With that thick wall-to-wall carpet in the room, she could have been anywhere. But wherever she was in that hotel room he knew she'd be looking at him in his naked bondage. He knew she'd be looking at his blindfolded face and gagged mouth, his lips pulled apart by the ball gag; at his palms held together against the small of his back by his metal handcuffs; at his taut, curved backside, ripe for a beating.

Then David heard Isabella moving, coming closer to him, coming so close he could smell her perfume, could hear her breathing right against his ear. A warm thrill swept through him. There was a long silence and then she spoke.

'I know the way it is with you now, David,' Isabella whispered hotly into his ear as he continued to breathe in her perfume. 'I know what I've done to you. You can't live without me, can you. You wait constantly for me to call you, desperate for me to call you, prepared to do anything I demand of you when I do call you. That is your life now: waiting for me, needing me, obsessing about me all the time and the things you'd like me to do to you, the things you *fear* I'll do to you. All of that's true, isn't it.'

David nodded his blindfolded head in agreement and gurgled as affirmatively as he could into his ball gag. '*Esh*,' it came out.

'Turn on to your back,' she instructed then and he obeyed, the metal cuffs still digging into his wrists. His breathing was spasmodic, his body shaking, his pulsing cock stiffly erect.

'I know that you want me to give you pain,' Isabella said next and he could feel her fingers on his nipples, squeezing them with increasing strength and causing a wave of pain to

22

shudder through his body. And she didn't stop, didn't let up on the pressure she was applying either: Isabella's fingers were pinching his two fleshy nubs harder and harder. David was shaking more than ever at the pain she was inflicting on him, at the *thought* of the pain to come. Then she stopped abruptly, removing her fingers from his nipples … and he heard a match strike.

'There are so many ways I can bring you pain,' Isabella said. A long moment passed and then he felt it: the hot molten wax, dripping down onto his chest, around his punished nipples and onto his stomach. It was stinging his flesh and exciting him more and more as he felt its burning splashes on his body.

David heard Isabella blow out the candle, and then she spoke to him again. 'You want me to bring you pure pleasure too of course,' she said, sliding her right hand to his erection and gripping its base. David uttered a low groan from under his gag as she began to masturbate him. Her fingers worked away up and down, sometimes gently, and sometimes hard, making him writhe helplessly in his bonds with delight. Isabella stroked and pulled at David's erection until it was on the point of exploding. Then the pulse came and he began to shudder and shake without control as his orgasm took him. And as David climaxed, his cries of pleasure muffled by the ball gag, semen shot out of his aching cock in spurts, warm and silky.

'Turn on to your stomach again,' Isabella then ordered and he obeyed, his body still shaking. 'I'll be in touch again soon,' she added as she unlocked and removed his handcuffs. And with that she was gone as suddenly as she'd arrived, the door opening and shutting to announce her departure. Her perfume still hung seductively in the air.

It had all happened so fast, David said to himself as he removed the blindfold and gag. And Isabella hadn't inflicted much more than token pain on his body, which he had to admit had been a little disappointing. But he realised that it hadn't been about whether or not he could take pain. No, essentially it had all been about those handcuffs, he was certain of it. Isabella had been testing him, seeing whether she could trust him to lock himself into them, whether she could trust him to trust her.

David was pleased that he hadn't failed Isabella, that she hadn't found him wanting. That feeling of pleasure at what he imagined he'd achieved lingered for a while but it didn't last.

Chapter Five

'I'll be in touch again soon,' Isabella had said. Those were her exact words. But damn it, she didn't get in touch soon, she didn't get in touch at all.

Clearly she'd made her promise merely to torment him, he decided, and it had worked. Every day that went by was an agony of unfulfilled expectations for David. The days and weeks passed and the agony he experienced intensified as her words persistently came back into his mind to mock and taunt him. They thrummed through his mind like the rhythm of rails beneath a train: *I'll be in touch soon, I'll be in touch soon, I'll be in touch soon.* Oh, why didn't Isabella contact him? Why, for God's sake? *I'll be in touch soon. I'll be in touch soon, I'll be in touch once in a fucking blue moon.* Then she phoned. 'Come to my place at eight tomorrow evening,' Isabella told him. And with that she hung up.

The next morning David awoke at the crack of dawn, thinking about Isabella, like he'd been doing in his dreams all night, like he did every night. Like he'd doubtless be doing tonight too, except that tonight, he knew that before going to his solitary bed he'd also be seeing her in person. David felt a jumble of emotions: fear, excitement, impatience, and, above all, readiness. He knew he was ready for anything she wanted to do to him. Sodomy and nipple torture and wax play had been just the start and he welcomed whatever she wanted to do to him next.

The hours passed that day as if on leaden feet; it was excruciating. At long last it was seven in the evening. David got into his car. He'd given himself ample time to get to

Isabella by eight; it was no great distance to drive from his house to hers. At 7.30 he found himself stuck in a huge traffic jam. The road was clogged both ways with a mess of cars, vans, motorcycles, and seemingly the entire population of the city. It was a nightmare.

As the traffic continued to gather thickly around him David got himself into an increasingly panicky state. At 7.50 his car was still crawling along bumper to bumper in the same huge traffic jam and he was by now in a total panic. He could hear the blood beating in his ears; his palms on the steering wheel had become slick with sweat. Then, at 7.55, miraculously the slow procession of traffic in which he'd been enmeshed cleared as he got past the road construction works that had caused the problem in the first place. At 8.05, after a drive that seemed to have lasted only a fraction less than for ever, David parked and rushed, breathless, to Isabella's door.

Isabella let him in, wearing a short black leather dress that was incredibly seductive, hugging her figure like a coat of emulsion. Her expression, though, was frosty. David was about to explain to her about the awful traffic jam he'd been stuck in but she didn't give him a chance. 'You're late,' she said coldly. 'I'm going to have to punish you for that.'

David could have said something then, uttered some words in his own defence. But he didn't say anything. It wasn't that he was lost for words. It wasn't that at all. He wanted Isabella to punish him, wanted her to beat him, ill-treat him all she liked. He wanted to start really proving himself to Isabella Stern at last. He wanted to show that he could take a lot more from her than being kept hanging around for weeks on end in a state of constant sexual longing, being fucked in the arse by her with a big strap-on dildo and having his nipples tortured with her fingers and his torso with hot wax – a hell of a lot more.

When they'd arrived in the living room Isabella's eyes fastened on David, dark and hard. 'Strip off,' she told him and as soon as he was naked he became stiffly erect. Isabella brought her fingers not to David's cock but to his nipples, and began pinching them with pincer-like force, markedly harder than that last time in the hotel room. She squeezed his nipples more and more viciously, causing him to shake all over with pain. And all David knew was that he wanted more, much more. He wanted to be thoroughly mistreated by this woman he barely knew but to whom he felt he belonged, body and soul.

Isabella seemed to read his mind. She stopped torturing his nipples and took a leather whip out of the top drawer of a nearby bureau. She told David to turn, bend forward and put his hands in front of him on top of the table that was now before him. This was it, David thought, breathing hard. Everything comes to those who wait.

And wait.

And wait.

Each moment passed with almost unbearable slowness and the anticipation he felt became so intense it hurt.

But not half as much as the first lash of Isabella's whip. Or the second or third or fourth or fifth...

On and on she berated David's back and rear with savage blows. Each one was a flash of pure pain that made him tense and squirm more and more as the full effect of the whipping spread through his body. Isabella kept on beating David in this ferocious way until the pain that was lacing through him was overwhelming. He felt as if his agonized body was on fire and he began whimpering, he couldn't help himself.

'No whimpering,' Isabella admonished calmly from behind him. 'You must make a different noise. I know you want to be beaten. Well, sound as if you want it.' And with that she brought the whip down with extra savagery on his backside. David did his very best to do as he'd been instructed, moaning orgasmically in response to the savage lash.

Isabella brought the whip down again and he made the orgasmic sound once more. Another lash, harsher still, and David moaned orgasmically again. Another blow, and another, fell on his body, leaving deep lacerations on his skin. With each increasingly savage blow, David's cries came louder and more orgasmic.

Isabella continued to rain down lashing blows until his back and rear were scored with livid red weals and he was in searing pain that also felt like the most exquisite pleasure; it was amazing. David felt the blood roaring through his body; his heart hammering; his head thundering; his shaft throbbing. Then he stopped feeling pain, stopped feeling pleasure. This was neither pain nor pleasure any longer. Isabella had taken him somewhere else, taken him to some other place where all boundaries of pain and pleasure had dissolved. It was a place he'd never been to before … and it was paradise.

David began to shudder without control. He closed his eyes and his mind darkened for a second and then imploded with glittering flashes of colour. He opened his eyes and let out yet another orgasmic cry that this time became a self-fulfilling prophecy as, delirious with ecstasy, he ejaculated spasm after spasm of creamy come that splattered onto the polished oak floor beneath him.

'Get on your knees and lick that up,' Isabella ordered harshly, putting the whip to one side. 'Lick up every last drop of your spilled come and swallow it all down.' Which he did, wallowing in the degradation, the delicious humiliation of what he was doing at her command.

'Stand up and face me,' she said when David had finished, and he did.

'You are always to address me as 'Mistress' from now on,' Isabella ordered, her dark eyes reaching for his and holding them, vice-like.

'Yes, Mistress,' David replied with a gasp, thinking ecstatically: This is so wonderful, this is what I want.

'And don't you ever dare to be late for an appointment with me again,' Isabella added. 'You are always to do exactly what your Mistress tells you to do without exception. Understood, *slave*?'

'Yes, Mistress,' David replied, thrilled beyond all expression at what she had just called him.

Chapter Six

David realised that none of this would ever have happened if he hadn't accepted his invitation to Matthew King's dinner party. David didn't go in for dinner parties and would never have contemplated hosting one himself. Indeed, although he was handsome and charismatic and exceptionally highly sexed and had experienced a string of raunchy affairs for those very reasons, David was essentially antisocial. When he received the invitation his natural instinct was to decline it.

But Matthew was David's oldest and his best friend even if they saw relatively little of one another these days. As good-looking as David and as blond as he was dark haired, Matthew's most striking feature was his eyes, which were pale blue like a tropical lagoon. You could fall into his eyes they were so blue. He also had an attractive crooked grin and was generally something of a charmer. But what of the man beneath that appealing exterior? Matthew was a great guy, in David's view. He was generous, open, intelligent and sensitive. He was also very reliable. He'd never let David down in the past – quite the reverse in fact on one notable, life-changing occasion recently – and David didn't want to let him down either. He felt honour bound to accept the invitation.

The dinner party had been organised mainly so that Matthew's friends could make the acquaintance of the new love in his life, Caroline Hunt. Matthew was clearly besotted with Caroline, a smart, sexy redhead who was the current manager of Brighton's now well-established fetish store: *La Fetishista.*

The guests at the dinner party included a well known fashion photographer. A handsome, olive-skinned man with a close cropped beard, he was accompanied by his beautiful girlfriend who was also one of his models. She was tall and rangy with perfect long chestnut hair. There was a successful financier, stocky with thick grey-templed hair, who had definitely proved that he had the Midas touch. He was rumoured to have made more than a billion pounds in derivatives – whatever they were – and had gone on to amuse himself by buying up and developing businesses he judged to have further potential.

Matthew had introduced him to David six months before, something for which David had come to be extremely grateful. That was because the financier had ended up buying David's thriving specialist IT company in a win-win situation for both of them that had left David in the enviable situation in his mid 30s of never needing to work for a living again as long as he was reasonably sensible with his money.

As to the other guests at Matthew's dinner party: There was an attractive brunette in her early 20s, her short hair cut fashionably dishevelled and spiky, who claimed to be gay but who kept shooting David the hottest looks. There was a ruggedly handsome television actor, with a huge female fan base, who was actually gay and who'd once seduced the bisexual Matthew. There was a quietly spoken male novelist with strangely simian good-looks, who wrote highly imaginative erotic fiction for pleasure and clichéd potboilers for money. And there was Isabella Stern.

Caroline hadn't met any of the other guests before but she did know Isabella – because Caroline worked for her. Isabella was Caroline's ultimate boss given that she and her husband, Alan Stern, owned the whole chain of *La Fetishista* stores. These kinky but classy establishments were evidently an idea whose time had come, catering very effectively for a growing niche market. It was one that the Sterns understood extremely well as it very much reflected their own sexual tastes.

The first of the stores had been opened in Brighton seven years ago. Others had been opened in many other cities in the UK subsequently, making a mint for the couple in the process, and expansion into the United States in the near future was very much in the offing. Internet sales were going from strength to strength too and all-in-all the business was booming. The Sterns owned a fine Regency home in Brighton, a big house in the country and a glamorous villa in Italy, all purchased by them with just some of the proceeds of their highly successful enterprise.

Isabella, who was unaccompanied by her husband or anyone else for that matter on this occasion, was the last to arrive at the dinner party. But what an arrival! She didn't so much walk into the room as slink in like a panther. David had never seen a woman move like that or have that kind of electrifying presence. She seemed predatory, as if she was on the prowl, and she made an instant and dramatic impact on him. As soon as David laid eyes on her, he felt a surge of excitement run through him and his heart started racing, the hairs on his arms stood up. His cock tried to stand up too, straining against his pants.

Isabella took the seat opposite David at the table, sat back and ran her fingers through her lustrous black hair. She arched her eyebrows and looked back at him with deeply disdainful eyes, looked at him as if he was the lowest of the low. It made his erection throb. Why did that look make him feel so sexually excited? It was because it said something else as well: it said that she lusted after him *because* he was such a lowly creature. No woman had ever looked at him that way before and he found to his amazement that it turned him on immensely. David tried to get a grip on his emotions and to control his sexual excitement. He looked away from Isabella for a moment, took a deep breath to regain his composure, and then looked back. She was no longer looking in his direction.

The dinner party went by for David in something of a blur after that. The food was good, the wine was good, the talk around him lively and animated. The unconvincing lesbian continued to give him the eye while making conversation with both the model and the writer who were seated on either side of her at the table. As for Isabella, she took no further notice of David whatsoever. She studiously ignored him throughout the meal, seemed to talk to everyone but him. It wasn't until the end of the evening that she handed him her card, taking his in return, and told him, out of the earshot of anyone else, to wait for her call. David had thought of that as a one-off "instruction" at the time. He had no idea at all that it was to become a complete way of life.

Chapter Seven

Those words uttered by Isabella immediately after she'd tortured David to orgasm and then made him lick up and swallow his own ejaculate echoed through his mind again and again and every time they did it filled him with the utmost delight. She was his Mistress, she'd told him that with her own lips, and he was her slave, she'd told him that too. And she'd proved it to him. She'd marked his body to prove that she was his Mistress and he was her slave. The weals and bruises left on his back and rear were fading with each passing day, but they still retained a residual tingling sensation of pain, which aroused him and brought the memory of her back to him. David concentrated on the pain as it wore off, it connected him to Isabella. He missed it when it finally disappeared altogether and she still hadn't called.

David hadn't heard from Isabella in weeks, disappointingly but all too predictably. She hadn't phoned and told him she was going to come to him; she hadn't sent for him either or anything else. His life once again was reduced to waiting and wanking. David masturbated as he remembered Isabella ramming her big strap-on dildo into him. He remembered how she'd forced it into his tight anus, vigorously plunging it in and out as she buggered and jacked him to climax. He jacked away and climaxed again, remembering it. David masturbated as he remembered how Isabella had squeezed his nipples and poured hot wax on his body before masturbating him to orgasm in that plush hotel room. He masturbated to orgasm, remembering it all, every second of it. He remembered how viciously Isabella had whipped him the last time she'd seen him, viciously enough to make him come. He stroked his cock as he brought that whipping to mind for the umpteenth time, and he came again for the umpteenth time too. David remembered how Isabella had put her mark on him by beating him in this savage way before telling him that he must always call her "Mistress", always obey her instructions to the letter because he was her "slave".

His mind kept spooling out those scenes as in an S&M movie, one kinky frame after another as he wanked and wanked. But memories and masturbation weren't enough. He wanted her to take out her sadistic frenzy on him again and to go even further this time.

So, phone, Isabella. Please, please phone.

Eventually she did, she phoned. 'Be outside *La Fetishista* at half past five this afternoon,' she said. Then the call terminated.

David had time to kill before 5.30 – not a huge amount but enough – and decided to take a circuitous route to his destination, going by foot. He didn't want to risk taking the car anyway, not after what had happened the last time. David left his house, and walked in a westward direction, zigzagging through familiar side streets before dropping down to the seafront. He crossed over the busy dual carriageway, then walked across the lawns and hit the promenade.

He paused for a moment and looked out beyond the shingle beach at the broad expanse of the sea, its waves slowly ebbing and flowing. Above him gulls soared, swooped and cried out in a sky that was bright blue and almost cloudless. David breathed in the sea air, tasting the tang of salt on his lips.

He began to walk eastwards along the promenade, and as he did he thought about his best friend Matthew. Before Matthew had invited him to his dinner party David hadn't heard from him for ages and it had been the same since then, no contact at all. But that was nothing new. It was the way it had been for years between the two friends, who'd known one another since schooldays. But, as is so often the case with really good friends, whenever they did get together they picked up right where they'd left off, like it had been only yesterday since they'd last met.

David would have liked to have confided in Matthew about his relationship with Isabella. He'd have liked to have explained to him how irresistibly drawn he'd been to her from the very first moment he'd seen her at his dinner party, and what a delight it was to now be her slave; that's right, Matthew, you heard me correctly: her slave.

David would have liked to have explained to Matthew that he worshipped Isabella, wanted nothing more than to bow down before her and take whatever punishment she chose to dish out to him. He'd have liked to have explained to his friend that this magnificent woman – sadistic Goddess that she was – had managed to transform him into a degraded and submissive creature, willing to obey her every perverted command. He'd have liked to have explained to him too what utter joy it brought him to be such a lowly creature. He'd have liked to have explained to Matthew how it felt to give himself to his cruel Mistress in this way, what it was like to surrender to her totally, to submit to her, to forget about everything except trying to be worthy of her.

But how could one explain such things? I mean *how*, realistically? He couldn't talk to Matthew that way. His friend simply wouldn't understand; nobody would. If he tried to have such a conversation with Matthew, he would think he'd lost his mind, taken leave of his senses completely. No, it was a crying shame but he couldn't confide in his best friend about all this. Or could he? After all, Matthew was a very open minded person and had always been completely up-front about his own bisexuality. He was also currently living with a woman who managed a fetish store, for God's sake – the very store David himself would be visiting in about half an hour. She'd be there too presumably and would doubtless report back to Matthew on whatever she observed. So, David concluded, all this agonizing on his part over whether or not to confide in Matthew could well prove to be entirely academic.

David stopped and gazed out to sea again for a short time, at the sad rusting spars rising from the Channel, which were all that remained of the West Pier. It was less sunny now, starting to cloud over, and the wind was picking up. David glanced at his watch, confirming that he was still in good time for his appointment with Isabella, and resumed his walk. As he strode along the promenade he looked at the people around him: a mash-up of straight and gay, students, couples, groups of friends, the usual spill of tourists. David felt alone amidst the throng. He'd never felt so apart. None of these people could have known the things Isabella had inflicted on him. Nobody had ever treated them the way she treated him. They'd never felt this desire, this pleasure of belonging, of giving themselves, submitting themselves entirely to someone as powerful and sadistic as her.

David saw the handsome façade of the Old Ship Hotel coming up on his left. He mounted the steps to the upper promenade and crossed the dual carriageway. He made his way through the beating downtown heart of the city, through the narrow passages and cobbled streets that made up the Old Lanes where all the antique dealers were centred. David was nearly at the *La Fetishista* store now. It was on the edge of the North Lanes district of Brighton, an area filled with trendy shops and restaurants and tiny terraced houses fronting directly on to the street. A blustery wind was blowing and the sky had clouded right over now. Seagulls wailed and shrieked and circled overhead.

David stood outside the dark-windowed store that was the Brighton branch of *La Fetishista*. He was on time. *Of course* he was on time. And feeling incredibly nervous. His mouth was dry and his skin felt moist and clammy. He told himself to get a grip and took several deep breaths to try and calm himself down. It was a little after 5.30 now but there was no sign of Isabella yet.

5.35, 5.40, 5.45 and still no Isabella. Christ, David thought, the place shuts at six. He stood there in front of the store waiting, waiting. He lowered his eyes and looked down at the pavement. When he looked up he saw Isabella. She was approaching him, just a few feet away, looking fabulous in black leather: a short figure-hugging dress and high stiletto-heeled boots that were polished to a fine shine.

'Come,' Isabella said, gesturing in the direction of the entrance door to *La Fetishista*. Forget about hello-how-are-you or anything like that.

'Yes, Mistress,' David said and they went in.

'Caroline's not here,' Isabella said. 'She's at a meeting at our head office, which started late and isn't expected to finish until mid-evening.' David wondered if that was deliberate. Was there some reason Isabella didn't want Caroline – and Matthew – to know about the way things were between them? He hadn't been sure whether or not he would be able to confide in Matthew about his relationship with Isabella. Maybe *she* didn't want him to know about it. There was a thought.

David's eyes travelled around the store, which had black softly-lit walls, and was full of BDSM gear. He could see whips, crops, handcuffs, clamps, various items of rubber and leather fetish wear, masks, collars, reels of bondage tape, a variety of bamboo canes, an assortment of butt plugs, harnesses, leads, body bags ...

A small handful of people were in the store, looking at the products. There was one assistant on duty, a slim dark-haired girl in a red rubber mini dress that was so tight it looked as if it had been sprayed on. David thought that she couldn't conceivably have had any underwear on underneath it. Her eyes, brown with a hint of green, were large and wide-spread and she had broad, high cheekbones. She greeted Isabella with deference, clearly well aware of who she was.

Isabella fingered several black leather items before picking out a slave's collar, wrist and ankle cuffs, and a cock corset. 'I'd like my slave to try these on,' she said.

'Certainly, Mrs. Stern,' the assistant replied, her tone as deferential as it had been before. 'All the fitting rooms are free at the moment.'

'We also need a chained collar with a padlock and key, a large black silicone butt plug, a black leather g-string, a steel genital ring, and a set of single-chain clover clamps,' she said. 'Pick them out, will you please.'

'I'll do it straight away, Mrs. Stern,' the assistant replied and immediately began selecting the items.

The fitting rooms were at the back of the store and Isabella strode towards them, with David following close behind. His cock began to swell as she pulled the curtain shut behind them both. He undressed in front of Isabella, his pulse racing, and by the time he was naked he was displaying a raging hard-on. The mirrors all around the wall reflected every part of his body, which aroused him even more. David put on the wrist and ankle cuffs, then the chained collar and finally the cock corset, which he buckled tightly into place over his erection, leaving its bulbous head exposed. Isabella looked him up and down appraisingly, running her eyes over his fine body. 'You look good, slave,' she said.

'Thank you, Mistress,' David replied, smiling. It was the first time she had ever said anything remotely complimentary to him and he bathed in the glow of these few brief words of approval from her.

Then the assistant's voice came from behind the curtain, telling Isabella that she had now closed the store. They were the only ones there.

'Thanks for letting me know,' Isabella replied. 'I am going to take my slave downstairs now.'

David was highly intrigued, highly excited too. His skin was tingling, his heart pounding, his leather-corseted erection throbbing. What was downstairs? He would soon find out. They left the fitting room and descended some stairs into the basement area, which was decked out as a sort of retail dungeon. All the equipment – the St. Andrews cross, the horse, the metal cage, the whipping bench, the suspension machine, the two winched chains hanging from the ceiling – had its price indicated to one side of it. The walls with the exception of one, which contained a wooden rack lined with whips, paddles and other disciplinary implements, again all priced, were mirrored to increase the sense of space on this floor of the sales area.

Isabella motioned for David to stand next to the chains hanging from the ceiling. 'Put your hands together in front of you,' she ordered. He joined his hands in front of him and she clipped his wrist cuffs together by means of a metal trigger clip and then attached them with another clip to the end of one of the chains, which she winched up so that his hands were held above his head. The chain held firm and Isabella pronounced herself satisfied with this piece of equipment.

'Put your legs together,' she then instructed.

'Yes, Mistress,' David replied and when he'd done this Isabella used a trigger clip to attach his ankle cuffs one to the other.

'I think I'll quality test one of my other items of merchandise,' Isabella said next, picking out a heavy leather flogger from the display rack – and losing no time at all in putting it to use. She brought the whip down swiftly onto David's backside. The pain was intense, the leather penetrating his skin like a rapier. He could not hold back his cry of pain. She brought the flogger down again, sharper and harder still, and he cried out once more.

'Silence, slave,' Isabella rasped as she brought down the flogger once again with even more vigour, and he duly obeyed, crying out inside instead. David's eyes blurred with tears of pain as Isabella continued to beat him, the blows succeeding one another with ever increasing violence.

And then David entered *the zone*, started to scream inside his head in pain, or pleasure, he didn't know which it was. He was desperate for Isabella to stop beating him and he was desperate for her to go on.

David became acutely conscious of the mirror in front of him, the one behind and the one at the side of him too. He saw his arched back reflected in the glass; saw his lacerated backside as Isabella continued to rain down blow after vicious blow with the heavy leather flogger. He saw his anguished face, his tear-filled eyes, saw his cock straining against its tight leather corset, its mushroom-shaped head purple and wet and drizzling precome constantly.

David was both terrified and immensely excited by the sight of his naked, lacerated body, by the sight of Isabella, her expression the very personification of cruelty, whipping and whipping him with such fury. He wanted to beg her to show him mercy, he was in so much agony. But if he did that she might stop beating him. And David didn't want that to happen because when Isabella was beating him it meant that he deserved her. She was showing him that he deserved her by beating him and he was showing her that he deserved her by taking his beating like a good slave.

Each of Isabella's savage blows was showing David that she thought he deserved her and he was immensely grateful to her for it and wanted to show that gratitude. So he wouldn't beg her for mercy, he wouldn't. But it hurt so fucking much. The pain was intense. So was the pleasure. He was in agony that was also ecstasy.

David reached the point where agony and ecstasy transformed themselves into purest ecstasy. Convulsions began to shake his body and he climaxed, ejaculating spurt after spurt of silvery come from his corseted cock. But before he'd quite finished coming David did something else. He fainted. Darkness rolled in behind the bright lines of orgasmic sensation he was still experiencing and he swooned down into a huge black void. His body collapsed when he fainted, except it didn't. It couldn't collapse because his wrists were secured above him to the chain.

When David came round it took him a few seconds to realise where he was. For how long he'd been dead to the world in this mirrored dungeon, he had no idea. All he knew when he awoke from his faint was that his backside felt extremely sore and painful, that he was still hanging by the wrists from the chain, and that he was alone.

'Mistress, Mistress,' he called out but Isabella didn't answer him and he knew somehow that she wouldn't. She wasn't there in the basement, he could see that clearly enough. But he'd bet she wasn't in the store either. He was all alone where he was, alone and in bondage and in great pain. David didn't call out for Isabella again. He knew she'd left the store, and he must leave too, but he couldn't. He tried – tried very hard – but he was unable to get his wrist cuffs loose of the chain.

David hoped against hope that Isabella would take pity on him and come back for him, but he knew in his heart that she wouldn't come, and he was right: she didn't. The dark haired assistant in the spray-on red rubber mini dress came instead. With a deadpan expression on her attractive face worthy of a poker player and without saying a single word, she removed his cock corset and collar, unclipped and removed his ankle and wrist cuffs, and freed him from the chain. With the items she had removed from David's body held in her slender hands, she went back upstairs and he followed her. He went into the fitting room to get dressed, feeling completely wiped out, shattered.

The assistant showed David all the items that she'd selected earlier at Isabella's behest, and she put them into a black carrier bag for him. She then added the collar and cuffs and cock corset he'd been wearing, dropping these into the bag too. David reached for his wallet to pay for the contents of the bag.

'That won't be necessary,' the assistant said, her voice as expressionless as was the set of her features. 'Mrs. Stern says they're on the house.'

'Right,' David mumbled distractedly, unable to meet her eye. She unlocked the entrance to the store and let him out into the grey dusk, the sky now the colour of dirty cotton wool. He went straight home, still very shaky but with only one thought in mind: When would Isabella get in touch with him next?

Chapter Eight

You might have thought that having left David hanging in a dead faint like that, Isabella would have contacted him soon afterwards to see how he was. Not a bit of it. She didn't bother to call, evidently didn't care one way or the other what state he was in.

Hours passed, days passed, weeks passed. There continued to be no word from her. It was the same old waiting game for David. Once in a while, he'd wake up and gaze out of the window at another day, and think despairingly, I cannot play this game any more. I cannot spend all day every day fending off the fact that Isabella isn't going to call and doing this by jerking off all the time, kidding myself that today's the day she *will* call.

Hell, she might very well not be in Brighton a lot of the time for all he knew, might even be out of the country altogether. Waiting for her constantly and libidinously like this was pointless, absurd, ridiculous.

It was all so utterly hopeless. This was a woman David worshipped and adored and for whom he'd do anything, but who didn't even care a damn for him, never mind love him; a woman who hardly ever wanted to actually be with him, and who kept him in this priapic state of suspended animation all the time.

He ought to give Isabella up; David understood that at some level. But he knew that he couldn't give her up, it was impossible. He was powerless to resist her because she'd changed him into someone else. She'd changed him into a person for whom she was everything, a person who wouldn't really exist without her.

David thought about just how much Isabella had changed him. His obsession with her consumed his waking hours, his sleeping ones too. Life went on of course but it unfolded around him in a haze. He thought about the extent to which his view of the world had been transformed, narrowed into nothing more nor less than his obsession with Isabella. David found that he spoke to hardly anyone nowadays. He had a naturally antisocial nature anyway but he had now become a lot more than antisocial: he'd become positively reclusive. David wanted to concentrate all his thought on Isabella. He didn't want the distraction of talking to anyone else if he could possibly avoid it. And that even included Matthew – not that he ever called anyway.

David didn't understand quite how Isabella had reduced him to this state and didn't actually care. All he knew was that she was his Mistress and he was her slave, she'd told him so. He knew that she could do anything she liked with him, no matter how sadistic and perverted, and that as long as she wanted to keep him as her slave he'd do anything to satisfy her demands.

Because David didn't take anything for granted, you see. He knew that any time Isabella chose to she could decide that she no longer wanted him as her slave and that would be the end of that. Finito, end of story. The thought of it made his stomach churn, made him feel sick, nauseous.

David knew only too well that every time Isabella contacted him it could be the last time. One of these fine days she'd set him free, he feared – no, dreaded. And from then on all he would have left would be memories: memories of the delicious torment of waiting for her calls, of the intense pain and pleasure – the *pleasure-pain* he'd experienced as a result of the fierce beatings she'd administered to him; of the way she'd stretched his anus with a big strap-on dildo and tortured his nipples and marked his body with livid welts; of the incredibly cruel way she'd always treated him; of the way she had displayed almost complete indifference to him right up to the end when that indifference had finally become total and she'd dumped him altogether.

Perhaps, David thought, slipping into despair, Isabella had

already got to that point already and had decided to finish with him, give him his wholly unwanted freedom. Perhaps he'd never hear from her again. Perhaps she was already gone from his life. Gone. The thought twisted inside him like barbed wire, it was awful. But no, he mustn't think like that, he told himself. He must continue to wait for Isabella to call, continue to hide away naked in his house, masturbating constantly, thinking only of her.

One evening, before he started jacking again, David decided to enhance his nudity and increase his sense of connectedness to Isabella by donning a couple of the items she'd gifted to him from *La Fetishista*. He lay on his leather couch, next to the phone needless to say, naked except for the chained collar, which he'd padlocked at the front, and the tight metal ring that encircled his genitals. His fingers were wrapped around his hard cock and he was letting thoughts of Isabella and what she might do to him – what she'd *already* done to him – permeate his mind thoroughly while he jacked away.

David imagined Isabella's hands on the back of his neck as she blindfolded him, like she'd done that first time. He imagined her buggering him with her big strap-on dildo while jerking him off, like she'd done that second time. He imagined her torturing his nipples and dripping hot candle wax onto him before bringing him off like she'd done the time after that. He imagined her whipping him so savagely that it brought him to a shuddering climax like she'd done the next time; imagined her going on to insist he lick up and swallow his come like she'd also done on that occasion. He imagined her whipping him with so much savagery that he fainted immediately he'd been brought to climax, like she'd done the last time he'd been with her.

Wouldn't it be truly wonderful, David said to himself, if Isabella would let him bring her to climax for once. Maybe she would sit before him, her legs spread and her pussy bare, and allow him to kneel submissively between her thighs, push the warm tip of his tongue between her pussy lips and lick her to orgasm. He would give her such pleasure she'd be in heaven. It would go like this, David imagined: He would kneel and take

44

her open pussy between his lips and start moving his tongue around her clitoris, licking it and licking it. Then he'd suck her juices, plunging his tongue into her pussy as far as it would go, licking and lapping inside her sex until she threw her head back with a loud groan and surrendered to the most deliciously protracted of orgasms.

Isabella had come nowhere near granting David such a huge privilege yet, there was no denying that. Jesus, she'd never even let him touch her. He'd never even seen her naked body, had never seen her other than when she was fully – albeit erotically – clothed. But it was early days; at least that's what David hoped. It could be the end. No, don't even go there, he told himself, retreating from the awful thought before it had a chance to take hold. Live in hope, that's what he must do: live in hope that if he kept being a good slave to Isabella she'd arrive one day at a point where she had become as addicted to his enslavement to her as he was to being her slave. She would then regularly require him to pleasure her pussy with his mouth and he'd be so amazingly good at it that soon she'd become addicted to that too, addicted to him pleasuring her in that way.

The idea of it was thrilling, causing a surge of desire to run through him. It made David masturbate all the harder, his fingers moving in increasingly feverish strokes. His handsome face distorted and his heart pounded faster as he stroked his cock ever more vigorously, imagining that he was licking Isabella's pussy with equal vigour. The hard nub of her clitoris would be caught between his lips, David imagined; her pussy would shudder as he licked it. Bringing these images vividly to mind, he worked his fist up and down fast, his erection moistened lavishly now by his precome. David jacked and jacked until erotic pleasure was coursing through him and his shaft was pulsing convulsively just like Isabella's wet pussy would have been under the skilful ministrations of his tongue as he pushed it in even deeper.

As David jerked more and more forcefully at his cock, fantasising all the while about performing equally energetic cunnilingus on Isabella, he felt himself on the verge of climaxing. His breathing was short and shallow, his heart was beating loudly and there was a roar like the ocean in his ears. His arousal had tightened now into something painful, desperate. He was ready to burst, nearly ready to come, right on the brink of his orgasm. Almost there. Then the phone rang and it was Isabella. 'Stop what you're doing at once,' she said.

Chapter Nine

David stopped what he was doing at once. It wasn't easy, wasn't easy *at all*. But that's what he did, because that's what Isabella had told him to do. He was still breathing rapidly, his chest rising and falling.

'Do you know *Latin in the Lanes*?' Isabella asked.

'Yes, Mistress.' It was an Italian restaurant just off the Brighton seafront and David had dined there on a number of occasions in the past, though not since meeting Isabella, not since becoming the onanistic recluse he now was thanks to her.

'I'll meet you outside the place just before nine,' she said. 'I've booked a table for two.'

'Yes, Mistress,' David said, his breathing a little less laboured now. 'Thank you so much.'

'There's more,' Isabella said. 'I want you to fit the butt plug inside you and keep it there all evening. I also want you to attach the clover clamps to your nipples. Keep them on all evening too. Put on the chained collar, the metal genital ring and the leather g-string as well. Wear them under your outer clothing.'

The phone went dead at that point and David immediately began to reflect on the ramifications of what he'd just been told. This evening was going to be a challenge, that was for damn sure, but it also represented to his mind real progress in his relationship with Isabella. Going out for a meal together in public was, from that viewpoint at any rate, a definite step up from his visit with her to *La Fetishista* to be disciplined. On the other hand, he smiled to himself, let's not get carried away here – it plainly wasn't going to be any ordinary meal, not by a long way!

David had plenty of time before he had to be at the restaurant but he felt it would be prudent to get ready sooner rather than later. It was better to be safe than sorry. David went up to his bedroom, took off the genital ring and unlocked the padlock to his chained collar, which he then removed. Then he headed for the bathroom. He stood in the shower, letting the warm water flow over his body, and soaped himself thoroughly. He got out of the shower, towelled off and reached for the enema kit ...

When he'd finished in the bathroom, David returned to his bedroom and put the chained collar back round his neck, going on to padlock it. He also put the tight genital ring back on. Now came the difficult part. David opened one of his bedroom drawers and pulled out a tube of lubricant, the large butt plug, and the nipple clamps. He lubricated the butt plug and pushed the rubber object into his narrow anus. It hurt as much as he'd known it would, which is to say that it hurt like hell. Next he attached the clamps to the clustered flesh of his nipples. That hurt a hell of a lot too, hurt as much as if the clamps had been burning pliers.

His anus now filled painfully by the butt plug and his nipples constricted equally painfully by the clover clamps, David proceeded to get dressed. First he put on the tiny leather g-string, which barely contained his metal-encircled genitals. He then donned a silky black T-shirt that disguised the telltale padlock to the front of his loose-chained slave's collar. Finally he put on a watch with a black leather strap, black socks, a lightweight midnight-blue suit that was casual in style, and shiny black loafers.

Under normal circumstances David might well have walked to the restaurant, the weather being particularly fine that evening. But the circumstances were anything but normal and this was certainly not an option on this occasion. David booked a taxi and when it arrived he walked unsteadily from the front door of his house to the waiting Streamline vehicle with its familiar turquoise-and-white livery. He noticed that the taxi driver looked more than a little bemused by the hesitant way he was walking. He probably thought his latest passenger had suffered a sports injury or something similar. He wouldn't have had even the faintest notion that between each unsteady step David was making toward his taxi he felt a sharp pain in his anus because of the large foreign object that was rammed up there. He got painfully into the back of the car, the cheeks of his backside pulled apart by the large butt plug, his nipples gripped painfully by the clover clamps.

The taxi ground through the evening traffic towards the seafront. It was one of those sunny evenings that can lift even the gloomiest of spirits. The sky was a pure blue and David could see through the gaps between buildings a shimmering strip of the English Channel on the horizon. On an evening like tonight Brighton was at its best, David thought. The place had a great atmosphere, with people sitting out at its numerous cafés and restaurants, talking, chilling out, flirting, listening to the cries of gulls ripping through the warm, briny air.

The taxi dropped David off and he walked uncomfortably towards the entrance to *Latin in the Lanes*. It was 8.45. He didn't see Isabella, didn't actually expect to see her for perhaps another ten minutes or so. Then he did see her, striding towards the restaurant. She looked stunning in a tight-fitting short black dress, which both revealed a daring amount of décolletage and showed off her terrific figure to perfection. Her breasts bobbed and her hips swayed enticingly as she moved.

Isabella arrived at the entrance to the restaurant where David was waiting for her. 'Are you wearing the nipple clamps and is that big butt plug in place, slave?' That was what she said to him in lieu of a greeting.

'Yes, Mistress,' he replied.

'Are they very painful?'

'Yes, Mistress.'

'That's good to hear,' she said, a crooked gleam in her eye. 'Do you like being in such pain?'

'Yes, Mistress,' he replied, for it was true.

They entered the restaurant together, a little early for their reservation, but that did not present any difficulties as luck would have it: the place was not too busy and their table was free and already set. As they threaded their way through the

49

other tables David concentrated on trying to walk as naturally as possible, which was no easy task. They were seated at their table by the waiter who said that he'd be back shortly to attend to them.

David shifted position in his seat to try and lessen the pain from the butt plug. The pain to his nipples was starting to diminish, though. He must be getting used to the clover clamps, David assumed. Perhaps he'd start to get used to the butt plug soon too; he certainly hoped so. Fuck, it was painful.

The waiter came back promptly and asked them if they would like a drink while deciding what they wanted to select from the menu. Isabella ordered a vodka tonic with ice and lemon and David a scotch on the rocks. The waiter then hurried off to get their drinks as they scrutinised their menus.

After a short while David looked up from his menu and across the table, across the shiny cutlery and the sparkling glasses, at Isabella. He thought she looked more gorgeous than ever. Her dark hair was shimmering and her eyes were shining. She looked smoulderingly sexy, super-erotic, darkly alluring. And she was here on a dinner date with him. The other diners couldn't keep their eyes off Isabella; she was by far the most beautiful woman in the restaurant. But hers was a cruel beauty. Because she was a cruel woman. She was a cruel woman who had made her dinner companion attach clover clamps to his nipples and insert a great big butt plug into his anus before allowing him to join her for a meal at *Latin in the Lanes*.

David's nipples felt OK now, not painful at all, just numb. But his anus was a different matter. He tried again to find a position that would make him less aware of the size of the object crammed inside him. But each time he moved, his insides seemed to swell even more, crying out in protest.

Their waiter returned, holding two glasses of spirit, ice cubes clinking. Isabella raised her glass and took a long pull and David did likewise, thinking: That's what I need – some liquid pain killer. The whisky felt good, giving him an instant buzz. He looked at his sadistic Mistress, then down at his drink, rattling the ice cubes. He drank some more whisky, feeling a warm glow begin suffusing itself through his body. The pain in his backside was starting to ease off now. When the effect of the scotch fully kicked in, David told himself, that would help further reduce his discomfort.

After briefly conferring with David Isabella took over the ordering of the food and wine. Neither of them would have a starter, she told the waiter, and they would both have the seafood salad, share a bottle of the house white.

Their meal arrived promptly and they ate it in silence for a while, Isabella choosing not to speak and David knowing instinctively that wherever possible he should only speak to his Mistress when spoken to. Then Isabella broke the silence. 'Do you find me a cruel Mistress?' she asked, studying him over the rim of her wine glass. There was nobody at the table adjacent to theirs or anywhere else in the immediate vicinity to overhear her words.

'Very cruel, Mistress,' David replied.

'But hard to resist, huh?'

'Impossible to resist,' David said. 'I couldn't imagine any slave trying to resist you.'

'It has been known,' Isabella said.

'Really, Mistress?' David sounded incredulous.

'There was this young slave called Dee who tried to resist me not so very long ago,' Isabella said, pouring them both some more wine. 'Would you like to hear about it?'

'Yes please, Mistress.'

'It happened last summer' Isabella said, commencing her account. 'You'll remember how lousy the weather was that season right from the start...'

Outside the sky was heavy with black clouds and it was raining hard. The wind was blowing branches around and gulls shrieked, almost inaudible in the storm. Isabella ushered her windswept friend John – or Master John as he was known on the Brighton fetish scene – into her beautifully furnished living room. She fixed her guest a drink and gestured with an elegant hand for him to come and sit with her on the black leather couch.

'Thanks for seeing me,' John said, a worried frown creasing

51

his handsome features. 'I didn't know who to turn to for advice about the problem I've got with my new slave Dee but you seemed the best person.'

'No thanks are necessary,' Isabella replied and waited for him to elaborate.

'You haven't met Dee yet, have you,' John said.

'I haven't, no,' Isabella agreed.

'She's lovely, stunning,' John enthused. 'I'm absolutely nuts about her.'

'So far so good,' Isabella said. 'Where's the problem?'

John took a sip from his drink and glanced out of the window. It really was wild out there. The weather had been like this for the last week – and it was supposed to be the beginning of summer in sunny Brighton. So far the weather had been foul, a south-westerly twisting off the English Channel day after stormy day. The seaside city was definitely not at its best. Nor was John. He looked back at Isabella, cleared his throat and said, 'In a nutshell, I'm finding Dee increasingly difficult to control.'

'Feisty at times is she?' Isabella asked.

'Yes, and obstinate, argumentative, truculent, opinionated, disobedient …'

'I get the picture,' Isabella interjected with a smile. 'But don't you perhaps think that by behaving like that she's just trying to goad you into disciplining her more strictly.'

'You think?'

'It seems a distinct possibility,' Isabella said. She liked John but to her mind he was less than convincing as a dominator. Not exactly the type. He was an amiable sort, never exactly pushy. 'In fact, if you want my honest opinion, John,' she went on, 'I think you're probably too damn nice to keep such an obviously wilful character under control. I hope you don't mind me saying that.' Isabella valued John's friendship and didn't want to offend him. On the other hand there was no point in beating about the bush.

'I've had a lot worse insults,' John replied with a wry smile. 'But I must admit being too nice, as you put it, isn't exactly an ideal trait in a Master – particularly with a handful like Dee to try and keep in order.'

'The way I see it, you've got some of the best characteristics of a great Dom,' Isabella went on, sugaring the pill a little for her friend. 'You're brilliant at Japanese rope bondage and wax play too, and you can certainly administer a good whipping. But you don't have that fundamentally cruel streak that's needed to be a truly effective dominator.'

'You're right, although I hate to admit it,' John said. 'The trouble is I can't make myself into something I'm not, I know that. Yet I'm genuinely worried that the whole situation could lead to Dee and me splitting up and I really don't want that to happen – I'm madly in love with the girl. What on earth am I going to do, Isabella?'

The dominatrix frowned. 'There must be a solution to this,' she said, pausing to think for a few moments, 'and … yes … I think I know what it is.'

'Go on.'

'What if Dee could be handed over to someone who's not only extremely sadistic but is also someone you personally feel you can trust,' Isabella said. 'This would only be for a brief session so she can be given a short sharp shock, so to speak. That might well do the trick with your Dee, don't you think?'

'What, bring her to heel?'

'Yes,' Isabella replied. 'And make her realise just how well off she is with you as her Master.'

'I think you might well be on to something,' John said, brightening. 'What you're suggesting's got quite a ring about it.'

'Also,' Isabella continued, 'there'd be an added bonus for you if you went ahead with my suggestion.'

'What's that?'

'You could threaten Dee with further sessions with the person concerned if she gets out of line in the future. That would be a good way of keeping her under control longer term, don't you agree?'

'I do, Isabella,' John said. 'In fact the whole idea sounds increasingly good to me the more you explain it. Did you have somebody specifically in mind to discipline Dee in this cruel and ingenious way?'

'Yes,' Isabella replied simply. 'Me.'

Chapter Ten

Isabella and Dee were in Isabella's luxurious living room. Its tall windows were curtained in heavy linen and net. Outside the sky was leaden with dark clouds and the rain was coming down in fierce grey sheets. Leaves clogged the gullies and lay in swathes across the pavement. The summer weather remained dreadful. It was definitely better to be indoors – for some people at any rate.

Isabella was seated in a black leather armchair. Wearing only a chain mail bra that barely contained her beautiful breasts, a tiny side-split mini skirt also of chain mail, and high-heeled shoes, she looked magnificent. Immediately adjacent to the chair in which she was seated was a side table that had a selection of whips, paddles, canes and other disciplinary implements neatly lined up on its surface.

Dee, the expression on her face as blank a mask as she could make it, was standing before the formidable dominatrix so that she could inspect her. Isabella noted the stubborn set of her jaw and the glint of disobedience in her big lustrous brown eyes. She was also struck by the almost perfect symmetry of her features and how lovely looking she was.

Dee had dark hair, which was shiny and straight and hung to her shoulders. Small earrings glittered at her ears. She had full breasts and tight tan legs. Her glorious figure was enhanced by the flesh toned mini dress she was wearing, which left nothing to the imagination. Her nipples were plainly visible beneath the dress and she was obviously nude underneath it. As well as being low cut, showing a large expanse of her ample bosom, the dress was miniscule and diaphanous. If anything it seemed to make her more naked.

'That's a nice dress you're nearly wearing,' Isabella said with a throaty chuckle. 'Mind you, I'm one to talk!'

Dee kept her expression impassive, thinking: What's she trying to do here? Just be friendly? Break the ice? Lull me into a false sense of security?

'Dee, I know what you're thinking,' Isabella said suddenly, unnerving the slave. 'Just stop it, all right.' She got out of her chair to stand in front of Dee and her dark eyes bored into her with piercing severity.

'Undo the top of your dress,' she ordered brusquely. 'Take your breasts out and be quick about it.'

'Yes, Mistress,' Dee replied and immediately did as she'd been told.

'They're nice and full, it's true.' Isabella stroked and lifted Dee's breasts approvingly. 'But I see no sign of any recent discipline. That concerns me.' She shook her head in apparent dismay.

'These are lovely too,' she continued, pinching Dee's pinkish-brown nipples, which protruded urgently in response. 'Tell me, do you have sensitive nipples?'

Dee did not at first reply and kept her expression impassive. But Isabella saw the defiance that flickered in her eyes.

'Well?' Isabella asked again, an edge to her voice. 'Do you have sensitive nipples?'

'Yes, Mistress,' Dee replied apprehensively, 'I do – very.'

'Good,' Isabella said, viciously squeezing the slave's engorged buds, 'Then you won't like me doing this.' Dee gasped with pain and hunched forward, her head bowed, her dark hair falling across her face.

'Don't slouch like that, Dee. Stand up straight,' Isabella told her as she herself returned to her seat. 'Now lift up your dress at the front. I want to examine your pussy.'

'Yes, Mistress.'

'Mmmm, very nice,' Isabella commented. 'No pubic hair at all … labia distended – lovely, like two petals … clitoris pronounced. Tell me, I've been reliably informed you keep your sex clean-shaven at all times. Is that so?'

'Yes, Mistress.'

'Well, at least you're doing one of the things expected of a good slave, but precious little else, I'm given to understand.'

'But …'

'No buts, slave. The only butt I'm interested in is this one.' Isabella gestured with an impatient twirl of her hand that she wished Dee to turn her back to her. 'Lift your dress again.'

'Yes, Mistress.'

'You have a lovely round behind,' she told her. 'It's eminently spankable.'

'Thank you, Mistress,' Dee replied, looking over her shoulder at Isabella and smiling for the first time. It was an engaging smile, very sexy. Her brown eyes glittered seductively.

'That doesn't mean I'm happy with it,' Isabella said, refusing to connect with that sexy smile, that seductive gaze, and fixing Dee with another sharp stare instead. She then looked back at the young woman's backside. 'Where's the evidence of recent punishment to this lovely rear of yours? The bruises, the weals, and the welts? I'll have to put that right *tout de suite*. Come across my knee, slave, now.'

Dee bent over Isabella's lap, placing her hands on the floor in front of her. The cheeks of her backside tensed as the dominatrix flicked the bottom of her insubstantial dress out of the way to fully reveal her comely rear again. Isabella stroked its beautiful soft globes with one hand and moved her other hand to Dee's sex.

Her fingers slipped inside her slippery wet vagina and as she moved to touch the pink thorn of her clitoris Dee let out a moan of pleasure.

'You're extremely wet down here,' Isabella said. 'I hope that doesn't mean you're expecting to enjoy this.' Isabella suddenly squeezed Dee's clit hood, causing the slave to cringe in startled agony.

'You must understand something, Dee,' the dominatrix explained, moving the hand that had been stroking the slave's rear to her breasts and squeezing hard on both her nipples for a second time, making her squeal. 'We're here so you can be severely disciplined, not for you to derive pleasure.

Understood?'

'Understood, Mistress,' Dee replied, shivering with pain.

'On the other hand,' Isabella went on, plunging her fingers into Dee's dripping pussy and starting to masturbate her, 'if at any time you find yourself on the verge of climaxing, you must get my permission to come. Clear?'

'Clear, Mistress,' the slave replied, gasping. She became increasingly frantic as Isabella's fingers worked more vigorously between the lips of her sex.

'I … ah … oh … permission to come, Mistress,' Dee cried out suddenly.

'Say "please",' Isabella taunted, increasing even more the rough finger-fucking she was giving the slave.

'Permission to come, please, Mistress, oh please …' Dee begged.

'Permission granted,' Isabella replied and the young slave climaxed in great shuddering spasms.

'See how good I am to you,' Isabella said next. 'Here, lick.' She put her fingers, sticky with Dee's love juices, across her lips and the slave kissed and licked them. 'Now suck them.' She slowly pushed two fingers into Dee's mouth and she sucked them greedily as Isabella slid them back and forth between her lips.

'Look Dee, fair's fair,' Isabella said, withdrawing her fingers from the young woman's mouth. 'You've just enjoyed some real pleasure. Now you must endure some real pain. Agreed?'

'Yes, Mistress,' she replied uncertainly.

Isabella paused for a moment to admire Dee's backside again, all round and bare and vulnerable, before beginning her spanking. Smack! The crisp sound announced that the spanking had begun and the red palm print on Dee's backside bore witness to the cruel accuracy of that first stroke. Smack! Isabella's hand cracked down again on the curved cheeks with another harsh spank.

After many more robust smacks, when that luxurious living room rang with the sound of hand on naked flesh, Isabella told Dee that her backside was reddening impressively. She then increased the frequency and harshness of her blows. She continued unremittingly, cracking her hand down onto Dee's backside with relentless vigour, following one smack after another in swift succession. The cheeks of the young slave's rear smarted with a fire that made her tense and squirm in pain, and with each slap her tensing and squirming increased.

'I can see a nice red glow now,' Isabella said, pausing briefly to admire her handiwork before returning to her task with a will. When she increased the momentum of the spanking still further Dee reached back with a hand to try and protect herself.

'Stop that this instant, bitch,' Isabella snapped, brushing the hand away. She did actually stop beating Dee for a short time and gently stroked her backside but only to quickly resume spanking her, this time with even greater ferocity. She now also included her upper thighs in the thrashing and did not stop until that whole area of her body was coloured an even red. Dee let out an involuntary wail of pain as the full effect of the spanking spread through her body.

'Ooh, poor baby,' Isabella cooed in mock solicitude. 'Does that hurt?'

'Yes, Mistress,' came the halting reply.

'Tough shit,' her tormentor retorted, adding ominously, 'For goodness sake, girl, I've barely even started.'

Isabella then suddenly pulled Dee off her lap by the hair. 'Stand up and take off your dress and shoes,' she demanded. Isabella got to her feet herself once Dee was nude. She instructed her to turn round so she could examine her punished rear. When she'd done this Isabella told her to turn back and face her. She looked the young slave in the eye.

Dee looked back at Isabella, again trying to keep any emotion from showing on her face. But inside she remained defiant, repeating to herself over and over her own determined chant, *I won't let her win, I won't let her win, I won't let her win, I won't ...*

Isabella interrupted this inner mantra, 'You know, Dee,' she said, shooting her an incendiary look, 'I can tell you – having myself just carried out an inspection – that you now have two lovely red cheeks.' Isabella had again noted the gleam of rebellion in the young woman's eyes that her expressionless face was unable to disguise. 'No, sorry, three red cheeks' she added, suddenly slapping her round the face hard.

'Look, I've told you before,' Isabella said in a patient tone as she watched the red rose of a bruise begin to bloom on the young slave's cheek, 'I know what you're thinking. So, please don't kid yourself you can beat me. Oh, and talking of beating ...' Isabella took hold of a red leather paddle from the selection of disciplinary implements on the side table, and weighed it in her hands. 'See my paddle, slave?'

'Yes, Mistress,' Dee replied, visibly shaken by the unexpected slap to the face that she'd received.

'I'm now going to use it to beat your backside an even redder shade of red – until it's as red as this paddle. No, thinking about it, redder still – as red as the reddest rose in a bunch of red, red roses. What colour would you say I am aiming for, slave?'

'Red, Mistress,' Dee muttered.

'Well spotted,' Isabella mocked. 'Now I want you to go over to that table.' Isabella gestured with the paddle. 'Lean over it with your arms in front of you, your back arched, legs parted and backside in the air. That's right ...Prepare to be punished further. But Dee,' she added, 'before we re-commence, please note that I've thoughtfully left a nice soft leather cushion on the table for you to rest your head on. You see, I'm not entirely cruel, now am I?'

'Yes, Mistress ... I mean, no,' responded the flustered slave, who found that she couldn't stop trembling.

When Dee bent forward, the cheeks of her quivering backside were stretched open. They presented Isabella with an exposed view of her puckered anus and the open lips of her sex. Her rear bore all too clear evidence of her punishment so far, and her anus and pussy just as clear evidence of its effect on her. Both were pulsating uncontrollably and her labia were swollen and wet. Trickles of love juice were running down her thighs.

'I'll start by beating your backside twenty times with the

paddle,' Isabella said. 'I want you to count off each strike and thank me for it in the proper respectful manner. Do you understand?'

'Yes, Mistress,' Dee replied, her voice unsteady.

Isabella raised her arm up to shoulder height and brought it down vigorously.

Thwack! That first blow nearly knocked all the breath out of the slave.

'One, thank you, Mistress,' Dee managed to pant.

Thwack!

'Two, thank you, Mistress.'

Thwack!

'Three, thank you, Mistress.'

Thwack! …. And on and relentlessly on.

'All right, Dee, you can keep quiet now,' Isabella said once the young slave had gasped her way through the full twenty strikes. The scorched cheeks of her backside were now flushed an even deeper and angrier shade of red. Isabella continued, 'Yes, you can keep quiet and you can stay quiet too. I don't want to hear another word out of you. From this point on you are to be obscene but not heard, *comprendre*?' Dee nodded her understanding.

Isabella carried on using the red paddle on her backside and upper thighs, beating her ever harder until she raised her back as an involuntary reflex action. 'Down, slave, down,' Isabella commanded, placing a hand in the small of her back and pushing her firmly down.

Isabella continued paddling Dee until she felt as if her backside and thighs were on fire. And then the dominatrix stopped, putting the paddle to one side.

'That makes a lovely picture, slave. You can take my word for it,' Isabella commented. 'But we don't want just a uniform red. Let's introduce some variety into the picture. I've just the thing – my braided leather flogger.'

Isabella picked up the vicious black and red whip from the top of the side table, positioned herself behind Dee again, and raised it. The whip hissed sharply when she swung it through the air and when it landed with a crack on its target the sudden pain that seared across Dee's backside nearly overwhelmed her. She was still trying to draw breath when Isabella brought the whip down again. It was even more agonizing. As the savage whipping continued, the furious pain Dee was suffering became almost unbearable. She raised her head and was about to register a protest.

'Stay put, you tiresome bitch,' Isabella demanded sharply, pushing Dee's head down before she had a chance to speak. 'I thought I'd already made it clear that you're to suffer in silence. You've got nothing to say that I want to hear unless it's to beg for mercy or ask for permission to come. Otherwise, just shut the fuck up and take your punishment.'

Isabella continued to thrash Dee's backside mercilessly, causing numerous welts to spring there like fresh cut stems. Finally she put the braided flogger back on the side table.

'Now I'm going to use my most vicious cane on you,' Isabella announced, her dark eyes glinting with malice as she picked up the thin length of smooth rattan and showed it to her victim. She gave the cane a couple of experimental strokes through the air. 'Listen to the sinister swishing noise it makes as it slices through the air,' she said, 'and feel its painful sting.'

And Dee did indeed hear the low swish as the cane was drawn back and the louder one as it descended and, oh, how she suffered the sharp sting of its first searing stroke as Isabella brought it down hard across the punished cheeks of her backside.

'Ow!' she squealed.

'Silence,' Isabella snapped. 'Be warned, I shan't tell you again.'

For a long time the room resounded once more with the sound of punishment, this time the swish and crack of cane against flesh. Isabella caned Dee's backside with unrelentingly hard rhythmic strokes until it was criss-crossed with clear stripes and the young slave's eyes were welling with tears of pain.

Isabella stopped and stroked the cane gently over Dee's rear, admiring the well-striped cheeks. She carried on rolling it tantalizingly over her backside and legs before recommencing the beating. This time the swipes of the cane she inflicted on her rear were less frequent but also much harsher as she brought her arm right back before striking. Three final vicious swipes in swift succession left Dee whimpering in agony. Isabella examined with cruel satisfaction the intensely painful red stripes that now covered her backside and thighs.

'On to your knees,' demanded the pitiless dominatrix, 'That's right, slave ... like that ... kiss the cane ... good ... keep your backside in the air ...' Dee's rear was burning ferociously and her breath was coming in little gasps as she put her lips to the thin hard rod.

'You've been exceptionally wilful and stubborn, Dee,' Isabella said 'But I trust you've learned your lesson now.'

'Yes, Mistress,' she responded meekly, looking up at her ruthless tormentor.

'I hope you're truly sorry for the disobedience and lack of respect you've shown to Master John,' Isabella continued, leaning down and gripping Dee by the hair so that she could look her directly in the eye.

'Yes, Mistress. I'm truly sorry.'

'And I really hope I don't have to see you here again,' Isabella added, staring at her with a gleam of pure menace in her eyes.

'Yes, Mistress,' Dee replied softly as she grovelled at Isabella's feet, her severely punished rear in the air. But what she was actually thinking as she looked up adoringly at Isabella was that she couldn't wait to see her cruel new Mistress again.

'I keep telling you, Dee,' Isabella rasped, harshly interrupting the slave's reverie, her eyes now flashing with anger, 'I know what you're thinking and, frankly, it simply won't fucking do.' With that she lifted the cane high above her head and rained blow after ferocious blow on Dee's backside, breaking the skin in numerous places.

'Mercy, Mistress, mercy,' the distraught slave screamed, weeping uncontrollably. 'Permission to come ... please, Mistress ... oh permission to come,' she begged in desperation. Isabella gave consent and Dee was utterly overwhelmed by an orgasm that was long and violent, the most savage climax she had ever experienced in her entire life.

Isabella paused for a while before speaking again, waiting for Dee's earth shattering orgasm to subside. 'I don't think you quite understood me,' she said calmly, looking down at the thoroughly chastened slave. Dee's face was stained with tears and she whimpered and shook pitifully at her feet. 'I really – and I do mean really – don't ever want to see you here again. Do you understand me now?'

'Yes, Mistress.' Dee looked up at her with her large brown eyes. They were tear-filled and thoroughly remorseful and, at long last, contained not even the smallest, not even the *tiniest* glimmer of disobedience. Job done, Isabella said to herself with satisfaction.

Chapter Eleven

'You are right,' Isabella said, concluding her much truncated, much censored account of the ruthless way in which she'd broken the wilful Dee. She turned her eyes directly on David's and he was struck anew by the almost inhuman power of her concentrated gaze. 'I really am very cruel indeed – as cruel as they come. I never take hostages. When a person is disciplined by me, they stay disciplined. Resistance is futile.'

'Yes, Mistress,' David replied with a shudder.

'Now, let's change the subject,' Isabella said, her eyes still fixed on his but much less intensely now. 'Is there anything you'd particularly like to know about me?'

David took a sip of wine as he thought about the question. 'Is Isabella Stern your real name, Mistress?' he asked, thinking as soon as the words had come out of his mouth: Surely you could have come up with a better question than that, you bloody fool. Talk about wasted opportunities. Still, he'd sometimes wondered. The name seemed almost too apt, a way of marketing *La Fetishista* maybe, a kind of stage name.

Isabella peered into her wine glass. 'Believe it or not, it is my real name, yes,' she said. 'My husband's surname has always been Stern – he's never felt any need for a name change; why would he have? And my birth name was Isabella Etorri. My mother was Japanese and my father was Italian, hence my rather exotic appearance. My parents emigrated from Italy to England before I was born. My father's family lived for generations on the Italian coast, which is perhaps why I'm so drawn to a seaside place like Brighton.'

'You are, Mistress?' David said, delighted to hear her say it.

'Absolutely,' Isabella said. 'Alan likes to play the squire in our country house and spends a great deal of his time there but I'm not personally a fan of the English countryside – all that *green*. Our villa in Italy is a great place to take a vacation occasionally and holidaying there gets me back to my roots but I wouldn't want to live out there for any length of time. Brighton is where we opened our first *La Fetishista* store; it's where we have our head office and where I live most of the time, the place I think of as home. Anything else you'd like to know, slave?'

'You mentioned your husband, Mistress,' David said.

'Ah, yes. I can understand that you would be curious about him,' Isabella said. 'He and I spend an awful lot of time apart, it's true. Is our marriage little more than a business partnership, you may be wondering? Well, sorry to disappoint you, slave, but Alan and I have a strong relationship, always have, although it is certainly a very unorthodox one. The major issue for us – and it's crucial – is that we are both extremely dominant and sadistic sexually, which has meant that we have had to seek … different solutions.'

'Thank you for the clarification, Mistress,' David said, thinking, so, what did that make him? – nobody of any great consequence to Isabella evidently. But it didn't always have to be that way, did it. If he kept on being a good slave to her … He didn't have time to pursue the thought.

'Let's go back to your house now,' Isabella said abruptly, summoning the waiter for the bill with an imperious wave of her hand. 'We'll take my car. It's not parked far away.' David was relieved to hear it, given what he had rammed up his backside. Walking wouldn't be as difficult as it had been earlier, he reckoned, but it still wouldn't be easy.

Isabella and David climbed out of her car. It was sleek and black and the Mercedes logo on the grille gleamed brightly in the steadily deepening twilight. As soon as they entered David's house and were in his living room, Isabella told him to put on the light and pull the curtains. When he'd done that she asked, 'What were you doing when I phoned you earlier, slave?'

'Masturbating, Mistress,' he answered truthfully.

'I thought as much,' Isabella said, her face twisting into a half smile. 'Take off your clothes and do it for me now. I want to watch you masturbating. Take off everything apart from your chained collar and genital ring. You must keep the nipple clamps and butt plug in place too.'

'Yes, Mistress,' David said and stripped off his outer clothing and the tiny leather g-string.

Isabella pointedly looked him over, her black eyes hard. 'Masturbate now, slave,' she said, focussing her gaze now exclusively on his crotch. 'Jerk yourself off right in front of me.' And he started to do as she'd told him to, stroking his initially semi-tumescent cock in smooth, regular movements until it was as hard as a rock.

'Do it faster,' Isabella then said, and he did, his heart pounding fast and his fist pounding faster as he jerked his cock in an increasingly insistent rhythm.

'Do it even faster,' she said next, and David obeyed, his pleasure mounting ever closer to boiling point as he jerked urgently at his erection.

Isabella's dark eyes were unreadable as she witnessed this uninhibited, this *feverish* solitary act that she herself had stage-managed. She followed David's every furious stroke, his every lustful expression, his every passionate gasp. Her own demeanour remained cool, calm and collected throughout, though, even when David reached his shuddering climax, spraying his fist with jism and letting out a guttural moan of release.

'You'd better go and clean yourself up now, slave,' Isabella said, the same impenetrable expression on her beautiful face. 'You can take off your nipple clamps and remove the butt plug while you're about it.'

David went up to the bathroom and washed his hands and genitals. Next he took off the nipple clamps, which hurt intensely as the blood rushed like quicksilver back into the previously constricted flesh. After that he removed the butt plug. Feeling the rubbery base of the object, he slowly extracted the monster from deep inside him. Oh, the incredible pain! Oh, the blessed relief!

When David returned downstairs to the living room Isabella had gone. His cruel and enigmatic Mistress had left him all alone once more.

Chapter Twelve

David was again left gazing at the phone, waiting desperately for Isabella to call him. There were times when he felt an almost overwhelming temptation to phone her instead. "I know you told me never to call you, Mistress," he'd say. "But this is urgent. It's a matter of life and death. You see, all this waiting around to hear from you is killing me, sucking the life blood out of me. I have to see you soon or I'll die. I have to feel your hands on me, feel the kiss of your whip on my skin, feel the ..."

But David knew he was being ridiculous, fantasising absurdly in his desperation to hear word from her. Isabella had made it perfectly clear right from the outset that she'd call him whenever it suited her and that he was never to call her. That was the deal, the only game in town for him. There was nothing he could do to change the situation.

Time continued to drag by as if it was infinitely elastic. Then at long last the moment David had been waiting for, *praying* for, arrived and she phoned again, her caller identification flashing up. He had the receiver in his hand before the second ring had ended. 'I want to see you, slave,' Isabella said.

'Thank goodness, Mistress,' David replied in relief, feeling the sensation almost as a physical force.

'Do you remember the first time I visited your home?'

'Yes, Mistress.' How could he ever forget it? The experience would be etched on his memory for ever.

'When preparing for my arrival today I want you to follow exactly the same routine you did then,' Isabella said. 'But this time when I arrive I want to find you kneeling on your hands and knees on the edge of your bed.'

Naked and blindfolded and on all fours on the bed, David heard Isabella's footsteps getting closer all the time as she mounted the stairs. They got closer still as she walked through the open door to his bedroom and crossed the room towards him. She was immediately behind David now, immediately behind his arched back, his splayed rear. He was trembling with excitement, the rosebud opening of his anus twitching, his cock rigidly erect and pulsing.

David was almost sure what it was that Isabella was going to do to him today and what she went on to do next only made him more certain about that. He felt the sensation of a tube emptying into his anal hole. The lubricant was cool as she squirted it into his anus, which tightened and then began to relax.

'I know what you're thinking, slave,' Isabella said. 'You think I'm going to fuck you in the arse again. And you're right, but I'm not going to do it with one of my strap-on dildos this time. I'm going to do it with my *fist*.'

Isabella moved her hand away from his body then. David gasped as he heard her snapping on the latex glove and gasped again at the liquid sound of her lubing up her fingers. She slid one, then two of them into the puckered opening of his hole and began to work them in and out of the darkness of his insides. It made him moan and squirm with pleasure.

Isabella concentrated on massaging the entrance to David's anal hole for a few moments, making it spasm as he pushed his hips back towards her wrist. She then returned to fucking him in the arse with the two fingers, making him breathe fast. Her fingers were really working his anus now and she twisted a third one in. Isabella drove all three of them inside him, plunging hard. David could feel his hole flex around her latex-covered fingers, gripping them, and he began whimpering with pleasure.

He shuddered as he felt Isabella add more lube, then ease her fourth finger into his wet anal hole and slowly start to fuck him there again. He was amazed her fingers were fitting inside him but it was now very far from being a comfortable fit despite all the lube. His thighs were tensed and he was in unbearable pain but was also experiencing intense pleasure – pleasure that was further intensified when Isabella reached around with her other hand and began to stroke his throbbing erection.

As Isabella eased her fingers into David's anus to the second knuckle, he groaned with pleasure-pain. He tightened his hole around her fingers as he realised she had added her thumb. He didn't think he'd have been able to take all her hand like this and yet he had. But, fuck, it really hurt and he was relieved when she started to ease right off. Isabella held the hand with which she was fisting David completely still inside him for a spell but she continued to stroke and pull at his stiff cock with the other one.

When she judged the time was right Isabella got to work with her latex-covered fingers again, started to ease her fist further into David's anus. She was nearly all the way inside him now, and it hurt *so* much. The pain was extreme ... and it was exquisite.

Continuing to massage his hard cock with her other hand, Isabella slid the hand with which she was buggering David further still into his anus. She did this oh so slowly, oh so gently and gradually his anal muscles began to loosen up a little more. As she slid her hand all the way in, he let out a loud cry and pushed backwards further onto her wrist.

His eyes closed tight behind the blindfold, David shuddered excitedly as he felt Isabella's hand right inside his anus, curled tightly into a fist as her other hand continued to work his hard pulsing cock, which was now spilling precome like a leaky faucet.

Then Isabella began to really bugger and wank David with a will, pressing the fist she had lodged up his lube-sodden anus backwards and forwards while her other fist moved up and down on his throbbing, precome drizzling erection. Each time she slid her fist back and forth inside his anal hole she pulled at his hard-on, making him groan aloud. David was intensely aroused, mad with desire. His blindfolded face was flushed, his mouth wide open, his breathing rough and ragged.

David pushed his hips back on Isabella's hand, feeling it slide even further in before she brought it back, feeling her other hand masturbate him in a complementary rhythm. On and on she wanked his precome-soaked erection with one fist. On and on she buggered his lube-soaked insides with the other. Her movements caused spears of pleasure to shoot through him as her latex-covered fingers made contact time and again with his prostate gland.

He groaned loudly with pleasure at each stroke of her fist inside his anus, at each stroke of her other fist over his stiff cock. Isabella worked her fingers faster and faster as David shuddered beneath her, on the edge of climaxing.

Then his orgasm came with full force, making him cry out loudly. Come spilled from his cock and out of control spasms spread through his body like a mighty wave. David felt like he never would stop coming. He didn't think of anything except the ecstatic sensations spreading through his body as he spilled his come in juddering spurts.

Finally David stopped ejaculating and Isabella slipped her hand out of his dilated anus, which was wet and sticky and dripping with lubricant. He was still breathing heavily, his body struggling against the spasms that continued to shudder through him.

For a while all was silence apart from the ragged sound of David's breathing. Then Isabella snapped off the latex glove and spoke. 'Remove the blindfold after a slow count to one hundred,' she said. It was word-for-word the same command she'd issued to him after she'd buggered him with the strap-on dildo all those months ago.

And by the time he'd completed his count and removed the blindfold Isabella was once again nowhere to be seen ... and it was back to playing the waiting game for David.

Chapter Thirteen

David couldn't call Isabella because she'd forbidden it. 'Don't ever call me,' she'd said. The instruction had been unequivocal. But she hadn't said, 'Don't ever write to me.' So maybe he could at a pinch do that, he thought. He could write her a letter. It would have to be a letter too, not an e-mail. A letter would be so much more appropriate than an e-mail, infinitely more respectful. David started to draft out a begging letter to Isabella.

I beg you most humbly to take pity on me and get in touch soon, Mistress, it went. *I'm desperate to hear from you again, desperate to be in your presence once more. I need so much to be ordered around by you, disciplined by you, whipped by you, fucked in the arse by you, made to suffer by you. I only really exist when I'm with you, Mistress; you must realise that. You are my whole world. Waiting for you to call me is tearing me apart and I can't wait any more. That's why I've resorted to writing you this letter.*

Please, please see me as soon as possible, Mistress, and treat me really sadistically when you do; be as rough as you like. It pleases you to hurt me. It makes you happy, I know that. But I can make you so much happier if you'll let me. I need you to torment my body again and you need to do that too – soon. You know you do. It would be in both our interests, Mistress, don't you see that. So, call me as soon as possible please, I'm begging you.

As first drafts went that was pretty pathetic, David had to acknowledge. It was suitably grovelling, yes, but it was all over the place, a hopelessly rambling effort. He couldn't possibly send it. David knew however that even if he scripted his begging letter to perfection he still couldn't send it to Isabella.

It was nothing more than another desperate flight of fancy on his part, a feeble grasping at straws.

Don't call me. Don't write to me. What difference did it make? He had let his fevered imagination take him into the realms of semantics and he knew it. There was no difference in this case; there certainly wouldn't be to Isabella. If he had the temerity to write such a letter it would more likely than not have the opposite effect to the one he'd intended.

After he'd disobeyed her orders in such a flagrant manner Isabella would leave it even longer before she got in touch again – if she did ever get in touch with him again that is, which she might very well not do. No, almost impossible to bear though it was, all David could do was to keep waiting with as much patience as he could muster for his cruel Mistress to call.

Eventually his patience was rewarded. His phone started ringing and her caller ID came up. 'I'm going to let you into Brighton's best kept secret tonight,' Isabella told David when he'd snatched up the phone and put it to his ear. 'I'll be taking you to a favourite haunt of mine, *Club Depravity*. It only opens its doors on the last Saturday of the month and I always try to go if I can. This time I intend to take you with me.' And that's exactly what she did – at eleven thirty that night to be precise. The club turned out to be, to say the least, aptly named.

Isabella punched in a number to the side of the tall metal-railed gate and the lock opened with a loud click. She pushed the gate open and took David down a spiral staircase and up to a thick metal door above which he could see a CCTV camera. She rang for entry and the door was opened by one of the club's hostesses, an attractive elfin-faced young woman. She had short dark brown hair with blonde highlights and was dressed in a shiny black leather mini dress that was skin-tight. 'Good evening, Mistress Isabella,' the hostess said.

'Hi there,' Isabella replied breezily. 'He's with me.' She gestured towards David as he followed her through the heavy door.

So, this is *Club Depravity*, David said to himself excitedly as Isabella led him into the cloakroom. He wondered how depraved things were going to get tonight, wondered what "Brighton's best kept secret" was actually like.

Isabella told him to strip naked and by the time he'd done so, his cock was standing stiffly erect. Isabella then removed her black leather coat to reveal what she'd had on beneath it: an extremely tight-fitting leather bodysuit, black too, with holes in the chest and crotch, from which her magnificent breasts and her shaven pussy protruded. 'You look superb, Mistress,' David said in awe-struck admiration, his erection throbbing.

'I know,' Isabella replied with a straight face.

As soon as they had come out of the cloakroom Isabella began to lead David down a dark corridor. It had one long continuous brick wall on one side and on the other side a series of large, dark chambers. The noises coming from these cavernous, brick-vaulted rooms – groaning, cries of passion and pain, the constant sounds of leather and rattan against bare flesh – gave the club an atmosphere of palpable lust and deviancy.

Isabella and David stopped on the threshold of the first chamber and gazed in. David gasped at the sight of a naked man lying flat on his back and spread eagled on a leather-covered bondage table. His wrists and ankles were lashed to its four corners with leather straps, the base of his erect cock was bound tightly with thin black rope and his scrotum was a mass of metal pegs. His nipples were clamped with clover clamps, which were being pulled hard by the voluptuous redhead, also nude, who was sitting on the man's face. He let out a muffled groan of pain beneath her comely thighs each time she tugged at his nipple clamps in this sadistic way.

In one corner of the room there was another naked man. He was kneeling over a leather bench where he was being caned ferociously by a statuesque black woman who was also naked. Her skin was so black and polished that she looked almost blue. Next to them there was a metal cage, the naked, rubber-hooded occupant of which was on his knees and masturbating furiously, his fist working away on himself in a blur.

Isabella and David continued down the dark corridor and

stood at the entrance to the next chamber. In the middle of the room was another naked man, this time standing in a spread eagled position with his wrists manacled to a spreader bar hanging from chains attached to the ceiling and his ankles manacled to a wooden hobble bar. He was blindfolded and gagged and his scrotum as well as his nipples were clamped. He was being savagely whipped on the back and rear by a leather clad dominatrix with slicked-back dark hair. Her vicious treatment of the man had made him hugely erect and his cock kept spitting out silvery jets of precome.

Another nude man was kneeling over a whipping bench nearby while a second leather dominatrix whipped his backside savagely hard with a flogger similar to the one being wielded by her fellow domme. As each of her blows landed with a sharp retort, another red streak appeared on the man's punished flesh, joining the pattern of angry-looking lines already there. The dominatrix, a strikingly beautiful woman with short ash-blonde hair, turned at one point and gave Isabella a wave, which she returned. 'That's my friend, Mistress Kate, and her slave, Tony,' Isabella told David, *sotto voce*. 'You'd never guess it to look at her now but Kate used to be my slave. I trained her to be a dominatrix once it became clear that she was a switch.' Isabella then added cryptically, 'But enough of Kate. We need to continue with this tour until we reach our destination.'

She steered David back into the corridor and they approached the next cavernous chamber. They could hear groans of pleasure and heavy breathing and wet, sexual sounds coming from the room but they could see precious little because it was only very dimly lit. Their eyes gradually adjusted to the dark and they made out what was going on in the centre of the room. A woman was sucking a man's cock, while she knelt on her haunches with her pussy over the face of another man who was being sucked off by another kneeling woman who was in turn being fucked from behind.

There was still more to be seen as Isabella and David's eyes adjusted further to the dark. To the left of this human chain, a man was lying on his back and two women were sucking and masturbating him, and to the right a woman was being fucked doggie-style by one man while sucking off another man who was standing before her. What was going on in that chamber, it was evident, was nothing less than a full-blown orgy.

Isabella and David moved on to the next entrance. Straight ahead of them was a wall-mounted cross with a naked man strapped to it on his back and next to that was a horizontal torture chair with another naked man secured to it in a similar fashion. The two men were on their own, apparently deserted for the time being, and both sported throbbing hard-ons that leaked precome as they waited for their domme or dommes to return.

Isabella took David along the corridor to the next entrance. Virtually the whole of the chamber beyond was occupied by a huge circular bed. It was extremely dark here and they could hardly see anything at all, just the undulating outlines of various naked bodies sucking and fucking. Clearly another steamy orgy was in progress.

Isabella steered David out to the corridor again and they made their way to the last of the entrances. This presumably was their destination, David thought excitedly. They went into the chamber, which was better lit than the last one and held a smaller bed. Also the room was occupied by far less bodies than the one before – only three in fact, two of them female. A tall, darkly handsome man stood, buck naked, masturbating languorously as he watched the action on the bed. There, a shapely blonde in a leather g-string was vigorously licking the pussy of a beautiful young woman with big sparkling blue eyes who was also blonde and who had an equally well shaped figure. She was on her back, her legs wide apart, arching her upper body, her lovely face contorting as her pleasure mounted. 'Yeah, lover,' she was murmuring enthusiastically, holding onto the back of the other woman's neck. 'Oh yeah.'

The tall handsome man stopped masturbating and came over to Isabella and David. The man would have been somewhere in his mid 40s, David guessed. He had a tanned, muscular body, a saturnine appearance and deep-set eyes that were almost as dark as Isabella's. He also had a big cock, which remained proudly erect.

'Hello, Alan,' Isabella said.

'Hello, dear,' he said warmly. 'I take it this is your new slave, David,' he added, managing to say this without even looking at him. And you must be Alan Stern, David thought. We meet at last – even if you can't actually bring yourself to look at me.

'That's right,' Isabella said. 'This is David.'

Alan Stern still did not look at David, never mind make any kind of eye contact with him. Instead he looked over at the two young women, who were still making love. 'Stop what you are doing, slaves,' he called out sharply and they stopped straight away.

The young woman who had been so heavily engaged in licking her companion's pussy turned round to reveal two things: first, that she was wearing a strap-on dildo attached to her leather g-string, and secondly that she was the spitting image of the blue-eyed blonde she'd been making love to. They had to be twin sisters, David thought – incestuous twin sisters.

'You, Stephanie,' Alan Stern said, 'Come and pleasure Mistress Isabella.'

'Yes, Master,' replied the sister who had been being pleasured so voraciously only a moment ago.

'Eve,' the man went on.

'Yes, Master,' replied the sister who'd been doing all the voracious pleasuring, her lips still wet from her sister's love juice.

Alan Stern pointed at David. 'When I say the word I want you to fuck this slave in the arse with your strap-on.'

'Yes, Master,' Eve said, sitting up and reaching for a bottle of lubricant that was beside the bed. She applied a generous amount of it to the dildo jutting from her groin.

Stephanie got up and stood in front of Isabella, who leaned forward and kissed her passionately on the mouth and began stroking her breasts and pressing her body to hers. She then ran her hands through her blonde hair, stroked her shoulders and moved her hands down her back and onto her rear where she cupped her smooth curves. Stephanie responded by touching Isabella's pussy, gently at first but soon with increasingly insistent fingers. She then got on to her knees to lick and suck her, moving her tongue around Isabella's clitoris, sucking it constantly. Isabella opened her legs to let her tongue enter her sex more fully.

'David, get on to all fours on the bed with your head right near the edge,' Alan Stern ordered. 'Eve get up there behind him and fuck him in the arse.' David got on to his hands and knees as instructed and Eve positioned herself behind him. She began pushing herself against him, ready to enter his anus at any moment. He lifted his hips slightly in order to meet her imminent thrust.

At the mention of her sister's name Stephanie took her mouth away from between Isabella's thighs momentarily in order to glance over in the direction of her sibling. But Isabella was having none of it. She immediately tugged on Stephanie's hair roughly and brought her mouth back to her pussy where the girl began to dig in deeper with her tongue to compensate for her brief transgression.

That was when Eve pushed in. Her strap-on dildo found its mark and began to sink past David's anal entrance. She pushed with a sudden groan, and he was impaled on half the dildo. Then she began to sodomize him good and hard. And David tried not to think, tried to blank out his mind, as Eve plunged in and out of him, each time going deeper into his anus.

Soon she had her strap-on dildo really deep inside him and was thrusting against his buttocks, squeezing his hips with her hands. She was fucking him even harder now, his sphincter clamping and possessing with each of her powerful thrusts.

David's eyes clouded over as Eve continued to sodomize him, moving her strap-on in and out of his anus, harder, faster. Then his eyesight cleared, only to find that Alan Stern's big cock, all stiff and purple and twitching, had appeared before his face. *What the fuck!* David almost said it out loud.

'Suck him off, David,' Isabella called over, the crouching Stephanie licking ever more energetically between her thighs. 'Do it now, make him come down your throat. I want to see you make my husband climax with your mouth. Come on, give him a really good blow job.' And that's what David did, God help him. He opened his lips wide and took Alan Stern's hard cock into his mouth. In and out he drew his erection, sucking it down, the entire length swallowing into him. He tried not to think about what he was doing, just obediently got on with doing it as well as he could.

David kept blowing Alan vigorously, moving his cock in and out of his mouth, while at the same time Eve continued ploughing inside his anus with her strap-on dildo. He was shaking, his mouth working faster, stronger. He could feel Alan Stern's mounting excitement and he knew he was about to climax when the man suddenly dug his fingers into his hair. He clung to it, bracing himself, and suddenly he cried out. His orgasm exploded in a forceful and abundant stream that filled David's mouth. David made his tongue keep working over his cock, dragging and drawing every last drop of his jism out and down into his throat.

David stopped moving his head as he swallowed his last mouthful of come, the other man's spent cock still in his mouth. Eve stopped buggering him but left the dildo deep inside his orifice. Alan Stern waited, David waited, Eve waited. They all waited for Isabella to climax. Then they heard it, heard Isabella's cry mounting, escalating, becoming more ecstatic, and then drifting away in a moan. Alan Stern withdrew his cock from David's mouth then. Eve withdrew the dildo from his gaping anus at the same time and Stephanie removed her lips from Isabella's pussy. The three slaves had not climaxed. But the Master and the Mistress had. That was all that mattered.

'You didn't want to suck my husband off, did you?' Isabella said to David a little later as the pair of them walked away from the club into the dark night. Alan Stern and the twins had remained at the club to do ... who knew what.

'No, Mistress,' David said. 'I didn't want to suck your husband off.' He had never before had any kind of homosexual experience, not even in the spirit of experimentation. Now look what Isabella had made him do. He would have liked to have eradicated what had happened from his memory. But he knew he'd never be able to do that. He was now officially a cocksucker.

'Do you know what would have happened if you'd refused to suck him off?' Isabella asked.

'No, Mistress.'

'I'd have dumped you,' she said. 'As it is, you've just passed your first major test.'

My *first* major test, David said or rather thought. What about all the ordeals Isabella had put him through before tonight? Didn't they count for anything? What did they amount to – no more than a mere bagatelle? And, Christ Almighty, considering what she'd insisted on him doing tonight, what else did she have in mind for him in the future? He felt a sudden cold shiver run through him.

Chapter Fourteen

The fact that he'd been required to suck off the husband of the woman who was his Mistress while another woman performed cunnilingus on her couldn't help but get David wondering some more about Mr and Mrs Stern. Isabella had told David that, notwithstanding the fact that they were apart an awful lot of the time, she and her husband's highly unorthodox relationship was a strong one and that this was the case even though sexually both of them were extremely dominant and sadistic. But he wondered exactly what kind of relationship the couple did have, given that they were both evidently bisexual as well.

Did the pair of them have multiple partners of both sexes or were they highly selective? Was David actually one of many or should he feel honoured to be one of the chosen few? How much did Isabella and Alan Stern confide in one another? Had Isabella told her husband about all the outlandish things she'd done to David? Had he told her all the outlandish things he'd doubtless done to "the twins"?

Where were Isabella and Alan Stern now? Maybe they were with Stephanie and Eve. What were they doing with them? Were they having sex with the incestuous twins? Were they enjoying some kind of foursome with them, involving lashings, yes *lashings* of S&M? Did Isabella ever think about David when she was having sex with other people? He certainly thought about her when he was having sex with himself. He did nothing but think about her, keeping himself going until her next call with memories and fantasies and masturbation – constant masturbation.

There were gnawing doubts too, about his own relationship

with Isabella – if indeed you could call it that, he thought ruefully. Whatever it was that Isabella and he had was based solely on sex and sadomasochism – when she could be bothered to see him at all, that is. How could you call that a relationship in any meaningful sense of the word, especially as it was so one-sided? He worshiped Isabella but she certainly didn't love him, maybe didn't even like him. Possibly she actually hated him.

The thought, barbed as a fish hook, twisted in his mind as he contemplated it further. The more Isabella harmed him, the more pleasure she felt, that was certainly clear. She also delighted in keeping him hanging around waiting to hear from her because she knew all the waiting was agony for him. Maybe she wouldn't be satisfied until she'd slowly but surely destroyed him altogether.

Perhaps that was where all this was leading. Look what she'd done to him already, after all. And how had she done it anyway? How, for Christ's sake? He had a mind of his own – a damn good mind at that; he had free will. How had she reduced him to the person he now was, a compulsive onanist who was cut off from everyone else?

But, hang on a moment, David said to himself. It wasn't as if Isabella had ordered him to wank himself stupid all the time she wasn't there. She hadn't ordered him either to avoid other people like the plague while waiting for her to call. These were things he'd done to himself, when all was said and done.

They weren't the only things he'd done to himself either, were they, and over a much longer period of time too. That was what the voice inside his head decided to tell David all of a sudden. And that voice – that unbidden thought – was like an incendiary device, setting off a depth charge that caused something truly startling to come hurtling up from the very deepest recesses of his memory. It was something David had blanked out completely from his consciousness a very long time ago because it had been simply too awful to contemplate. Was that it? Was that the key to all this madness? Yes, it had to be …

Then the call came, not from Isabella this time but from

Matthew. 'We've not seen anything of each other since my dinner party,' he said. 'I'd really love to see you. How about coming over this evening? Caroline's away at a sales conference at the moment, so it would just be you and me.' And David said yes. Matthew's call couldn't have come at a more opportune time. He had to talk to his best friend about what it was that just that moment had emerged from the darkest depths of his subconscious. His mind was still reeling from the discovery, his pulse still racing. He *had* to tell Matthew about it. How much more he could confide in him, though, he still didn't know.

Matthew lived in Hove, a residential district that had not so many years ago been a separate town to Brighton, although the two places had always been very closely associated. Hove was quieter and more suburban than buzzy, cosmopolitan Brighton, but nonetheless they had always been joined at the hip.

It was a fine sunny evening, the sky crystal-clear, and David opened the window of his car a little to let in the warm, balmy air. He drove past the open, tree-lined recreation area of Hove Park, which still contained a fair smattering of people enjoying what remained of the day.

David drove into one of the most pleasant parts of Hove, a tranquil, hilly area of detached houses with in-and-out driveways and sizeable, nicely landscaped gardens. He arrived at Matthew's home, parked his car in the drive and walked towards the front door, which was opened before he'd even pressed the bell.

'Hello, stranger,' Matthew said amiably, his pale blue eyes shining. 'It's so good to see you.' Slim, tanned and handsome with shiny blond hair, he was looking relaxed in a crisp white T-shirt, loose-fitting jeans, espadrilles over bare feet.

'It's really good to see you too,' said David who was then ushered by Matthew through the hallway and into the large open-plan living room.

'First things first,' Matthew said. 'Would you like a drink?'

'Please.'

'Whisky on the rocks?'

'Great, thanks.'

Matthew mixed them both large whiskies in glass tumblers, adding ice cubes. He handed David one of the tumblers and they sat down together on the couch.

'What have you been up to since we last met?' Matthew said, taking a sip of his drink.

'You first,' David said, playing for time. He really didn't know what to say to his friend, still in two minds whether or not to confide in him about his enslavement to Isabella and all that went with it – particularly if Isabella herself didn't want him to, something about which he remained unclear. And then there was that other matter, the key to it all surely. He had to discuss that with Matthew some time this evening but, hell, there was no rush. He took a pull from his drink, ice cubes rattling.

'I'll do better than tell you what I've been up to. I'll show you,' Matthew said and, after putting his drink on a side table, he leant forward to open an expensive looking oak chest that was positioned close to the couch. To David's amazement he saw that it was full of various S&M artefacts. He could see a studded paddle, a bamboo cane, an assortment of whips, handcuffs, a muzzle, and several other restraints including a harness, some bondage rope and a couple of reels of bondage tape.

'Caroline doesn't just sell this stuff,' Matthew explained, giving David a crooked grin. 'She likes to use it. Boy, does she ever like to use it! She's a dominatrix in her private life for much of the time.'

He went on to tell David that Caroline, whenever the mood was upon her – and it ever more frequently was – liked nothing better than to make him submit to her sadistic desires. Matthew said that Caroline kept on pushing his limits further and further in the kinky games they played, and that he loved it. He'd found that he was a real pain-slut. 'Whenever I'm with her and she's in a sadistic mood I'm not the man you know, David,' he said. 'And I'm certainly not the man my business colleagues in the City *think* they know. What I am is Mistress Caroline's grovelling sex slave.'

'I see,' David said, giving his friend a small smile. 'How did all this start? What's the story?'

Matthew picked up his tumbler and tipped it side to side for a moment, watching the light play over the amber liquid. 'I'll tell you, David,' he replied.

Chapter Fifteen

'Looking back, I guess there was a degree of inevitability about what happened,' Matthew said, smiling reminiscently. 'I mean, when you've fallen head-over-heels in love with a horny redhead who happens to manage a fetish store you can be pretty sure of one thing: your sex-life is likely to get kinkier – and fast. And so it was with me.' He continued, 'we'd only been living together for about a week or two when Caroline introduced me to the pleasure of pain ...'

'You've got a seriously cute arse, Matthew,' Caroline announced out of the blue. She and he were naked and padding around the bedroom, getting ready for bed. 'I'd love to spank it.'

'What, right now?' Matthew replied with a chuckle – and more than a twinge of excitement.

'Why not,' Caroline replied, her green eyes doing a little dance. 'No time like the present. Come on,' she added, sitting on the edge of the four poster bed. 'Get over my knee.'

Matthew felt growing excitement at what was about to happen to him, his cock getting harder by the second. It was achingly erect by the time he positioned himself over Caroline's knee. He waited for the inevitable, his heart racing and his breathing quickening all the while. But Caroline took her own sweet time.

She stroked his muscular rear sensuously, tantalisingly, over and over again, teasing him unmercifully, and then: Smack! The sharp sound announced that the first spanking Matthew's backside was ever to receive had finally begun – and the vivid red mark on his rear evidenced the cruel accuracy of that first stroke.

Smack! Caroline's hand smacked down again crisply on Matthew's backside with another harsh spank and his breath quickened further. His breath came even quicker with the third spank and when she spanked him a fourth time, this time even harder, he let out a loud groan of pain.

But there were many more hard smacks to come, when their bedroom echoed with the sound of hand on naked flesh. Over and over Caroline spanked Matthew. She didn't let-up and indeed increased the frequency and harshness of her blows. There was no let-up either in Matthew's erection; it was as throbbingly hard as ever.

Matthew let out a wail as the full effect of the spanking spread through his body. He was in acute pain yet he could never remember being as sexually excited as this in all his life.

Having finally stopped spanking Matthew, Caroline ordered him to get on the bed and lie on his back. When he did, his huge erection reared in the air invitingly.

'I can't wait any longer,' Caroline said, her voice breathless. 'Let's fuck.'

She straddled Matthew's thighs and sank down onto him, his cock forced deep and high. It drew a moan from him, from her too. Caroline's pussy muscles flexed around Matthew's stiff cock, rocking him, her pussy tight and soaking wet. Matthew carried on moaning with Caroline's movements and ran his hands over her thighs and her breasts as she rose and fell on him.

She shuddered hard and cried out loudly, pushing her pussy against his groin as her orgasm rolled through her in mighty waves. Feeling and hearing Caroline come made Matthew want to come too, urgently. He started to thrust his hips upwards fast, plunging into the wetness of her pussy until the sensation was heavy, intense, unrestrained. He climaxed then convulsively, filling her sex with hot spurts of come as he gave himself to the surging sensations that had taken over his body.

Caroline and Matthew lay damp and spent in each other's arms for a long while after that, lacquered together in the silence that surrounded them. Matthew knew that what Caroline had done to him that night was not going to be a "one off". He wondered where it was going to lead. His backside still ached with pain. It felt great.

Chapter Sixteen

'That turned out to be just the beginning,' Matthew said. 'After that spanking and the wonderful sex that followed it Caroline really started going to town on me.' He gestured towards the open box crammed with disciplinary items. 'Since then my sadistic lover Caroline – my beloved *dominatrix* Caroline – has used everything in there on me at one time or another and in the process I've become a complete pain junkie.' Matthew picked up his tumbler and took a pull of whisky. 'And that, my good friend, is my story,' he said. 'Now it's your turn. I happen to know that you've been seeing Isabella Stern and her sexual interests aren't exactly a closed book.' He shot David a knowing grin.

'How do you know I've been seeing her?' David asked, looking surprised.

'Because she told Caroline,' Matthew replied.

So, he'd got it wrong, David thought in relief. Isabella hadn't been keeping their relationship a secret from Caroline and Matthew, as he'd suspected. She was clearly quite happy for them to know about it, and thank goodness for that. 'Come on,' Matthew added conspiratorially. 'Tell your old friend all about it. Spare me none of the sordid details!'

David wondered what exactly to say. How far should he go in his reply? How explicit should he be? Matthew had been completely honest and open with him about his relationship with Caroline. David told himself that he should be similarly candid with him – and that meant being *completely* candid. And, taking a large swig of his whisky to give himself some Dutch courage, he decided that completely candid with Matthew was what he would be. And he knew now that there was no question about it – he definitely could confide in his friend about the nature of his relationship with Isabella, particularly under the circumstances he himself had just outlined to David. Matthew was, surely, bound to be *simpatico*.

'Isabella Stern is my Mistress and I am her slave,' David said. 'I've been blindfolded and gagged and put into bondage by her. I've been beaten by her and I've been buggered with a strap-on dildo by her. I've been taken out in public by her with my nipples clamped and a huge butt plug shoved up my arse. I've been made to masturbate in front of her. I've been made to lick up and swallow my own come by her. I've been fisted by her, paraded around a fetish club in the nude by her. I've been ...' David paused. He was going to say, "made to suck off her husband by her" but he faltered, couldn't quite get the words out.

Matthew unwittingly came to the rescue. 'What a dark horse you are,' he said, giving David's arm a friendly nudge. 'I didn't know you were into BDSM at all, never mind to the extent you obviously are. You know you can trust me. You should have said something.'

'I could say the same thing to you,' David replied. 'I knew you were bisexual because you told me you were years ago of course, but I had no idea you were a submissive masochist, no idea at all.'

'Nor did I before Caroline and I became lovers and she started dominating me,' Matthew said. 'That's the God's honest truth.'

'Snap! I didn't understand that about myself either until I met Isabella,' David said. 'She brought something to the surface, something I've managed to keep buried for too damn long, so deeply buried in its secret hiding place in my mind that it's only extremely recently – I mean, like, *today*, would you believe – that I've been able to bring myself to acknowledge it at all.'

'Do you want to talk about it?' Matthew asked, giving his friend a look of concern.

David rattled the ice cubes in his drink hard. He swallowed the rest of his whisky in one gulp and put down the tumbler. 'I think I need to talk about it – badly,' he said and began his story. 'It all goes back to the death of one of my parents...'

Actually, Matthew was well aware that both of David's parents were dead although he had only known one of them. Matthew could remember David's father quite well: a likeable enough man, he supposed, as self absorbed workaholics go. He had also been a very heavy smoker, David now reminded him, and had paid a cruel price for his nicotine addiction, dying at 47 from lung cancer. That had been a tragically early death and David, who had been in his late 20s at the time, had been very distressed by it. But the death of his mother had been considerably more devastating to him given that he had only been very young when it had happened. That had been awful enough but what had made it even worse was that the relationship she'd had with him before her tragic and untimely death had been a particularly complex one.

'I was a very difficult youngster and she was a sadist ... maybe ... perhaps ... I don't know,' David said, stumbling over the words. He still couldn't quite bear to acknowledge what his mother had been. 'What I do know – what I now remember at long last – is that she used to beat me constantly "on the bare", as they used to say, in order to try to get me to behave, but that it only made me worse because I found I liked being beaten; it made me feel all ... tingly. So I would go out of my way to misbehave again, so that she'd beat me again. I remember now, too, exactly how I used to feel, waiting to be beaten by her: all warm and expectant and deliciously shivery. And then there'd be the sensation of her open palm exploding painfully again and again against my bare bottom and afterwards that tingling afterglow. Then there'd be the next incident of bad behaviour on my part, the next beating on the bare bottom from her, and so we both went on. It was like a game we'd play. Then she went and ruined everything. She died.'

'How did she die?' Matthew asked, looking intently at him. 'Do you mind me asking?'

'It was a stupid accident,' David said, a gleam of moisture in his eye. 'She was in hospital for a routine operation – really minor, you wouldn't believe – but there was some screw up with the anaesthetic. She never came round. She was so young, barely 30.'

David explained that immediately afterwards and obviously deeply traumatised by the event, he'd got it into his young head that somehow his mother's death had been all his fault, that if he hadn't been so badly behaved she wouldn't have died. He resolved after that to always be a "good boy", to live his life as his mother would have wanted him to. Therefore all through the rest of his time at school and at Sixth Form College and university David had done exactly what he thought his mother would have wanted from him, excelling in his studies and on the playing field, and always behaving impeccably.

He wasn't being himself though, this young paragon of virtue. What he was doing instead was impersonating the person he thought his mother had wanted him to be. David got exceptionally good exam results at secondary school where he also met a certain Matthew King who became his closest friend. David went on from sixth form to attend one of the best universities in the country at which he studied technology, and he obtained a first class honours degree in the subject. And there were girlfriends, lots and lots of girlfriends; because David discovered that he had an extraordinarily powerful sex drive. But he always had the most conventional – and short lived – of relationships with these girls. Anyway, no mere girlfriend could hold a candle to his dear departed mother.

David went on from university to pursue a highly successful career in Information Technology, leading a few years down the line to the formation of his own company. This led in turn a few more years down the line, and with the assistance of Matthew's timely intervention, to the sale of that company to a hot shot financier for millions of pounds. What a success story! What a "good boy"!

It was only after meeting Isabella Stern and falling so thoroughly under her spell that David had started to realise that there was something unresolved at the very core of his being. Now, at last, after the startling epiphany he'd experienced earlier that day, he knew what it was that had been lodged so deep in some recess of his memory that he'd had no idea it was there at all. He'd buried it as deep as could be, tucked away in some small place in that young boy's mind. But he remembered it now, felt it tear in his soul. David knew exactly what it was that, as the ultimate coping mechanism, his subconscious mind had blocked out of his memory completely ever since the trauma of his mother's death, blocked it out because it was simply too painful to acknowledge.

'OK, I'll say it right out,' David said, taking a deep breath. 'My mother was sadistic towards me ... and I loved it. I showed my sadistic mother how much I loved her by misbehaving all the time. That way I created situations where she could beat me and at the same time show me how much she loved me. Now I am giving myself to a woman who expresses her feelings for me by beating the shit out of me and otherwise mistreating me – and I love that too, fucking love it.

'At its root it's Oedipal, I can't deny it, but it's made me feel like the real me for the first time since my mother died. When I first submitted myself to Isabella's sadistic will I was convinced she'd somehow turned me into another person by the power of her mind. I was wrong, so very wrong. What she'd done was to release the person I really am. I see that now. Because of her I'm no longer living a lie.'

David stopped speaking and there was a long silence. Finally Matthew spoke. 'You know what, David,' he said, grabbing the whisky bottle. 'I think we could both do with another drink.'

'Just a small one for me this time,' David said. 'I'm driving, don't forget.'

'Still being a good boy?' Matthew said, with an ironic lift of the eyebrow.

'Not at all,' David smiled. 'I'm a bad boy who needs to be punished ... severely.'

Chapter Seventeen

Knowledge is power, they say. Not in David's case it wasn't. He may have been clear now about the root cause both of his masochism and of his dependence on Isabella. But it gave him no sense of empowerment, only a greater sense of powerlessness. What David felt most acutely as he went back to staring at his phone, waiting desperately for Isabella to call, was fear. He was afraid, terrified of losing her.

David was afraid that he wasn't a "bad boy" at all, not to his Mistress. He jumped to attention in response to every one of her orders, after all. He never resisted her in any way, not one iota. What if she wanted him to put up a bit of resistance sometimes? What if she found the wholeheartedness of his submission to her tedious, no sort of a challenge to her? But then again, she'd told him quite clearly that if he'd refused to suck off her husband that she'd have dumped him. No, David concluded, his safest bet if he didn't want to lose Isabella was to keep doing exactly what she told him to do, no matter how unpalatable to him that might sometimes be.

But he couldn't do as Isabella told him until she actually got in contact with him again, and he wondered when on earth that was going to be. God, how he yearned to hear from her, to see her, to have her near to him. His body ached for the lash of her whip, for the feel of her hand on his cock, for … The phone rang and Isabella's caller ID flashed up. David's heart was already racing as he pressed the button to take the call. 'I want you to come over to my place tonight,' Isabella said. 'I'll phone again when I'm ready for you.'

David glanced at the clock on the wall. It was just past 6 p.m. He waited for Isabella to call again, his heart still beating hard. As the time passed – one hour, two hours, three hours – David felt more and more on edge, more and more agitated. His nerves were as taut as violin strings and there was a knot of tension in his stomach that refused to unclench. Isabella didn't call until 10 p.m. 'Come straight over,' she told him.

Some 15 minutes later David parked his car in her quiet, affluent street. He was feeling intensely excited but agitated still too – incredibly keyed up, he couldn't really understand it. Isabella let him into her house, taking his hand in hers. She squeezed his fingers with apparent affection although the greeting she gave him was neutrally pitched. It gave away no more than did her cool unflinching gaze.

Isabella was barefoot and wearing a long kimono, which was patterned black and red. Underneath this shimmering silken garment she was obviously nude. David admired the sway and jiggle of her unbound breasts and the lazy sway of her hips as she sashayed down the hall with him. His heart began to beat harder still, pounding through his shirt.

'Strip naked and kneel before your Mistress,' Isabella said when they had entered her living room. David held his breath as he stripped off and then knelt at her feet as she had instructed, his cock already hard.

'Good slave,' Isabella said and began to stroke his hair. It was another display of what looked suspiciously like affection from her and it filled David with delight. What a joy it was to have his Mistress all to himself, he thought.

Which was when a door at the end of the room opened and in walked the blonde twins, Eve and Stephanie. They were hand in hand and as nude as David was. He looked enquiringly at Isabella, whose only response was to let her kimono fall to the ground. Now all four of them were as naked as nature intended. David could feel his cock getting even harder. He would have preferred to have had Isabella all to himself, that was for sure, but he was also enjoying the way things were starting to unfold. His enjoyment was very short lived.

'Kneel where you are, slave,' Isabella told him, her voice sharp, and that's what he did. David felt the green monster of jealousy creep up on him all too quickly as he watched what happened next. First, Isabella wrapped her arms around Stephanie's shoulders and the two women kissed with great passion, their tongues engaging wetly. Isabella had never once kissed David and yet this was the second time he'd witnessed her kissing Stephanie, witnessed her gorging herself on her mouth.

As the two women continued to lose themselves in that wet passionate kiss, Eve got on to her knees behind Isabella. She then prised open the domme's shapely buttocks and pressed her lips to her anus, her taut red tongue flicking in and out. Eve used her tongue to lick its magic over Isabella's anal hole until she squirmed in delight. And all the while David carried on doing as he'd been told, just kneeling there like a spare part – and wishing against wish that it was him and not Eve licking his Mistress's anus so assiduously.

Did Isabella have any idea how much it hurt him to watch her making love to these two women, he wondered despairingly. David knew – of course he did – that he had nothing remotely approaching an exclusive claim on his Mistress. But now, suddenly, he felt this desperate need to be on his own with her. All David wanted was for Isabella to get rid of these two interlopers so that he and she could be alone together, so that she could kiss him and not Stephanie, so that he not Eve could lick deep into her anal hole, so that he could make her come like that with his lips and his probing tongue.

And Isabella could, needless to say, do anything she wanted to do to him. She could fuck him in the arse with her strap-on dildo or fist him with her latex-covered hand. She could beat him harder than she'd ever done before, beat him to kingdom come. She could do anything in the world to him she wanted to, just as long as the two of them could be alone together, just as long as the desire she displayed was for him and him alone.

But Isabella didn't even look his way. It was as if he was a stranger to her; no, less to her even than that, it was as if he wasn't there at all. He was an invisible witness, a helpless onlooker as his privileged position with Isabella was usurped by two horny blonde sisters. The sense of rejection was more excruciating now; it was cutting right into him like a knife.

David was overwhelmed by feelings of jealousy at what Isabella was doing with such fulsome passion with these two deeply perverted young women.

David wished – oh how he wished – that Isabella would kick the twins out, or if she wouldn't do this, that she would at least throw a crumb of comfort his way. It wouldn't take much, just a bit of contact, just one little touch, anything to give him back something of his old status, make him feel he was important to her again.

Isabella stopped kissing Stephanie. 'I suppose you want a beating, slave,' she said, finally looking over at David.

'Yes, Mistress,' he replied and his heart lifted, but only momentarily. It sank like a stone at what she had to say next.

'Eve, do the honours, will you,' Isabella said, looking over her shoulder at the arsehole-licking blonde. 'You'll find a whip in the top drawer of the bureau.'

'Yes, Mistress,' Eve replied as she got up from her knees.

'I want your sister to eat my pussy now,' Isabella said, settling down onto the couch with Stephanie. 'She does it so well. And I'm going to lick her pussy too.' She guided Stephanie's mouth to her sex and then swivelled so that her own lips were fastened to the blonde girl's sex. The two of them began to lap at each other's pussies, at first gently and then lustily, drinking from one another.

David got on to all fours and awaited his beating, with blackness in his heart. Isabella had delegated his discipline to one of the twins, the same one who last time had fucked him in the arse; it was so ignominious for him.

And Eve was a vicious bitch, too – a vicious switch and a vicious bitch. David felt the whip she was wielding strike his backside for the first time and it stung like crazy, as it did also the second and third and fourth times. Each time the leather thongs of the whip penetrated his skin they left yet another collection of vivid red marks in their wake, but not the slightest sensation of erotic pleasure, which couldn't help but bug him.

There was another thing that bugged him too: Every time that whip landed, Isabella and Stephanie seemed to move in time to it as if the music of the leather strands lacerating

David's backside so viciously was giving a rhythm to their lovemaking, increasing their mutual desire. And, in the process, it was killing any desire David might have had. The beating Eve was giving him hurt, it hurt one hell of a lot. But it was pure pain, not pleasure-pain. It was doing him no good at all.

Eve's blows succeeded one another with increasing savagery, making David cry out, making him scream for mercy in the end because the pain was so unbearable. 'Stop now, Eve,' Isabella demanded, pulling her love juice-smeared lips away from Stephanie's pussy. 'Come and join me and your sister. Let's have some girl on girl *on girl* action.'

'Yes, Mistress,' Eve replied lasciviously. She put the whip back in the bureau drawer and moved towards the two other women.

'David,' Isabella then called out, gazing at him and through him with a look of almost complete indifference.

'Yes, Mistress,' he said. There was a tremor in his voice

'Get dressed and fuck off.'

And that's what David did. He did exactly what he'd been told to do by his Mistress, as he always did. Isabella didn't even look at him when he went to leave; she only had eyes – and fingers and lips – for the incestuous blonde twins. On his way out of the room David mumbled a disconsolate 'Goodnight, Mistress', which was also ignored.

Leaving Isabella's house, he walked down the dark street to where he'd parked his car. His shoulders were slumped. He felt desolate, felt black despair penetrating him, overpowering him, spreading through his body and working its way inside his soul. He felt like an abandoned child, his neglectful mother cruelly unconcerned about his fate. Why had Isabella decided to treat him like this? Why?

David sat in his car but did not start the engine. He felt his face crumple inwards and his breath became broken and jagged. His eyes were suddenly blinded by hot tears that started to roll down his cheeks as he began to sob. The tears ran down his neck now too and reached the collar of his shirt, as he sobbed and sobbed. His body shook with the force of the sobs.

The emotion he was experiencing was intense, extreme, and disproportionate.

He realised that he was not crying about what had happened to him tonight, about the way that Isabella had treated him, which was, let's face it, only par for the course for such an exceptionally cruel Mistress. No, he was crying about something else entirely. He was crying about something, *someone* he'd lost a very long time ago.

Chapter Eighteen

David didn't sleep a wink that night and spent much of it in tears, a whole reservoir of grief and loss overflowing. Right at the break of day, when the dawn light had dimmed all but the brightest stars, he walked down to Brighton beach to try and pull himself together. He was jittery from lack of sleep and his eyes were swollen from crying. There was nobody about at that early hour and the air was cool and clean. David wandered along the promenade at the edge of the pebbled shore, watching the rhythmical coming and going of the waves. And he gave himself a really serious talking to.

Now that he had unlocked from deep within himself the secret of Isabella's powerful hold over him, did he want to continue being her docile slave, her fucking doormat? Did he want to keep meeting her ever more sadistic tests and challenges? I mean, did he *really* want to live such a thoroughly perverted, degraded kind of life? You bet your sweet life he did! Isabella was the very embodiment of sadism and sexual deviancy and she meant the world to him for precisely those reasons. That being the case, David told himself decisively, he must never again allow himself to become jealous when she had other sexual partners or to become resentful of her exceptionally cruel treatment of him. He couldn't have it both ways, now could he.

David stood on the empty promenade, still staring at the water. He gazed at the waves, which crested as they moved towards the shore before pounding down. They sent trails of white foam up the beach, and then pulled back, turning the stones with them. A few solitary gulls swooped into the sea for fish and a row of moored boats bobbed up and down on the swell. David turned away from the shore and walked back towards his home, back to his Isabella-obsessed life, which was the only life he wanted.

Isabella phoned a couple of weeks later. Fantastic, wonderful, marvellous, David thought; he'd be seeing her again. Wrong. 'I'm handing you over to Mistress Caroline for a night or two,' she said. 'Be at her and Matthew's house at eight o' clock tonight. And, David ...'
'Yes, Mistress.'
'I've told Caroline you're a cocksucker.'
And Caroline will have been bound to have told Matthew, David said to himself, which was more than he had been able to bring himself to do when he'd had the opportunity. He regretted that now because he'd promised himself that he'd be completely candid with his friend that last time they'd met and he hadn't quite made it, had fallen at the last hurdle. It would have been a good thing to have got out of the way between them. Under the circumstances this latest challenge Isabella had dreamt up for him was going to be ... ehm ... interesting.

When David arrived at Caroline and Matthew's place that evening he was dressed all in black – leather jacket, snug-fitting T-shirt, and even snugger fitting leather jeans with which he wasn't wearing any underwear. Matthew opened the front door a fraction, stood back to let David into the hallway, and shut the door. He smiled knowingly at David who smiled back, the air suddenly crackling between them like electricity. Matthew was wearing nothing but a see-through black mesh top and tight black leather shorts which, David noted when he turned to usher him through to the living room, were backless.

His friend's naked buttocks looked good to David – they looked more than good. They had a harmonious shape, curving gracefully from the small of his back. A tight feeling spread down to David's crotch and his cock began to pulse beneath his tight leather jeans. He'd never thought he'd see the day that he was sexually attracted to another man, least of all to his old friend. But never say never: that day had come. He felt another

102

jolt of desire, a twitching of his cock inside his leather jeans. He could imagine masturbating Matthew, could see himself sucking his cock while caressing his muscular backside. Where were these thoughts coming from? Where were they taking him? His cock twitched again, pushing against the tightness of his jeans.

Matthew showed David into the living room where Caroline was seated in a black leather armchair. What an extraordinarily beautiful woman she was, David thought. She had a porcelain-perfect complexion, glittering emerald green eyes that were lit from the inside and full sensuous lips. Her shoulder length red hair had a glossy sheen and she had a wonderfully well-shaped body, which was minimally dressed on this occasion. What few clothes she was wearing – a halter top that barely contained her full breasts and a tiny skirt – were of soft black leather. The oak chest full of BDSM items was open before her.

'Hello there, David,' Caroline said in friendly greeting. 'Nice to see you again.'

'You too, Mistress,' David said. 'You look really lovely in that outfit, if you don't mind me saying so.'

'Why, thank you,' she replied, turning the full force of her smile on him. She ran a hand through her silky mane of hair as she added, 'You're looking pretty darned attractive yourself come to that, but you're wearing way too much for my purposes this evening. Matthew, take him into the next room. I want the pair of you to strip naked there and then return to me.'

Once in the other room Matthew and David removed their clothes and their cocks instantly became rock-hard. 'Mistress is right,' Matthew said, giving his friend a hot look. 'You're looking very attractive.'

'Thanks Matthew,' David replied. 'So are you.' He was aware of electricity in the air between them again: crackling, shimmering, vibrating.

Matthew then pulled David into him, causing a sharp tremor in his hard cock, in Matthew's too. Both men's shafts were now pulsing. Matthew put a hand down and gripped it round David's erection; he began slowly pulling it up and down. David found himself doing the same to Matthew, taking hold of his shaft with a firm grip, and the two men masturbated one another excitedly. Before getting too carried away, though, they remembered what Caroline had said to them and stopped as quickly as they'd started.

When the two men returned to the living room, Caroline narrowed her eyes suspiciously and remarked on their throbbing, precome-coated hard-ons. 'I strongly suspect that you two have been playing with each other's cocks without first obtaining my permission,' she said sternly. 'That is clearly grounds for punishment. Stand side by side, turn round and reach towards your toes.'

Caroline started as she obviously meant to go on, spanking the two friends relentlessly – spank, spank, spank, spank, spank – each of her blows landing explosively on their rears in swift succession. She did not stop until both their backsides had coloured a deep and painful red.

The dominatrix then demanded that they kneel down and face one another and that David kiss Matthew's right hand. 'That's right, slave,' she said, 'lick and suck his fingers – make believe you're sucking his cock.' And that's what David did. He was a cocksucker, after all. Isabella had *made* him a cocksucker. But this thought occurred to him: perhaps he'd always been a cocksucker, deep down, just like he'd always been a submissive masochist without ever realising it.

Matthew had quite probably always lusted after him, David guessed, although up to this evening he'd certainly never indicated as much. But David realised, thinking back, that there had always been an element of the homoerotic on his own part in his friendship with Matthew. The trouble was that previously his own buttoned-up persona had prevented him from contemplating such a thing for even a second.

Well, he was liberated from all that bullshit now. He was the real David Alexander at last: bisexual when it came right down to it, as well as being profoundly submissive and masochistic. That was what he was, who he was. And that was that. He carried on sucking Matthew's fingers, imagining that he was sucking his cock, hoping that he would soon *be* sucking his cock.

'I want to move on to some serious discipline now,' said Caroline impatiently. 'After all, I wouldn't want to disappoint Mistress Isabella by not thoroughly punishing her slave this evening. And what's good for one slave is, of course, good for two.'

Caroline got the two men to kneel besides each other on all fours, and then extracted from the oak chest two white candles, which she lit. David and Matthew whimpered as she poured the molten wax from the candles onto their backs and rears – drip, drip, drip, drip, drip – and soon the two of them began to tremble, their bodies twitching and writhing in pain.

Caroline blew out the candles, put them to one side, and withdrew a heavy leather flogger from the oak chest. She used it to whip their backsides – whip, whip, whip, whip, whip – beating them without mercy until they were both finding it almost too agonizing to bear. Then she stopped.

She got them to kneel upright as she delved back in the oak chest, this time taking from it a box full of black pegs, a rattan cane and a cat o' nine tails. Caroline attached a peg to each of David's nipples and six more to his scrotum and did the same to Matthew. This caused both men to shudder and shake with pain.

'Get on to your hands and knees again,' she told the two men, going on to take the rattan cane to their backsides. She caned them so hard – swish, swish, swish, swish, swish – that in the end they had to beg for mercy, both of them sobbing with agony.

Caroline ceased caning them, got them to kneel upright again and removed the pegs from their bodies. 'Remain on your knees and turn to face one another,' she commanded of the two tearful slaves. 'Now, David, I want you to wank Matthew.' David did as he was told, did it gladly. He enclosed his friend's shaft in his fingers and began to stroke it, working up a steady rhythm.

'Lean forward and suck Matthew's cock,' Caroline then instructed and that's what David did. He closed his lips around Matthew's shaft and started to blow him. His friend's cock felt meaty and tasted tangy in his mouth. It tasted very good and so did the precome that was leaking constantly from its tip.

As David luxuriated in sucking Matthew's cock Caroline picked up the heavy leather flogger again and beat her slave hard on the backside with it – whip, whip, whip, whip, whip – chanting all the while, 'cocksucker, cocksucker, cocksucker ...'

'I want you to change positions now,' Caroline said after a while. 'You're to lie on your back, David, and Matthew is to kneel at your side and suck your cock.' She used the cat o' nine tails to lash Matthew's back and rear – lash, lash, lash, lash, lash – while he blew David for all he was worth. She resumed her chant, 'cocksucker, cocksucker, cocksucker ...'

Caroline got completely naked next, removing her miniscule leather outfit. She then straddled David's face. 'Use your tongue and fingers on my pussy,' she told him and he obeyed, snaking out his tongue and pushing it between the lips of her sex as he used his fingers to stroke her clitoris.

After a while Caroline climbed off David's face and moved away from him and the kneeling Matthew to forage in the oak chest once more where this time she selected a double dildo strap-on and a bottle of lubricant. The naked dominatrix lubricated both dildos and first inserted the internal one into the wetness of her sex, letting out a lustful groan of pleasure as she did so. Then she buckled up the leather harness of the strap-on so that she now effectively had her own hard cock.

She ordered David to remain flat on his back and Matthew to change his position so that they were sixty-nineing one another. 'You are not permitted to come under any circumstances unless and until I give you permission,' she told them.

Caroline eased the dildo into Matthew's anus. David heard him grunt with pain and at the same time felt his cock become even harder and pulse as he squirted a throb of precome into his mouth. Caroline used the strap-on to fuck Matthew hard – thrust, thrust, thrust, thrust, thrust. She did this in time with her chant, which had moved into the plural, 'cocksuckers, cocksuckers, cocksuckers ...'

She speeded up her thrusts still more and with each push of

her hips she penetrated Matthew further. The harder she fucked him – furiously entering and re-entering his anus with her strap-on as she continued her cocksucking chant – the more violently this made the two men suck each other's cocks and it was only with great difficulty that they managed to hold themselves off from climaxing.

Finally Caroline, moaning and shivering with lust, built to a frenzied orgasm. While in the throws of her climax she managed to gasp out that Matthew and David were now allowed to come. At long last the two best friends – the two *cocksucking* best friends – enjoyed their shuddering release, spilling their seed in spasm after spasm into one another's waiting throats.

Eventually Caroline and the two slaves disengaged their bodies. 'Get dressed and go home now, David,' Caroline ordered, staring coolly at him. 'I'd like you to return tomorrow evening when I shall dominate you and Matthew again.'

Chapter Nineteen

Fast forward a day. Caroline stood at the window tightening the curtain. She was wearing a choker, a miniscule bra that left her gorgeous breasts entirely exposed, merely framing them; a tiny slit-sided skirt, beneath which she was naked, and very high-heeled boots.

Caroline turned away from the curtained window and looked at Matthew and David. Matthew was standing near the middle of the room with his arms hanging loosely by his side and his blond head bowed submissively. He was nude but for several black leather items: a slave's collar, wrist and ankle cuffs and a tight cock restrainer that held his erect shaft upright. There was a chest of drawers next to him on top of which there was a leather whip and a red fibreglass cane. David was kneeling with his back to the wall. He was completely naked and had a sizeable erection.

'Be a voyeur for a while, David,' Caroline said as she strode towards Matthew with measured steps, the high heels of her boots decisive on the oak floor. Her exposed breasts jiggled, her nipples as hard as bullets, and her hips swayed seductively as she moved.

Caroline told Matthew to bend over and reach towards his toes. He obeyed immediately, his backside raised high, its muscular cheeks offered for punishment. Caroline went on to pick up the leather whip and beat his rear with it, every stroke planting a line of fire on his flesh. Matthew responded to each harsh strike with a gasp of breath that was both pain and pleasure. A red heat seemed to be burning into his skin, sinking deeper and deeper. Matthew pressed his chin into his neck, trying to ride out the pain of the beating as best he could.

Caroline then put the whip back on top of the chest of drawers and picked up the red fibreglass cane instead, giving the savage implement a couple of practice swipes. Matthew readied himself for what he was about to receive, tensing his body and gritting his teeth. The sharp stinging pain swept through him as Caroline brought the cane down. He barely had time to catch his breath before her second strike landed. Again, the razor sharp pain swept through him as the fibreglass cane landed on his rear. He could feel the heat burning on the cheeks of his backside, the skin raised and imprinted with the pattern of the cane.

On and on Caroline berated Matthew's rear with the vicious fibreglass cane, her arm flashing up and down. Matthew closed his eyes, feeling that he was unable to endure the severity of his punishment any longer. But he had to, because still she went on. His backside ached, the smarting pain of each impact merging with the ones that had preceded it and seeping through his body.

David, kneeling with his back to the wall, watched wide-eyed what Caroline was doing to Matthew and it was making him grow more and more sexually aroused. His breathing became short and shallow and his cock even more rigidly erect. Be a voyeur for a while, that was what Caroline had said to him. It would be his turn to be disciplined like this soon, he thought excitedly. It would be his turn soon.

Caroline eventually stopped beating Matthew, replacing the fibreglass cane on the top of the chest of drawers, and instructed the much relieved slave to turn round. After that she removed his penis restrainer and when she did his hard cock stiffened still more.

Caroline then said, 'Now, Matthew, for something you tell me you've been fantasising about for years but never thought would actually ever happen. I want you to start by lubing up your cock.' She opened the top drawer of the chest on which the heavily used whip and fibreglass cane had been replaced and took out a tube of lubricant, which she handed to him. Matthew unscrewed the tube before coating his shaft with a liberal amount of its contents. He then screwed the top of the tube back on.

'David,' Caroline called out to the kneeling slave, looking not at his handsome face but at his huge throbbing erection.

'Yes, Mistress,' he replied, his voice hoarse.

'Crawl over here,' she ordered and he did so immediately. 'Now arch your back and spread your legs.'

'Yes, Mistress,' David replied. By now he was almost certain what was coming next – and it wasn't what he'd been expecting at all. Yet somewhat to his surprise his erection remained throbbingly hard. He wanted what was coming next, that was the truth of the matter – if what he was now assuming was correct, that is.

It was. 'Matthew,' Caroline ordered, 'I want you to fuck David in the arse.'

'Yes, Mistress,' Matthew replied excitedly, positioning himself behind David. He still had the tube of lubricant in his hand.

'David,' Caroline went on, 'prepare yourself to be sodomized by your best friend.' David reached behind him and parted the cheeks of his backside with his fingertips, exposing the pink opening of his anus.

Matthew unscrewed the top of the tube of lubricant again and dribbled a cold stream of lube into David's anal hole. He opened him up with his fingers in preparation for his buggering.

And David, he had to admit to himself, could hardly wait. The thought of it was making his head swim and his heart race. He could hear his breath coming in shallow gasps and could feel his cock stiffen even further. It was pulsing with even more insistence as Matthew probed his anal channel with his fingers.

Matthew eased his erection into David's anal hole. In response David pushed up against him, his fingers still parting his cheeks wide. Then he let out a strangled moan of pleasure as his anus clenched rhythmically around Matthew's shaft, tightening and relaxing its muscles to accommodate it. Matthew's hard cock was stretching him now, filling him. And it was ecstatically pleasurable. David's sphincter constricted suddenly and he felt a pulsing throb deep in his anus. He put his hands back onto the floor before him, the sinews standing out in his arms.

'Wank him too, Matthew,' Caroline ordered.

'Yes, Mistress,' Matthew gasped as he reached under David. He started to squeeze his erection, his fingers curled around its base, while pushing again with his cock into his body.

Matthew then began to pump hard in and out of David's anal channel. Over and over he drove his thick cock into him, his shaft filling him as he rocked his hips up to meet his thrusts. And all the while Matthew was masturbating David hard too, just as instructed, his hand moving in swift urgent rhythm over his stiff pulsing cock until it was dripping constantly with precome.

'Come for me now, slaves,' Caroline then ordered.

And they obeyed. Matthew, his breath coming faster and louder, climaxed in huge spasms, spraying streams of sticky wetness deep into David's rear as he too erupted into orgasm, spilling his creamy load onto the oak floor beneath him.

Caroline waited several beats and then said, 'How was that for you, David?'

He looked up at her with shining eyes. 'Amazing, Mistress,' he replied.

'It was Isabella's idea,' Caroline smirked.

'I see, Mistress.' It figured.

Chapter Twenty

It was back to playing the waiting game for David. He'd allowed himself to be sodomized by Matthew, something which might have been expected to prey on his mind to some degree. But it didn't, not a bit. *Isabella* preyed on David's mind and only Isabella as he waited obsessively for her to call him. She continued to occupy his every thought, to affect his every breath. One, two weeks went by; no call. All David thought about was Isabella. He belonged to her, that was the only thing that mattered. She was his Mistress and he was her slave. Three, four weeks went by; no call from her. He wished Isabella would hurry up and call, wished desperately that she would. Five, six weeks went by; still no call.

Then an alarming thought occurred to David. Why had Isabella handed him over to Caroline? Had she been sending him a subtle message by doing that, one that he'd been painfully slow to recognise? Had it been her way of telling him it was over between them, that she'd lost interest in him; her way of saying she'd moved on and that he should do likewise? Was that it? Was it all over between them after everything she'd put him through, he asked himself, spiralling further down into despair. After all the waiting around, all the hoping and dreaming, was it all over? Oh God, was it? Was it?

No it wasn't. She phoned. 'Do you know where the head office of *La Fetishista* is?' Isabella asked.

'Yes, Mistress,' he replied. It was in a side road off Russell Square near the seafront.

'Be there in one hour – exactly on the hour,' she ordered. 'My PA, Sandra, will meet you at our reception area and will bring you up to my office. I've told her that you are a potential investor in the company. Make sure you maintain that fiction when you meet her.' And the call was ended.

David parked his car in the NCP underground car park at Russell Square and, emerging from its main exit, glanced in the direction of the seafront. It was a fine day, sunny and bright, and the usually murky English Channel was giving a fair approximation to Mediterranean blue.

He checked his watch and walked the short distance to the head office of *La Fetishista*. After lingering outside the entrance to the building for a few minutes until it was exactly on the hour, he went straight to the reception area. There he was met by Isabella's PA, Sandra, with briskly businesslike amiability. Sandra was young, blonde and pretty in an understated way and had a tidy, efficient air about her. She looked bright and astute and David wondered how much she knew of her employer's private life. He concluded that she would be aware of everything that was in the public domain – which was pretty general when all was said and done – and anything else Isabella may have chosen to share with her. And what did that tell him? Next to nothing, he decided.

Sandra brought David up in the lift to Isabella's outer office and invited him to take a seat. She then sat down behind her desk, buzzed and spoke into an intercom to let Isabella know her visitor had arrived. As he waited for her to make an appearance, David could feel his heart beating faster with anticipation. He hadn't heard from Isabella in six weeks, hadn't seen her for longer than that – two months.

When Isabella emerged from her elegantly appointed office David held his breath. She was wearing an appropriately severe tailored suit of dark grey and high heeled black leather shoes – and she was all business. 'Hello, Mister Alexander. Good to see you,' she smiled, holding out her hand to him formally. 'I'm afraid our meeting will have to be fairly brief as I need to go off to an appointment at the bank in about 30 minutes.'

David played his part. 'Not a problem, that's perfectly fine,' he replied, pretending that it was. Two months he'd waited to see Isabella, two whole months, and she was only prepared to give him half an hour of her precious time. Still, beggars can't be choosers, he told himself, trying to be philosophical about the situation.

Before taking David into her office Isabella turned to Sandra. 'I don't want any interruptions during my meeting with Mister Alexander,' she said briskly.

'Understood,' Sandra replied, echoing her employer's brisk tone.

Once they'd entered Isabella's office she took a few steps back and looked at David. As always with Isabella it wasn't just the coldness and blackness of her eyes, it was their steady, piercing scrutiny that was so unsettling to David. 'Pleased to see me, slave?' she asked.

'More than words can say, Mistress,' he replied with feeling. His whole body, his whole *being* felt tense with wanting her. 'I've been dreaming about this moment for weeks and weeks'.

'I'm sure you have,' Isabella said, walking to the office's big picture window as she spoke. A silence hung in the air between them as she lowered the Venetian blinds and then adjusted them so that the office was obscured from outside. Isabella stood silently in the half-light for a moment and then spoke again. 'Strip naked and be quick about it,' she said. 'We don't have much time, as you're aware.'

Isabella came back to where she'd been standing before she'd adjusted the blind. Her eyes lingered on David as he hastily took off his jacket and unbuttoned and removed his shirt. The rest of his clothing swiftly followed and he stood before her, naked and erect.

What next, he wondered excitedly and very soon had his answer when Isabella suddenly grabbed him by the hair and pulled him down on to his knees. 'So, you're pleased to see me, are you, slave,' she said. 'Show me how pleased you are by bowing at my feet.'

'Yes, Mistress,' David replied softly. He remained where he was on the carpet and pressed his forehead to the ground in front of her feet.

'Now lick my shoes,' Isabella demanded crisply. David

lifted his head a little and pressed his lips against the pointed toe of the shoe that she presented to him. He slid his tongue along the smooth leather, his lips caressing the sensuous feel of it, lingering over the instep and then up the sharp heel. She presented her other foot to him and he repeated the process. He could feel his erection throbbing.

Isabella then told David to get up from his knees and stand before her again. 'Join your wrists behind your back,' she commanded.

'Yes, Mistress,' David replied and when he had done this Isabella brought her right hand to his pulsing erection. He uttered a low groan of pleasure as she began to masturbate him, pushing her fist up and down in a steady rhythm.

'Clearly you have missed me, slave,' she said, continuing to pull rhythmically at his shaft. 'But how much have you missed me?'

'Immensely, Mistress,' David replied. He wanted to ask her why she'd left it so long before contacting him and why she was only seeing him for such a brief period this time; but he didn't of course.

Isabella continued to pull his hard cock with her right hand and then began to stroke the cheeks of his backside with her left. 'Have you missed being tortured by me, slave?' she asked, pinching one of his buttocks as sharply as she could.

'Yes, Mistress,' he whispered on a breath of pain.

'A lot?'

'A lot, Mistress.'

'Let's see what we can do about that,' Isabella said, removing her hands from his body. 'Don't move,' she added.

She went behind David and he heard her open and then close one of her desk drawers. He waited, not daring to move a muscle, and in a few moments Isabella was back in front of him again. David had to hold back a shudder when he saw what she had in her hand. 'Now for a little of that torture you've been missing so much,' she announced as she attached the vicious looking nipple clamps to his chest. A jolt ran through him and his face contorted with the snaking pain – and pleasure – it brought in its wake.

Isabella began to yank at the clamps with her left hand, making David gasp with pleasure-pain. He moved his shoulders, offering his clamped nipples to the fingers that were pulling at them. She yanked again, and again, and again and he moaned continuously in response – but quietly, always conscious of Sandra's presence outside the door, at her desk in the outer office.

Isabella then returned her right hand to the hard throbbing flesh of David's cock while continuing to pull at the nipple clamps with her left hand. She started to rub her fingers fast and hard over his erection. She was pulling the nipple clamps, pulling his hard cock, and it was making him frantic. David wanted to offer himself fully to Isabella as she yanked harder at the clamps with her left hand and stroked and pulled at his erection more insistently with her right, her fist moving furiously now.

What Isabella was doing to David with both her hands drove him so mad with desire that he got very close indeed to climaxing. Then she abruptly stopped pumping her hand over his shaft although she continued yanking at his clamps. 'Bring your hands to the front of you and ejaculate into your palms,' she ordered, at the same time pulling extra hard at his nipple clamps. And he obeyed, shuddering and jerking without control as his creamy come spilled in abundance into his waiting palms.

Isabella then stopped pulling David's nipple clamps and removed them from his chest. She went behind him again and he heard first the sound of her desk drawer opening and shutting as she replaced the clamps, and then a short buzzing noise followed by the sound of her voice. 'Sandra, I'm going off to that appointment at the bank now,' she said into the intercom. 'Come and help Mister Alexander to clean himself up, please, and then send him on his way.' And with that Isabella left her office without uttering another word. The door made barely a click as she closed it behind her.

What followed with Sandra when the door opened again was as excruciatingly embarrassing and humiliating for David as Isabella had clearly intended it to be. It made his cheeks flush red and sweat pearl his forehead. Sandra however appeared to take it entirely in her stride. It was all in a day's work, the expression on her pretty face seemed to say.

Chapter Twenty-one

The next phone call David received from Isabella came only three days later, much to his surprise, delight … and confusion. Why would she want him to go with her to her office at eleven o' clock at night, he wondered. What bizarre humiliation did she intend to inflict on him there this time? It didn't bear thinking about and wasn't worth thinking about anyway. It was not as if there was anything he could do to influence whatever it was that she was going to do to him there. Isabella was his Mistress and could treat him exactly as she saw fit. That was the way it was between them, the way it had to be.

'So we're going to your office, Mistress,' David said when Isabella climbed into the passenger seat of his car at 10.45 that night. The dominatrix was looking radiant in a tight black leather mini-dress and a pair of tall boots with high heels. She was carrying a small holdall, also of black leather.

'You misunderstood me, slave,' she said. 'We are not going to my office. We are going to *The Office*.'

'Mistress?'

'*The Office*,' Isabella repeated. 'It's a swingers club up past Brighton Station. They specialise in themed parties. Tonight's is called *swings both ways*. Need I say more?'

'No, Mistress,' David gulped. He put the car into gear and set off northwards in the direction of Brighton railway station. David tried to concentrate on his driving but his mind kept straying. What in God's name was Isabella getting him into now? He could feel a heady mixture of anxiety and sexual anticipation rising up within him.

With Isabella giving directions once they'd got to the enormous cast-iron structure of Brighton station, they soon arrived at *The Office*. It was a nondescript single storey building within a business park. David brought his car to a standstill and switched off the ignition and lights. He and Isabella climbed out and walked towards the building's main entrance, which had a bell to the side of it. Isabella rang it and a few seconds later, the door was opened by a heavy-set security guard who ushered them inside good humouredly. He directed them to a good looking young Asian man with hair as intensely black as Isabella's. He was seated behind a metal desk and greeted Isabella by name with a broad smile. Returning his smile, she handed the entrance fee to him and he put it into the cash box beside his laptop.

With Isabella leading the way, she and David then walked through a set of doors and into a long, dimly-lit corridor. A brief way down the corridor they went through an open entrance and into a largish room. It too was dark and contained a bar and a dance floor on which people were moving their bodies sinuously to soft sexy music, swaying back and forth. There were men dancing with women, women dancing with women and men with men. '*Swings both ways* indeed,' David said to himself with a shiver of excitement.

Isabella led David to the bar, which was the only part of the room that was well illuminated. 'Drink, slave?' she asked.

'Allow me, Mistress,' David said, reaching for his wallet.

'No, I insist,' Isabella said. 'Whisky on the rocks?'

'Thank you, Mistress,' he replied.

'One whisky on the rocks and one vodka tonic with ice and lemon, please,' Isabella told the unobtrusive barman.

David could have done with a stiff drink, he had to admit. He was very nervous and felt the alcohol would help him relax a little. Isabella handed him his drink and clinked glasses with him. She sat down on a stool to the side of the bar and told him to take the one next to it. Sipping at his whisky, David looked around the room but found that he couldn't really see much of anything, not even the people on the dance floor, because the room was so dark. But it didn't matter to David. He only had eyes for one person in that room: the woman seated beside him, the magnificent cruel dominatrix to whom he belonged.

After a while Isabella got to her feet. 'Drink up and follow me, slave,' she ordered. 'This is where things are going to get interesting,' she added, a flash of fire in her eyes. David swallowed down the last of his whisky and stood up. He could feel his cock stiffening as he followed Isabella out of the room.

They re-entered the corridor, a short way along which was a row of good sized lockers. 'Strip off,' Isabella ordered and he did. She did likewise at the same time. Isabella was flawless in her nudity, David thought: a naked Goddess beyond compare. She put their clothes into one of the lockers and closed its key in the lock. The key was on a strap which she buckled around her wrist.

Isabella picked up the small leather holdall with her left hand and not for the first time David wondered what was in it. She grabbed him by his erect cock with her right hand and pulled him after her. 'Make me proud of you tonight, slave,' she told David, looking back at him with shining eyes.

'Yes, Mistress,' David replied. You bet he would, he told himself resolutely. He was ready for anything his beloved Mistress wanted to make him do tonight in this decadent sex club, no matter how outrageous it might prove to be, no matter how depraved.

With Isabella still pulling David along by his erection, they arrived at the entrance to another doorless room. It was very dark and seemed to consist of no more than a couple of big couches and a large bed. On both of these a number of bodies were entwined: embracing, stroking, fondling, and God knows what else.

'This is the groping room,' Isabella whispered as she worked her fist up and down David's shaft. They gazed for a short time into the room at the writhing bodies, which were all but obscured by the encompassing darkness. Then the couple were on the move again and walking along the corridor once more. Isabella was still leading David by the cock with her right hand, the leather holdall in her left.

They arrived at another doorless room, which was smaller and better illuminated than the previous one, although it was still quite dark. It contained only one bed and only one couple, both of them naked. A lithe young man with an all-over-tanned body and cropped sandy-blond hair was knelt on the floor with his mouth in the pussy of a dark haired beauty with long shapely legs and big firm breasts. She was on her back, her quivering thighs wide open and her head thrown back, as her partner pleasured her sex eagerly with his lips and tongue.

Isabella began to stroke David's erection again, pushing her fist up and down its length, as they stood there watching this sumptuous young woman being pleasured by her partner.

Isabella then let go of David's cock. 'Go and join them,' she whispered in his ear. 'Sit on the bed by their side and see what happens.'

David began to tremble with panic, a reaction he quickly realised was pointless. I mean, what options did he have here? He had to obey the order Isabella had just given him, come what may. More than that, he wanted to obey that order, was eager to obey it, because he wished so much to make Isabella proud of him tonight. She'd said that that was what she wanted of him and he wanted it too – desperately.

He padded towards the bed, still shaking with nerves, sat down beside the couple, and waited. He was finding it hard to breathe. Before long the young woman turned her head in David's direction, giving him an encouraging smile. Her eyes glittered with desire. She then snaked out her hand towards his throbbing erection and began to masturbate him. In contrast to the woman's actions, David's presence barely seemed to register with her partner who kept on energetically licking her pussy as if the pair of them were still on their own together.

David enjoyed the softness of the young woman's hand against the hardness of his pulsing erection as she stroked and pulled it with her fingers. She then let go of his cock, sat up and drew his face to hers, kissing him. He felt her tongue in his mouth, her lips merging with his as she kissed him more insistently. And all the while her single-minded lover kept vigorously pleasuring her sex with his own lips and tongue, still seemingly oblivious to the fact that she and he very much had company now.

David was oblivious in his own way too, because he wasn't

thinking about the girl who was kissing him or the man knelt between her quivering thighs, licking her pussy. He was thinking about Isabella. He could feel her behind him, feel her eyes on him. He could feel too somehow or other that she was pleased with him and that invigorated him, made his senses race. Then the young woman stopped kissing him and spoke. 'I'd like you to fuck my husband in the arse,' she said huskily. And this caused David to panic all over again. He didn't know what to do.

He glanced quickly at the man who even then didn't budge from what he was doing despite what his wife had just said – although he did grab hold of his own cock and begin slowly masturbating. David then looked back at Isabella anxiously, hesitantly... and saw that she had put on a buckled black leather belt that went round her narrow waist. A strap that was in a V-shape hung down from the front and went up snugly between her shapely thighs. It was evident that she'd extracted the item she was now wearing from the leather holdall.

'It's my favourite double dildo strap-on harness,' Isabella explained, addressing her words to David and also to the young woman. 'It already has one of the dildos in place, the one facing inwards. Now I'll complete the ensemble', she added, pulling out of the leather bag a black rubber dildo, which she affixed to the outer fitting on the strap, and also a bottle of lubricant with which she doused the dildo.

'Now, slave, I believe this beautiful young creature wants you to fuck her husband in the arse,' Isabella went on, staring directly at David now. 'Is that not so?'

David moistened his lips. 'Yes, Mistress,' he confirmed.

'Well, do what she wants,' Isabella ordered, handing David the lubricant. 'You fuck him in his arse and I'll fuck you in yours.'

David began to breathe heavily. He got off the bed, lubed up his erection, and positioned himself behind the man. David put his hand on the small of the man's back and moved his hard cock slowly into his anal hole, pushing against the tight ring of muscles. It caused the man to issue a pussy-muffled groan of pleasure-pain and to masturbate harder. Then it was

Isabella's turn. She glided her hands up David's thighs, parted the cheeks of his backside and with a couple of skilful thrusts, plunged the dildo deep into his anus, which made the other dildo shift inside her excitingly.

The man kept pulling at his erection and lapping at his wife's sex. She was now flat on her back again and groaning with pleasure, her pelvis strained towards his mouth. At the same time David kept fucking him, moving his hard cock in and out of his anus. He felt the pressure of his mucous membrane on his shaft as he continued pushing inside him. He could feel too the strong thrust of Isabella's dildo ploughing deep inside him as he arched his back, offering himself up to her as the dildo inside her slid ever faster.

It was as if Isabella was not just fucking herself and fucking David but fucking the man and the woman as well and the excitement all four of them were experiencing mounted fast. The woman was the first to climax, her body shaking as her husband's tongue worked fast and hard on her clit. Then he succumbed too and spurted extravagantly into his fist, his climax overwhelming him and causing David to climax as well in an orgasm that swept over him uncontrollably. He heard his own cry as he ejaculated deep inside the man's anus. Then he heard and felt Isabella climax with a loud moan and convulsive spasm around the dildo rammed into her sex.

And then it was all over – and far too quickly as far as David was concerned. He didn't want that, didn't want that at all. His body was still aching to be fucked by Isabella. He wanted her to fuck him for ever, do it without stopping, never let him go.

The moon glowed full overhead as David pulled his car over to the side of the street outside Isabella's house where he was about to drop her off. He was feeling down, couldn't help himself. He'd only been with Isabella for a short while again – two, three hours on this occasion – and the time had flown by. Now she was about to leave him once more and the prospect of it filled him with deep dismay. He could feel a chasm of despair start to unfold in his stomach.

David watched Isabella as she opened the car door, the dome light blazing white on the porcelain smoothness of her skin. Before she got out, she turned to him. 'You made me proud of you tonight, slave,' she said. Then she was gone ... and so was David's attack of the blues. He thought he was going to burst with happiness at what Isabella had just said to him.

Chapter Twenty-two

David went straight to bed when he got home but didn't sleep much, didn't even try. He couldn't get Isabella's words out of his mind; they kept dancing round and round in his head in a whirl. 'You made me proud of you tonight, slave.' That was what she'd said to him. 'You made me proud of you ...' He was thoroughly elated. And things got even better. She phoned him that afternoon. That *very afternoon*, would you believe.

'Caroline's just invited me round for drinks tonight with her and Matthew and has suggested that I bring you,' she said. 'I've accepted her invitation on behalf of us both.'

'That's great, Mistress,' David replied, thrilled. 'Thank you very much.'

'You know that smart-casual outfit you wore when I took you to *Latin in the Lanes*,' Isabella said.

'Yes, Mistress,' he replied.

'I liked it.'

'Thank you, Mistress.'

'I would like you to wear it tonight,' Isabella went on. 'There's no need for the nipple clamps and butt plug this time though. It's not going to be that kind of an evening. I've agreed with Caroline that it will be purely social. I'll pick you up at eight thirty.'

'Yes, Mi ...' He didn't get the words out, Isabella had already hung up. He replaced his own receiver on its cradle with a feeling of exhilaration.

David had high hopes for the evening, which he could see going very well. Its main potential for him lay in the fact that the four of them shared so much common ground. There'd be much to discuss on the subject of BDSM. Also, he reflected sardonically, they all actually knew one another, which was more than could be said about last night's depraved foursome – not that you'd find him complaining. *"You made me proud of you tonight, slave"*.

David had been right. No sooner had the four of them sat down in the living room, drinks in hand, than the conversation turned to the delights of domination and submission. Caroline looked on approvingly, her green eyes sparkling, as Matthew told Isabella and David about how she was the love of his life and how happy they were together. He said that being Caroline's slave was the most fitting way he could imagine of showing her how much he adored her.

David was very pleased that his friend had found such happiness with Caroline, but what he had to say gave him pause for thought too. He knew things were very different between Isabella and himself because with her it was all one-sided. He wasn't even allowed to contact her, and she never showed him any affection to speak of. But perhaps all that was about to change, David told himself optimistically. Those words of praise she'd given him last night might have meant she was starting to have tender feelings towards him at long last. Why, only today she'd complimented him on the outfit he'd worn when they'd dined out at *Latin in the Lanes*, the same one he was wearing tonight on her instruction.

David was brought rapidly down to earth by what Isabella then had to say. Her relationship with him was very different to the one Caroline and Matthew enjoyed, she said. It was not a love affair like theirs. It was a diversion on her part, that was all.

David felt crestfallen to hear Isabella say these words. It was a blast of reality from her after his optimistic flight of fancy and it made his head drop. Of course it was all just one-sided. Of course she didn't have tender feelings towards him. He couldn't help envying Caroline and Matthew the love they had for one another. And yet that loving relationship was also strongly sadomasochistic and certainly was not monogamous. He of all people knew that after the two amazing BDSM sex sessions he'd had with them in this very room. There was something contradictory there, he suggested. How did they resolve it as a couple?

Caroline answered for them both. 'Matthew is the man I love and respect and take care of in all the conventional ways,' she said. 'But by my choosing him to be my slave and him agreeing willingly to that enslavement and all it implies we've achieved a whole new level of intimacy and togetherness in our relationship. Our sex life is kinky and it's pansexual and it's hardcore. It is all about pushing limits and heavy duty S&M. But in its essence it's about trust and love.

'I know Matthew has told you about the first time I spanked him,' Caroline went on. 'I hope that aspect of it came across in his account.' David assured her that it had. Caroline turned to Matthew. 'After that spanking came your first whipping. Needless to say, I have pushed your boundaries very much further since then, but I assume you still remember the first time I took a whip to you.'

Matthew remembered it all right. The details were still as sharp in his memory as if it had all happened yesterday, each moment vividly recalled as it flashed across his thoughts. The experience had been euphoric. In its own perverse way, its own perverted way, it had represented a profound expression of love on both their parts...

Matthew was naked and on his stomach in a spread eagled position, his wrists and ankles secured by black rope to the sturdy bedposts of the couple's four-poster bed. The blood was pounding in his veins and his throat was dry. Caroline, who was also nude, picked up a leather whip and brought it down hard on his backside. That first blow delivered pain to Matthew, sending a wave of agony through his body. It also delivered sexual excitement and anticipation. He wondered excitedly what Caroline would do next. Would her next blow be even harder? Could he handle it? Could he take the pain?

Caroline brought the whip down a second time, striking him even harder. Matthew felt pain and trepidation and excitement and anticipation. He felt something else too – complete confidence that he could trust Caroline. He was confident that even though this was the first time she'd ever taken a whip to him she would know innately what he could handle and what he could not. He knew he could trust her implicitly not to cross the line.

Caroline brought the whip down once more and the bed creaked and his body tensed and the pain bit deep. Then she brought it down again … and again and again until his body stopped tensing, instead giving itself up, yielding to the insistent lashing of the whip. Matthew began to rock his hips to the furious rhythm of Caroline's lashes as she brought the whip down on his skin hard, harder, harder still. Finally he was on the point of orgasm. 'Permission to come, Mistress,' he gasped. His spread eagled body was shaking in its bondage as though electric shocks were coursing through his veins.

'Not yet,' Caroline said. 'Not until you tell me what you are, who you belong to.'

'I am yours, only yours, Mistress,' Matthew replied in exaltation. 'I am your slave.'

'Come for me now, slave,' she said, bringing the whip down on his rear with one last ferocious blow. And he did. Matthew climaxed violently for Caroline, spilling his load in abundance as he shuddered without control within his rope bonds.

Chapter Twenty-three

'...reminder of your enslavement to me.'

At first lost in his reminiscence of that first whipping he'd received from his beloved Mistress, Matthew heard Caroline's voice only as a distant, disembodied sound. 'Sorry, Mistress,' he said, focussing on her. 'What did you just say?'

'I was telling our guests that I insist that you always wear the slave's collar you have on this evening when you're at work,' Caroline said, 'and that my reason for doing this is to give you a constant reminder while you're there of your enslavement to me. Show it to them, would you.'

'Yes, Mistress,' Matthew replied dutifully. He unbuttoned the top of his shirt to reveal the loose chained padlock he was wearing around his neck.

'Now you, slave,' Isabella said to David. 'Let's see the one you're wearing tonight.'

David's mouth fell open. 'B-but I'm not, Mistress,' he stammered. 'You told me it wasn't going to be that sort of evening.'

A tight, uncomfortable silence descended for a lengthy moment. 'Correction, slave,' Isabella finally replied, her face now hardened to a mask. 'I told you to wear the same outfit you wore when I took you to *Latin in the Lanes* but said you should omit the nipple clamps and butt plug. You'll be telling me next that you're not wearing the genital ring or leather g-string either.'

David lowered his eyes. 'N-no I'm not, Mistress,' he responded falteringly. 'I seem to have got the wrong end of the stick.'

'I don't know about that,' Isabella snapped. She deliberately stared at David, forcing him to look up and meet her gaze. 'I would have said that my instructions to you were perfectly clear. The bottom line here is that you didn't do what I told you to and that's simply not acceptable.'

David felt his Adam's apple bob. 'I apologise, M-mistress,' he said, his words still stilted. 'I meant no disrespect to you. I seem to have got the …'

'… wrong end of the stick, yes you've already said that,' Isabella cut in irritably. 'You accept that you must be punished for what you've done?'

'I do, Mistress,' David replied humbly. He felt mortified. 'Straight away, if you wish.'

'It's not up to me, is it, slave,' Isabella corrected David, fixing him with another withering gaze. 'This is not my house.'

David made an effort to swallow. 'No, Mistress,' he said. 'I'm sorry for being presumptuous.'

Isabella turned to Caroline. 'I'm in your hands, my dear,' she said. 'Actually I would like to punish him right now. But I don't want to abuse your hospitality. We did agree earlier between ourselves that this would be a purely social evening. What would you like me to do?'

'Punish him now,' Caroline said. 'It's what I'd want to do in your position.'

'Thank you for that,' Isabella said. 'I propose to tie him up and beat the crap out of him. Do you think you could loan me some bondage rope and a heavy leather strap.'

'Certainly,' Caroline replied. 'I have both in my box of tricks here.' She motioned towards the oak chest in which, as David already knew, she kept many of her BDSM items.

Isabella turned back to David. 'We appear to be all set, slave,' she said, gazing at him coldly. 'Get up, leave this room, go to the foot of the stairs and take off all your clothes. Then wait where you are and contemplate the punishment you're about to receive. I'll join you there in a few moments once I've spoken some more with Caroline and obtained from her the implements I'll be disciplining you with.'

'Yes, Mistress,' David said nervously. He took a deep breath, stood up and left the room, his head lowered. He shut the door behind him and stripped off at the bottom of the stairs. A shudder of fear ran up and down the length of his spine as he waited for Isabella to come through the door.

When she did she was holding the heavy leather strap and length of bondage rope she'd borrowed from Caroline. Isabella told David to put his hands together in front of him and cross them at the wrist. Once he'd done this she expertly tied them to the newel post of the banisters with the rope.

Isabella then grasped David's hair and put her face very close to his. 'I'm going to make you really suffer for what you've done, slave,' she said, her lip curling with displeasure. 'I'm more than a little pissed off with you, in case you hadn't noticed.'

Isabella let go of David's hair and he braced himself for the rigours of what lay ahead. Isabella moved behind him, raised the leather strap high and swished it through the air. It landed with a crack on its target, causing David to gasp at the sudden pain that seared across his backside. Immediately Isabella brought the strap down again. It was even more agonizing. When David felt the strap sting his backside for the third time he couldn't hold back a cry of pain. A fourth and fifth stroke followed in swift succession and then down came the heavy strap again. David's eyes blurred with tears of pain as the blows succeeded one another with increasing violence. Isabella carried on thrashing his backside mercilessly, causing numerous red streaks to appear there. David's naked, lacerated body glistened with sweat and burned with unbearable pain.

He was about to beg for mercy when Isabella suddenly stopped beating him. She moved briefly to his front, laying the heavy strap over the balustrade. Then she moved behind him again and shortly afterwards he heard her open and shut the front door of the house. He then heard the sounds of Isabella slamming the door of her Mercedes and of it growling away out of the drive and down the street.

David was left, tied to the banisters by his wrists, naked and in great pain and all alone. But he was not left like that for long. Matthew came out of the living room, freed his hands and retrieved the bondage rope and leather strap. David said how sorry he was for screwing up the evening the way he had but Matthew waved his apology away. 'These things happen,' he said gently. 'Everyone makes mistakes.'

'I'd better go,' David said, his voice subdued.

Matthew did not demur. 'I'll call you a taxi,' he said, reaching out and squeezing his shoulder.

Chapter Twenty-four

Isabella didn't call. No surprises there. After what had happened David didn't expect her to call any time soon. Indeed he strongly feared that she'd never call again.

Matthew did call though. He phoned the next day to check David was OK. David told Matthew that he thought he may have blown it permanently with Isabella. But his friend told him he was worrying needlessly. 'Think logically about this, David,' Matthew urged. 'It was a simple misunderstanding on your part, that's all. Isabella knows that perfectly well, so the chances of her wanting to finish with you because of it have got to be remote in the extreme. The incident was just a minor setback, no more than that, trust me.'

David was reassured by Matthew's advice, which on reflection made a lot of sense to him, and he managed to stop worrying. Even so, it soon became clear that Isabella was in anything but a rush to get back to him. As time went by and the painful welts on his backside slowly faded there wasn't a day David didn't spend thinking about Isabella and masturbating. And there wasn't a night that he didn't spend dreaming intensely vivid erotic dreams about her. Those dreams tended to follow something of a pattern.

In them Isabella took David to a club that seemed to be some sort of a cross between *Club Depravity* and *The Office*. She was dressed in a tight fitting leather body suit and he was naked and on his hands and knees beneath her. Isabella lost no time in handing David over to an Amazonian blonde beauty wearing nothing but a gigantic strap-on dildo. The Amazon lost even less time in putting her strap-on into use. She sodomized David vigorously, her hands on his hips, her sharp-nailed fingers digging into his flesh. Her stomach kept beating against his rear while she was pounding in and out of him. Time and again that rapacious Amazonian blonde penetrated him, plunged hard into his narrow anus then withdrew, then plunged in hard again. Over and over she hammered into him, making his insides scream in protest. David's body was so stretched, so damaged by this brutal onslaught, that it felt as if it was broken in pieces.

Eventually Isabella spirited the brutal Amazonian woman away and replaced her with a group of handsome young men with tanned, toned bodies. All of them were naked and hugely erect, their big cocks hard and eager. Having told David to kneel upright, she instructed the young men to form a circle around him and wank themselves off, telling them to make sure they ejaculated all over him.

They went about their task with gusto, licking their lips and gasping as they worked their hands fast along their hard cocks. They stroked and pulled and jerked forcefully at their erections until they climaxed as if as one, all of them convulsing in spasms. They squirted their hot seed over David's body and face and splashed it onto his hair in a real bukkaki-fest.

It was deeply humiliating, but David didn't mind. In truth he revelled in it. He was so submissive, so devoted to Isabella there was nothing he wouldn't do for her. He was hers to abuse as excessively as she saw fit. His battered, gaping anus and come-covered face and hair and body was the proof of it. It proved that he was worthy of her. Isabella was proud of him too, she kept on saying so over and over again ... in his dreams.

There was a slave auction at the club but Isabella didn't put David up for auction. Instead she made a successful bid for the most beautiful young man there. He was auburn haired and pretty, with a completely hairless body and a thick tight cock. He had been perfectly trained by his Mistress who had named him slut-boy. Isabella and David both kissed and sucked and fondled him languorously.

Isabella told David to prepare slut-boy's anal hole for her strap-on dildo. David filled slut-boy's anus with his saliva and then pressed his lips to it and licked, his taut wet tongue wiggling and wiggling. Isabella then pushed David aside and fucked slut-boy in the arse, penetrating deep inside him. She moved in and out, pushing the dildo all the way in each time, and he pushed back on it as his excitement grew and grew.

Then Isabella withdrew the strap-on from slut-boy's anus and handed him back to the kneeling David, telling him to give the young slave a blow job. David slid his lips around slut-boy's cock, taking its moist warmth into his mouth. The palms of his hands resting gently against slut-boy's thighs, David began sucking his cock with regular movements. From time to time, he withdrew his mouth and licked underneath, with little flicks of his tongue, back and forth. Isabella then told him to finger-fuck slut-boy at the same time as sucking him. David put three fingers inside slut-boy's dilated, lube-filled anus, sliding them in as far as he could and turning them, while he continued moving his mouth up and down his cock.

David concentrated, focusing on slut-boy's pleasure, which he could feel mounting. He began to stroke slut-boy's balls as he sucked voraciously at his slick, hard cock and worked his sodden anal hole with his fingers. When slut-boy came, crying out in ecstasy, David gulped down all the creamy come that spilled from his shaft, every last ounce. The young man's eyes were closed tight as he let David suck him dry. All that come had been the essence of slut-boy and he kind of *melted away* after that…

David next found himself gagged and tied on his front to a whipping bench. He was being beaten viciously by Isabella on the rear with a whip, which had leather strands that were inlaid with small pieces of *bone* for fucksake. Each time this extraordinarily savage whip landed, another red streak appeared on his flesh, joining the angry pattern of lacerations already there. And because David was gagged he couldn't sob or moan or scream in agony … and ecstasy.

A circle of beautiful naked women, all of them with short platinum-white hair and much tattooed bodies, began to form around the ultra-sadistic dominatrix and her craven victim. They gazed on rapturously at the damage Isabella was doing to David's backside with that terrifying whip and they all began to masturbate. As the multi-tattooed women watched they were soon wanking away like demons, their fingers plunging and plunging into the wetness between their legs. Isabella whipped David ever more furiously, her violence so incredibly sweet to him, and the women wanked ever more furiously too.

David could smell sex in the air, the delicious scent of pussy, and no wonder. The women's hands were glistening wetly, sticky from finger-fucking themselves so feverishly at the sight of him being tortured with such savagery by Isabella. Then one by one the tattooed women began to ejaculate in huge juddering spasms, clear fluid squirting from their urethras in abundance, each one gushing a glutinous deluge of sticky wetness...

David invariably found that he too had ejaculated copiously when he awoke from these incredibly torrid dreams, his hair damp and his heart still racing wildly in his chest. His torso was sticky with the sperm that covered it. It was further proof that Isabella controlled him. She controlled his thoughts and controlled his dreams. How he wished she would call, how he wished he could see her in person again instead of her phantasm. As David waited week after week for that time to finally arrive his mind reached constantly for thoughts of Isabella … and his hand reached constantly for his cock.

Chapter Twenty-five

'I am taking you to *Club Depravity* again tonight to further test your limits,' Isabella announced when she finally deigned to phone David again. It was the last Saturday of the month. She made no reference to what had happened at Caroline and Matthew's place as a result of his stupid faux pas. That was all now behind them, ancient history – or so David fervently hoped. 'We'll be joined this time by Mistress Kate and her slave, Tony,' Isabella added, 'and will be in one of the chambers, which I've booked for the evening.'

David could distinctly remember Mistress Kate from his first visit to the club. She had been the strikingly beautiful leather dominatrix with the short ash-blonde hair, the switch who'd once been Isabella's slave. But for the life of him David couldn't remember what Tony looked like. As it turned out, at least initially, he needn't have bothered trying.

Tony was wearing a red rubber mask with open eyes, nose and mouth holes and was on his knees in a locked cage. The chained lead attached to his collar was wrapped around one of the bars of the cage. Clover clamps hung from his nipples and a red leather ball stretcher pulled down his scrotum. His back and rear were criss-crossed with welts from a recent beating he had received from Kate, and his cock was hard.

David was looking out from a St. Andrews cross, which was set against one of the chamber's brick walls. His arms reached out on either side of him, the wrists firmly secured to the cross. His legs were immobilized too, strapped as they were to the base of the cross. His head and face were covered by a black leather hood. David could see and breathe through the eye and nose holes of the hood but he was gagged with a red ball gag.

His nipples had been clamped and six red pegs had been attached to his scrotum. David's back and rear were extremely sore from the heavy thrashing that Isabella had administered to him before strapping him to the cross; his shaft was as stiffly erect as Tony's.

The two mistresses both looked stunning. Isabella was wearing a very short, tight black leather dress and high-heeled shoes. Kate's outfit, black leather as well, consisted of a halter-top and tiny skin-tight shorts that revealed the cheeks of her well-shaped backside and outlined the lips of her shaven sex. In addition she was wearing knee-length boots with very high heels.

Isabella and Kate strode arm in arm across the vaulted dimness of the chamber and over to the cage. Isabella unlocked it and Kate unhooked Tony's lead. She used it to take him crawling over to kneel at the foot of the cross to which David was strapped.

'Masturbate David,' Kate demanded of Tony. The dominatrix had oval-shaped violet eyes, which shone like cut glass. Her slave obediently complied, gripping his hand round David's cock and pushing his fist up and down. He used brisk short strokes that caused David's excitement to mount but also made the pegs attached to his scrotum pull painfully … which added to his excitement. At the same time Isabella and Kate each used heavy leather floggers to add further welts to Tony's back and rear.

'Now suck David's cock,' Isabella commanded of Tony, as she moved over to pick up a candleholder from the floor. This contained three red candles, which she went on to light. The flames from the candles reflected in her gleaming ink-black eyes. As Tony sucked up and down on David's hard cock Kate continued to whip her slave's rear and Isabella poured hot wax on his punished back. He shivered with pain in response and his shaft began oozing a rivulet of pre-come.

Kate finally stopped beating Tony and put a strap-on over her miniscule leather shorts. The dominatrix lubricated the dildo before thrusting it into Tony's tight anal hole. She immediately began fucking him hard in the anus, pushing and pushing and pushing. As Kate sodomized Tony, Isabella returned to whipping his back and he continued sucking David's cock. Then, on Isabella's direction, they all stopped.

Kate withdrew the dildo from Tony's anus and dragged him away by his lead. After removing both the strap-on harness and her leather shorts, Kate detached Tony's lead and removed his nipple clamps and ball stretcher.

'Lie flat on your back on the floor, slave,' she commanded. 'Mistress Isabella is now going to use you as a human dildo while you lick me off. You're to keep your body completely still and are forbidden to come.'

Isabella sat on Tony's hard cock, letting its thickness impale her, and Kate straddled his face and began to lower herself towards him. She placed her dripping pussy over the open mouth of his red rubber hood, grinding her hips down. The two women kissed each other passionately on the lips as they pleasured themselves in this way.

What of David, though? What was going through his mind at this point? Was he feeling a twist or more of jealousy? Was he envious of Kate and Tony and the intimacy they were enjoying with his Mistress, as he viewed them all from the St. Andrews cross? No, he was not. He wouldn't allow himself to be jealous. As he'd told himself decisively before, as he was telling himself just as decisively now: he couldn't have it both ways.

Isabella and Kate carried on using Tony's body for their mutual pleasure until, panting and gasping, they climaxed simultaneously. By contrast Tony did not climax and continued to remain stock still, exactly as he had been instructed to do.

The two women climbed off the obedient slave. Kate told him to get back on his hands and knees and crawl over to the upright torture chair that was positioned in a corner of the dimly-lit chamber. She strapped him into it at the neck, wrists, thighs and ankles. Kate put the clover clamps back on his nipples and Isabella inserted a red ball gag in his mouth and buckled it into place.

The two dommes stood back to admire their handiwork for a moment and then Isabella asked, 'Do you ever think back to when you used to be my slave, Kate?'

'Frequently,' Kate replied, her violet eyes shining more brightly than ever. 'I worshipped you then and I always will.'

'If you worship me,' Isabella said, 'you should be on your knees.'

'Yes, Mistress,' responded Kate and immediately knelt. Old habits die hard.

'Now kiss my feet,' Isabella commanded and again Kate obeyed instantly, raining kisses onto the shiny leather of Isabella's high heeled shoes.

'On to all fours with you now, slave,' Isabella instructed next, taking hold of the heavy leather flogger once again. She went on to beat Kate's back and rear more and more savagely until she was forced to beg her to stop. Isabella ceased straight away, helped Kate to her feet and the two women masturbated one another frantically until they both climaxed in a noisy delirium of mutual lust.

They kissed and caressed tenderly in the afterglow for a while, then looked over at their two hooded and gagged slaves, noting their hugely engorged cocks. 'You know, Kate,' Isabella said, 'those two are enjoying themselves far too much.'

'I agree,' Kate replied. 'Don't you feel we should inflict some *real* punishment on them now?'

'I do indeed,' Isabella said. 'It's time for some needle play, I think.' She laughed then. It was a merciless sort of laugh.

Tony was chosen first. The clamps were removed from his punished nipples, causing him to squirm with pain. As Isabella pulled at his erection, Kate inserted a needle through one of his nipples. The ball gag muffled his agonized scream. When another needle was inserted through his other nipple he let out a further muffled scream and erupted into orgasm, sending a long spray of ejaculate into the air.

Kate carefully removed the needles from Tony's nipples. She gave him a few moments to compose himself, then freed him from the torture chair and took off his ball gag. 'Get on to your knees,' Kate demanded and the whimpering slave obeyed instantly.

By the time the two Mistresses made their way over to

140

David, leather-hooded, gagged, clamped, pegged and tightly strapped to the cross as he was, he was also something else: absolutely terrified. His eyes had gone very wide, his heart was pounding. Sweat was streaming down his skin, his whole body was shaking in its bonds. Kate knelt down again, this time to engulf David's swollen cock in her mouth and start to suck it.

Then Isabella got to work. As she drove the first needle through one of his nipples David let out a high-pitched strangled shriek, muffled by his gag, in response to the extreme pain he was experiencing. When she drove the second one through his other nipple, causing another muffled shriek, he was in an agony so extreme that it suddenly spilled over into a fierce climax. And as it unleashed its full orgasmic fury Kate sucked and sucked …

Chapter Twenty-six

A little later David and Tony found themselves alone together in the same dark chamber. Kate had removed Tony's hood to reveal a pleasant looking man with short brown hair, grey eyes that were tinged with green, and fine-featured good looks. David remembered him now from his first visit to *Club Depravity*.

Isabella had removed David's hood too, as well as his ball gag. She'd also removed the pegs that had been attached to his scrotum and the needles and clamps from his nipples.

The two men remained naked and were standing face to face, Isabella and Kate having manacled their wrists to either end of the same metal spreader bar that hung from the ceiling by chains.

'Jesus, that whole scene was very intense,' Tony said with feeling.

'It certainly was,' David agreed. 'And that last bit with the needles hurt like fuck didn't it.'

'No argument there,' Tony replied. The two of them had been left on their own in the dimly-lit chamber while Isabella and Kate had gone off to socialise at the bar and also to view the "kinky cabaret" that had been organised there for that evening. It involved a naked female contortionist who, among other tricks, was able to lick her own clitoris.

'The whole experience was a hell of a way for the two of us to get acquainted,' David smiled, showing strong, even teeth.

'A hell of a way,' Tony agreed, smiling back at him.

There was silence between the two men for a while, which David was the first to break. 'Tell me a bit about yourself, Tony,' he said.

'Sure,' he replied agreeably. 'I'll tell you anything you want to know.'

'I'd be interested to know how long you've been Mistress Kate's slave.' David asked. 'Has it been for a long time?'

'About three years,' Tony said. 'They've been the best three years of my life too. I love being enslaved to her, really love it. She's introduced me to some fascinating people on the Brighton fetish scene as well.'

'Have you met my friend, Matthew and his Mistress, Caroline?' David asked.

'Yes, I know them well. They're a great couple,' Tony replied. 'Mistress Caroline was the one that got Matthew into all this, wasn't she?'

'She was,' David said. 'And it was my Mistress who got me into it too. Was it Mistress Kate who first introduced you to BDSM?'

'No,' Tony replied. 'I started young. Would you like to hear my story?'

'I'd love to,' David said, 'if we have time.' It was anyone's guess when Isabella and Kate would return.

'OK,' Tony said. 'Well, to start by perhaps stating the obvious, given what you and I have just been doing, I'm bisexual. In fact, I used to be more attracted to guys than girls. The first boy I fell in lust with was called Paul. Actually, he and I had known each other for ages – since we'd been kids, when we'd often played together. One particular incident had stuck in my mind from that time.'

'What was that?' David asked.

'Paul and I were having one of those playful wrestles that young pals have,' Tony replied, 'when all of a sudden I became acutely aware of a kind of electrical charge between us, an exciting tingling feeling in my loins. I was certain Paul had experienced a similar sensation and it was with a sort of bewildered reluctance on both our parts that we managed to prise our bodies apart.

'I didn't understand at the time what that electric sensation had been but the memory of it stayed with me and as Paul and I both grew into adolescence so did our mutual sexual attraction.

143

Our friendship kept developing in that direction and we became 'jack-off buddies'. I used to love my mutual masturbation sessions with Paul. We'd wank each other off every opportunity we got. And it didn't stop at just mutual masturbation, far from it – not once we went into the woods on the edge of town ...'

Tony and Paul ventured off into the woods one day with nothing but sex on their minds. It was a relief to be away from prying eyes in those quiet woods, with nobody else about and the only sounds the murmurings and stirrings of nature: the occasional creaking of a bough, the shuffling of leaves under their feet. They made their way deep into the dark woods and the deeper they got the more sexually excited they became. As they walked along they began to fondle the bulges in one another's tight denim jeans.

They arrived at a fallen log not far from a clearing that was edged by a pebbled stream. The clearing seemed perfect for what Tony and Paul had in mind, and they stripped off all their clothing. Leaving their clothes on the log, they rushed stark naked into the clearing, their erect cocks bobbing ahead of them. Once there, they stood in each other's arms, caressing and kissing as their engorged shafts rubbed together, mingling their pre-come.

Paul then got on to his knees and stroked Tony's cock while sucking its head. Then he took its length into his mouth. He pulled on the smooth hardness of his own shaft at the same time and when Tony came into his mouth, this pushed him over the edge. As Paul swallowed Tony's jism, he climaxed convulsively as well, spilling out ropes of pearly come onto the soft grass beneath him.

'I was very much a novice compared to Paul when it came to gay sex,' Tony said, continuing his account.

'How so?' David asked.

'Let's just say he had a very close relationship with an uncle of his and leave it at that,' Tony replied enigmatically.

'Anyway, here's what happened the next time I went into the woods with my more experienced friend.'

It was a splendid day, the air lazy and mild and the trees speckled with sunlight. There was a freshwater pool not far from the clearing that they'd been to before and Paul had suggested to Tony that they go skinny dipping in it. Paul came prepared with a backpack containing a couple of towels for them to use.

When Tony and Paul got into the water they were both sporting gigantic hard-ons and happily played with one another's cocks as they splashed around in the sparkling water. At one point Paul took Tony into his arms and they kissed passionately, his hard cock pressing against Tony's as he gently caressed his back and rear.

Then he opened up Tony's anus with one, two fingers. That was a new experience for Tony and it felt really good, but there were more delights to come. After they'd got out of the water and towelled themselves dry, Paul asked Tony to bend forward with his legs apart. He knelt behind him and burrowed his face between the cheeks of his backside. Tony felt Paul's sinuous tongue begin to probe his anus and he squeezed and relaxed his hole as his tongue flicked in and out. That was another first for Tony – getting rimmed – and it felt great.

The two young men lay back on the soft grass for a few moments, staring up at the leafy trees and the blue vault of the sky above them. Both their cocks were still hugely erect. 'Get on to all fours, I want to fuck you,' Paul said next. 'Don't worry,' he added, taking a tube of lubricant from his bag. 'I know what I'm doing.'

Once Tony was in position Paul smeared lube onto his cock and eased it into his virgin anus until its head pushed through his tight sphincter. It hurt at first but, like Paul had said, he knew what he was doing and the pain soon turned to delirious pleasure as Tony savoured the throbbing hardness of Paul's erection pressing deep inside him. As Paul fucked Tony he also pulled at his shaft. When Paul finally climaxed, pumping his hot seed into Tony's anal hole, Tony couldn't contain himself any longer and came violently, spilling out one thick spurt of come after another as he yielded to the ecstasy of release.

Chapter Twenty-seven

'The next time Paul and I went into the woods together we could hardly wait to get to the clearing by the pebbled stream and have sex together again,' Tony continued. 'But you know what they say: the best laid plans ...'

Once Tony and Paul had stripped off and got almost to the clearing they were stopped in their tracks. There was a dry crack of wood and the careless rustle of undergrowth coming from where they were headed. It quickly became evident from the voices they heard next that others had beaten them to it.

Tony and Paul crept gingerly towards the clearing and, peering through a canopy of leaves, saw to their surprise half a dozen good looking young men who seemed to be about their age. They were all naked and erect, and were sitting on a slope by the stream, stroking their hard-ons. They seemed to be waiting for someone. There was also another young man there, a beautiful blond-haired Adonis. He was sitting on a rock slightly apart from the others, masturbating like them but with a noticeably pensive expression on his face. Then the person they'd evidently been waiting for arrived.

He had luxuriant dark hair and was well muscled. He was also incredibly handsome with the most piercing blue eyes Tony had ever seen. He began to think of him as 'Blue-eyes' and the blond Adonis as 'Blondie'. Like the others, Blue-eyes was buck naked and erect; the glans of his cock was wet with pre-come. He walked straight over to Blondie who stood up so that they could caress. However no sooner were they in each other's arms than Blondie broke their clinch and squeezed the other's nipples hard, causing him to gasp in pain.

Blondie gestured for Blue-eyes to get on to his knees and blow him. He pulled at the other's long hair as he sucked his cock and fondled his balls. Blue-eyes, now alternately licking the head of Blondie's cock and sucking his balls, seemed to be relishing his submissive role. But it soon became evident that it was all an act.

Blue-eyes got up from his knees and began to regain control in this brief power struggle – if he'd ever truly lost it, which Tony very much doubted when looking back on the whole extraordinary experience. Blue-eyes spun Blondie round, bent him over and spread the cheeks of his backside. He tongued his anus greedily while his lover/rival pulled on his own hard cock with brusque, short strokes.

Blue-eyes then began spanking Blondie's backside vigorously, each smack a sharp explosion of sound as he followed one stinging blow with another in rapid succession. By the time he spat into Blondie's open anus to lubricate it for entry, his rear was a fierce red from the spanking it had received.

Blue-eyes pounded his cock in and out of Blondie's anal hole, fucking him hard to the rhythm of his groans of pleasure. He obviously decided not to come, though, as Tony and Paul heard him say, "Let's save the best until last". At this point he withdrew his cock, which was as dripping with pre-come as Blondie's.

All the other young men then got into a huddle and began masturbating one another. By this time Tony and Paul were beside themselves with lust. It was time to reveal themselves, they decided, whatever the consequences of doing that might turn out to be. So they emerged from their hiding place and began to stride into the clearing, their hard cocks bobbing obscenely ahead of them.

'We seem to have company,' Blue-eyes announced to the assembled wankers who all looked in their direction. He added, addressing himself directly to Tony and Paul and surveying them with obvious approval, 'And what do you two horny boys want?' His impossibly blue eyes were gleaming with desire.

'We'd like to join in your sex games,' Tony replied boldly.

'I'll bet you would and we'd love to have you do that,' smiled Blue-eyes, resting his hand on Tony's arm. He had a once-in-a lifetime smile and his touch was electric; and as for those blue, blue eyes ... 'But there's an initiation ceremony for joining this select little group of perverts' he went on. 'Basically it involves either getting a face full of come from half a dozen hard cocks or taking a severe beating. As there are two of you, it'll be a case of one each. Now which one of you would be willing to take the heavy beating?'

'I would,' Tony replied unhesitatingly. 'I'd be willing to do that.'

'No, don't,' Paul said, his voice urgent, 'not for me, please. I'd never ask that of you.'

'You don't understand. I want to,' Tony responded firmly. 'You see, Paul, I really get off on the idea.' As the words came out of his mouth Tony realised that he'd never made a truer statement in his life. It was his eureka moment, no question.

And so the initiation ceremony began in earnest as a number of the young men used the leather belts from their discarded jeans to first tie Tony's wrists together and then upraise them and secure them to the sturdy branch of an oak tree. They also used a belt to tie his ankles together. Blue-eyes told Blondie to go and get his rucksack, and from that he took a come-caked handkerchief. He handed it round to all his companions to use to wipe off the pre-come from their hard cocks until the cloth was soaked with boy juice. He then gagged Tony by stuffing his mouth with it.

Blue-eyes delved into his rucksack again and this time brought out six clothes pegs. He attached two of these to Tony's nipples and the other four to his scrotum, causing him to tremble with pain. He then told Paul to kneel in front of Tony and suck his hard cock for all he was worth, instructing Tony that under no circumstances was he to allow himself to come. Paul wrapped his lips round Tony's shaft and obediently began to give him the four star blow-job that had been required of him. He swirled his tongue around the head of Tony's cock, flicked it round his come-slit, and then moved it up and down his shaft, tasting every throbbing inch of it. It was pleasure, pure pleasure for Tony.

'Now – pain,' Blue-eyes announced and the beating started. All the young men took it in turns to whip Tony's backside with leather belts, stroke after searing stroke as he struggled uselessly against his bonds. Blue-eyes took over next and beat him with a bamboo cane he'd just cut. Each of his swishing blows smarted vividly, until the pain Tony was enduring had become a fury burning agonizingly into his flesh and his eyes were glistening with tears.

Blue-eyes appeared to relent at this point and ceased caning Tony. He also told Paul to stop blowing him but to remain on his knees. He removed Tony's sodden gag from his mouth and the pegs from his nipples and scrotum; and lowered the belts that held his wrists together and to the branch, releasing his arms completely. He removed the belt from his ankles too and passed it to Blondie. He told him to use it to tie Paul's wrists behind his back.

Blue-eyes ordered the kneeling Paul to suck off Blondie and swallow his come. He also told the rest of the young men to come all over Paul's face. He then made Tony bend forward and spread his legs. He knelt behind him, pulled the cheeks of his backside apart and licked his anus, his anal muscles contracting around his sinuous tongue. Then he got up from his knees, leant down and took some lubricant from his rucksack. He next rubbed it on his hard cock, and pushed it into Tony's rear. The thrill of penetration edged with the pain Tony felt in his anus, and Blue-eyes started to fuck him, the strokes of his cock slow at first but building steadily in pace.

Tony panted with desire as Blue-eyes fucked him ever harder while pulling on his aching tumescence. He watched an ecstatic Paul gulping down Blondie's come, and then have all the other young men – now masturbating feverishly – each build themselves to a climax and come over his face in shuddering spasms.

Blue-eyes finally reached his own powerful climax, sending spurt after spurt of come deep into Tony's punished rear. At the same time he took Tony with him with his pumping hand around his cock, making him shudder to orgasm, right there in the middle of the deep, dark woods.

Chapter Twenty-eight

David and Tony were still up-close-and-personal in their naked bondage, their wrists manacled to the metal spreader bar that was hanging from the ceiling by chains. David had become very aroused during Tony's graphic account and Tony had become equally excited in the telling of it. Both men were therefore massively erect, their hard cocks rubbing together excitingly, by the time Isabella and Kate returned to the dimly-lit chamber.

'What do you think our two slaves have been doing while we've been away enjoying the company of our fellow perverts and the performance of that clit licking contortionist?' Isabella asked.

Kate shrugged. 'Bonding in their bondage?' she suggested with an amused smile.

The two women then pushed David and Tony right against each other, in the process pinning their hard cocks together. They then went on to manacle the men's ankles to the end of a metal spreader bar, which was identical to the one to which their wrists were already secured. Finally they blindfolded them and also gagged them again, buckling behind their heads the red ball gags they'd gagged them with earlier.

'We've brought our two naked slaves even closer together now,' Isabella said, taking hold of a couple of rattan canes and handing one of them to Kate. 'How about we give them a major beating and *really* make them come together.'

'Six of the best to start?' said Kate.

'To *start*, yes,' Isabella replied with heavy emphasis, her dark eyes shining sadistically through the shadows.

'Want to go first?' asked Kate.

Isabella nodded that she did. She then gave a practice swipe with her cane while David waited, his heart pounding with excitement, his erection pulsing against Tony's stiff cock. Then it began. Isabella sliced the cane through the air in a graceful arc that cracked hard across David's backside. It hurt like hell, a white flash of pure pain that caused him to inhale sharply behind his gag and left a red track across his backside.

The second stroke whistled through the air, cracking hard against David's rear. There was that white flash of sensation again and then a second track to join the first. A third stroke of the cane followed the second one before David had time to recover. Strikes four and five came down in even swifter succession, harsher and sharper still.

The sixth stroke bit hardest of all, a flash of pure agony. Isabella stopped then and the pain David was suffering started to dissolve, becoming a suffuse red heat that seeped through his body, connecting with the pulsing hardness of his cock as it throbbed against Tony's own pulsing erection.

'Over to you now, Kate,' Isabella said and it was Tony's turn for six of the best. The cane swished down and the fire followed an instant later. Then it happened a second time, a third, a fourth, a fifth and a sixth. Tony felt the blaze of each of the six strokes as Kate laid them carefully across his rear, the heat building in his backside and raging outwards through his cock as it rubbed and throbbed against David's shaft.

Then it was David's turn again, the blows landing agonizingly across the earlier strokes where the red welts had already risen. Each time Isabella caned him he bucked against Tony. Then it was Tony's turn, and then David's turn again. Then Isabella and Kate began to beat them both together. On and on the two women caned their blindfolded and gagged slaves, one vicious swipe after another, until excruciating pain burned like twin flames into their flesh.

Then pain suddenly turned to pure lust, throbbing and hot. David and Tony's nerves were on fire, every cell in their bodies on red alert. The heat of desire swept through their bodies and blood pulsed in their aching cocks, precipitating them both to orgasm. They came together – and voluminously.

Their shafts pumped thick waves of come over their torsos that were pressed so closely together as they writhed helplessly in their bondage, the mutual agony they were suffering finally outweighed by the ecstasy of mutual relief.

Chapter Twenty-nine

'Tonight you will face your biggest challenge yet,' Isabella informed David when she phoned him next, which was one month later to the day. As it was again the last Saturday of the month David's first thought was that it would take place at *Club Depravity*. He was wrong about that, as swiftly became clear. 'It will take place this evening when I christen my newly created dungeon,' Isabella went on. 'Ideally I would have liked my husband to jointly host the event with me but he and the twins are currently out of the country and will be for some while to come.'

David assumed that Alan Stern's absence from the UK was business related, and his assumption was correct. The Stern's company had been selling more and more merchandise via the web, especially to customers in the United States. To start to build on that success and further expand the company Alan Stern had gone out to the States for the duration to open up several flagship stores, the first one to be in New York.

He'd been gone three weeks already and during that time Isabella had supervised the completion of a personal project of hers that was especially dear to her heart: the creation of a superb dungeon in the basement of the Stern's Brighton home. Among other things, Isabella had arranged for the basement area to be soundproofed in its entirety and had had shower, washing and toilet facilities installed in one corner.

The work that she'd had carried out to the rest of the large space included the fitting of subdued lighting that focussed on various pieces of the *La Fetishista* dungeon equipment she'd had installed. Most of this was covered in soft black leather, like the horse, the padded bondage table, the horizontal torture chair, the vertical torture chair, the whipping bench and the St. Andrews cross. There was a cage in one corner and chains hung from the dungeon ceiling in a number of locations.

An open cabinet of dark wood had been fitted that was panelled up to the ceiling and extended the length of one of the walls. Upon the polished wood there now hung many of Isabella's large collection of disciplinary instruments. They ranged from simple straps to tawses, crops, whips, paddles, canes, gags, chains, handcuffs and a variety of clamps.

Once completed to her exacting standards, the whole space gave off the wonderfully sensuous aroma of leather and screamed out sadomasochistic sex. It was definitely time to give her brand "spanking" new dungeon the christening of which she had spoken.

Joining Isabella for this event, as well as David, were Caroline and Matthew, and Kate and Tony. The three men, all entirely naked and displaying impressive erections, were kneeling in a row with their backs against one of the dungeon walls while their respective Mistresses stood together nearby, conversing.

Tony's Mistress, Kate, her short ash-blonde hair brushed back from her beautiful face, was naked but for a tight corset and knee-length boots with high heels. Both the corset and the boots were of dark red leather. Isabella and Caroline were also virtually naked. Caroline was wearing only a skimpy black leather bra, which did little more than cover her erect nipples, and high heeled shoes. Isabella wore a tight black leather waistcoat, which she had left undone, and knee-length high heeled boots, also of black leather.

She was holding two objects, one in each hand. In her left she held a leather flogger that was the same dark shade of red as Kate's minimal outfit, and in her right, of all things, a cheap plastic battery-operated clock. It was black in colour and did its job of ticking the present into the past with noisy insistence. Isabella strode over and placed this last eccentric item on top of the whipping bench. She performed this last act with exaggerated ceremony, as if it were the crown jewels themselves she was handling.

'What have we here?' Caroline asked, her green eyes sparkling with amusement.

'I've thought up a game we can play to christen my dungeon,' Isabella said. 'I've called it "Last slave standing". The idea is that we three dommes all swap subs and then, each in turn, do our damndest to make our assigned slave climax, using a devilish mixture of pain and pleasure. The slaves must do their best to resist and the one who manages to retain his erection the longest, as timed on that clock over there, will be the winner. Do you like the sound of my game?'

'I like it a lot,' Kate enthused.

'Me too,' Caroline added. 'Are there any particular ground rules?'

'There are no gags or blindfolds allowed,' Isabella replied. 'And we'll all start our turn in the same place – with our slave's up-stretched arms attached by the wrists to the cuffs at the end of those two ceiling chains.' She pointed to the centre of the dungeon where two adjacent chains with black leather cuff attachments were hanging, approximately two feet apart. 'Also, the only disciplinary implement we can use is this one.' She held up the dark red whip. 'Beyond that, anything goes. We'll determine who gets which slave and so on with a quick game of dice.'

The first roll of the dice gave Caroline her choice of slave. She chose David, leaving Kate with Matthew, and Isabella with Tony. Another roll of the dice made Isabella the clock watcher except when it was her turn to torment Tony; and a final couple of shakes of the dice determined that Kate and Matthew would go first, Isabella and Tony after that, and then Caroline and David.

The result of that final roll of the dice, the one determining that David would be the last of the slaves to be tormented, troubled him greatly. It was psychologically the worst place to be, he was sure of it. That was because he would know exactly what time he had to exceed in order to win this sadistic game that Isabella had devised. And he desperately wanted to win it, desperately wanted to meet what Isabella had described as his "greatest challenge yet". All these tests and challenges must be leading somewhere surely, he told himself. If he won this big one – who knew? – he might even be promoted to being something more than a mere "diversion" in Isabella's life. He could but hope.

As David watched Kate take Matthew to the centre of the dungeon, he was struck yet again by the blonde domme's great beauty and by what a lovely body she had, with her firm breasts tipped with dark nipples that seemed always to be aroused, her shapely thighs and her prominent, hairless mound.

It was amazing to think that this truly formidable dominatrix, who was doubtless about to beat the living daylights out of his best friend Matthew, had once been Isabella's slave. Indeed she would always remain her slave when push came to shove, as he'd clearly witnessed a month ago at *Club Depravity*. To think that he'd actually been sucked off by Kate. To think that he'd actually been sucked off by Matthew as well, that he'd sucked him off too, and been buggered by him as well – all of it in the context of the kind of heavy duty S&M sessions that would have shocked most people in the vanilla world to the very core. It was all so surreal, so amazing. David felt himself utterly submerged now in a world of such extreme perversion and deviancy that almost anything was possible.

He watched as his best friend began to be put through his paces. Matthew placed his arms above his head and Kate attached his wrists to the leather cuffs on the ends of the two ceiling chains. She stood to his front and masturbated him for a while, her fingers expertly playing the length of his stiff cock, before suddenly moving her hands to his chest. Kate squeezed both of his nipples at the same time and very hard too, making him gasp with pain.

She then moved behind Matthew and told him to bend forward as far as the chains would allow. 'Time for a spanking,' she said before raising her hand high and bringing it down with a hard slap that made him cry out. Kate raised her hand again and brought it down a second time as swiftly and as hard as the first stroke and then kept on spanking Matthew until his backside glowed as red as an angry sunset.

Next Kate switched to the red leather flogger, which she went on to use remorselessly on Matthew's already punished rear, the whip landing each time with a sharp crack that resounded noisily around the dungeon. By the time she stopped whipping him, his backside was heavily marked with stripes and he was whimpering in agony.

Kate detached Matthew from the ceiling chains and told him to get on to his knees. His erection hung stiffly between his thighs as he knelt down. 'Lick the high heeled boot I am pointing at, slave,' she instructed, gesturing towards her right foot. 'Worship it with your mouth.' Matthew obeyed without hesitation, bending his head forward and pressing his lips against the pointed toe of the red boot. He slid his eager tongue along the leather, his lips caressing the smoothness of it.

'Lie on your back,' Kate ordered next. 'Suck the heels of my boots.' Again, he obeyed instantly, his throbbing shaft rearing in the air. Matthew sucked first one and then the other of the shiny red daggers that were Kate's high heels as she presented them to him in turn. He was utterly absorbed in this ritual, concentrating intently on worshipping Kate's high heels.

Matthew's climax came all of sudden, taking him completely unawares, when Kate quickly moved her boot away from his face to his crotch and dug its heel against his pulsing cock. The sharp pain combined straight away with the delirious pleasure of orgasm. Matthew called out, a wordless explosion of anguish and desire, as he spurted his climax across her heel. Kate brought the heel back to his lips. There was no need to wait for her command; Matthew took the hard point of her heel in his mouth, sucking off his come and swallowing it down as his erection began to subside.

'Thirty minutes, give or take a second or two,' Isabella announced as she handed over clock-watching duties to Caroline. She added with undisguised relish, 'It's my turn to do some serious tormenting now.' Isabella led Tony to the centre of the dungeon and secured his wrists to the ceiling chains above his head.

The dominatrix then took hold of the flogger and whipped Tony's chest, each blow stinging and sharp, before switching to his genitals, concentrating her blows on his helplessly exposed cockhead and causing him to yelp with pain. Isabella whipped Tony's rear next, every skilfully aimed lash striking him in a regular rhythm. She showered his backside with blows until it was covered in lacerations.

Isabella then detached Tony from the ceiling chains and led him over to the horizontal torture chair, telling him to get on to it on his back. She buckled his wrists behind his head, his knees up and his legs wide apart.

Isabella put on a sizeable strap-on dildo and coated it liberally with lubricant. She eased it into Tony's anus and he let out a groan, his cock throbbing and spurting out pre-come as his sphincter tightened and relaxed around the large intruder now lodged inside him. Isabella began to fuck Tony hard. As she built up ever greater momentum, she also started pulling his cock, her hand moving with a swift rhythm. Eventually Tony could take no more and he ejaculated, the come leaping out of his aching cock and spilling in pools across his stomach.

'Well done, Tony – 33 minutes,' Caroline proclaimed as she watched Isabella release him from the torture chair. The flame haired dominatrix, who was clearly more than a little impatient to get started herself by this stage, added, 'At last it's time for my turn and I can't fucking wait.'

Isabella moved back to her former position as she unbuckled her well used strap-on, and returned to watching the clock. Sweet Jesus, David said to himself in dismay. He would have to keep going for more than 33 minutes to win this game. That was a very tall order, a very tall order indeed. Isabella hadn't been exaggerating when she'd told him this would be his toughest challenge yet.

Caroline told David to get off his knees and as she strode briskly across the dungeon, pulling him along by the hair, it was evident that here was a woman who definitely meant business. She attached his wrists to the ceiling chain cuffs very quickly and immediately set-to with the dark red flogger like some sort of a whirling dervish. Caroline whipped David's chest, genitals, back and rear in an onslaught of fury that was unrelentingly cruel and seemed to him to go on for ever. On and on she flogged David until his body was thoroughly striped with the marks of the whip and he was enveloped in acute pain.

His wet-tipped cock was hugely erect, though, and Caroline began to masturbate him. She worked her hand urgently up and down the hard shaft that became increasingly smeared with pre-come until her fingers were covered with copious amounts of the fluid and David felt, despite his best efforts, on the verge of climaxing. 'Lick my fingers clean,' she told him. David opened his mouth and closed his lips around Caroline's fingers, sucking feverishly while desperately willing his impending orgasm to subside.

David then did something he instantly regretted: He looked over at the clock. He couldn't believe it. Only 20 minutes had passed since the start of his torment. He could have sworn it had been longer than that – at least half an hour, surely. Christ, it had felt like an eternity. David didn't look at the clock again, but from that point on he couldn't get its insistent ticking out of his head. The clock ticked with agonising slowness and seemed to him to become ever more audible.

Tick tock.

Tick tock.

Tick tock.

Tick tock.

That noise was like water torture to David. It was a constant reminder of how much longer he would have to hold out if he had any hope at all of winning this game. And David so much wanted to win. It was his chance to really prove himself to Isabella once and for all. But who was he trying to kid? He had almost ejaculated a moment ago. Time was most definitely not on his side. He was between a rock and a hard place. Correction, he was between a *clock* and a hard place.

Tick tock.

Tick tock.

Hard cock.

Hard cock.

Caroline began to whip him furiously between the legs, aiming her blows first at the insides of his thighs and between the anus, and then at his genitals, concentrating on his painfully hard cock. Each blow to his aching shaft made him flinch convulsively.

Tick tock.

Tick tock.

Whip cock.

Whip cock.

Caroline then detached David from the ceiling chains and led him over to the horizontal torture chair where she told him to lie on his back. Her fingers working very quickly indeed, she strapped his wrists behind his head and his legs wide apart.

David's whole body now ached with extreme pain yet was permeated as well with extreme pleasure as Caroline continued to do her very worst. She masturbated him again, her hand moving up and down the length of his stiffness quicker and quicker.

Tick tock.

Tick tock.

Pull cock.

Pull cock.

Caroline leant forward so that she could suck David's cock, rounding her lips and closing them around his hardness, taking it into her mouth, pressing against the head of his shaft with her tongue. She pushed herself further forward so that she could pull more of his length into her mouth. The up-and-down movement of her head went ever faster as she sucked his cock harder and harder.

Tick tock.

Tick tock.

Suck cock.

Suck cock.

While continuing to suck David's cock voraciously, Caroline pinched his nipples savagely hard. He felt great pain; he felt great pleasure. The clock was ticking; her mouth was sucking.

Tick tock.

Tick tock.

Suck cock.

Suck cock.

If he could just hold out, David told himself desperately, if he could just hold out, if he could … but he couldn't any more and finally reached the end of the line. He climaxed convulsively, pumping out great surging waves of come deep into Caroline's throat, the sound of that accursed clock even then still ticking in his head.

Tick tock.

Tick tock.

Tick tock.

Tick tock.

But had he made it? He looked over at Isabella. She looked at the clock and back at David, her expression betraying nothing. Finally, she said, 'Thirty five minutes.' He'd made it all right – just barely. He was the winner, the "Last slave standing".

A long moment passed. Then David took it upon himself to speak to Isabella, he simply had to. 'I wonder if I could ask you to do me a real favour, Mistress,' he said, his voice panting, his breathing laboured.

Tick tock.

Tick tock.

Tick tock.

Tick tock.

'What might that be, slave?' she asked, her face still unreadable.

Tick tock.

Tick tock.

Tick tock.

Tick tock.

'Could you please, please, *please* take the battery out of that clock!'

Tick tock.

Tick tock.

Kill clock.

Kill clock.

Tick tock.

Tick tock.

Ki …

Chapter Thirty

Shortly after that hard-won triumph things changed radically for David, changed more radically than he could have dared dream possible. The next time Isabella phoned, it was to tell him she wouldn't be phoning him again. His first reaction was to gasp in horror, his stomach lurching. David began to protest but Isabella immediately cut him short, telling him to let her finish what she'd started to say. There would be no need for her to phone him again, she went on. He had proved himself a good and loyal slave and had responded well to all the challenges she had thrown at him, not least that last one. Now the 'Last slave standing' could have his well deserved reward.

Isabella informed David that she wanted him to move into her Brighton home and be her full time house-slave. In this capacity he would be bound by a number of rules: He must, of course, continue to always call her "Mistress" and should avoid speaking to her unless directly addressed. He would be required to remain naked at all times in the house or its secluded rear garden unless she instructed him otherwise. He would be expected to clean her shoes and boots to a perfect, mirror-like finish, and undertake a whole range of other menial tasks for her to a similar high standard: cooking, cleaning, gardening, and so on. He was never to masturbate unless she had given her express permission for him to do so, Isabella emphasised.

She said that he would also be required to sign a slave contract, a copy of which she had just that minute e-mailed to him. Isabella told David to click on his e-mail and scan the contents of the agreement right there and then, which he did. The contract contained the following conditions, by which, the document made clear, David would be required to conscientiously abide all the time:

1. I will serve and please Isabella Stern, my Mistress and owner. I will always obey any instruction Mistress gives me without question, without fail and to the very best of my abilities.

2. Above everything else my first priority will always be to please Mistress, my most earnest desire being that she should find me pleasing in all that I do, whether I am in her presence or not.

3. I worship Mistress totally.

4. Mistress's power fills me with the utmost wonder and awe.

5. Both my body and my mind are entirely the property of Mistress.

6. I am always under the control of Mistress, whether or not I am in her presence, ready and willing to please her at any time, anywhere and under any circumstances, regardless of who may be present.

7. My place is kneeling before Mistress, for it is the greatest privilege and honour imaginable to be her house-slave

After allowing David enough time to peruse the document, Isabella gave him a couple of final pieces of information before telling him to put his affairs in order, lock up his house and get himself over to her place with minimum delay.

As her house-slave, she said, he would have his own modest quarters in her home. These would have a small en-suite bathroom and would be furnished with the bare essentials: a bed, a chest of drawers and a wardrobe. But such details were of little consequence, she went on to advise. This was because, apart from carrying out the various menial tasks he'd have to undertake, he could expect to spend pretty much the rest of his waking hours in her dungeon where she intended to discipline him constantly. Isabella proved only too true to her word. It was in that dungeon also that she and David finally became lovers. Of sorts

Isabella, her face pale and luminous in the half-light of the dungeon, was a vision of loveliness in black leather. She was wearing a choker, a bra that merely framed her magnificent breasts, leaving them completely exposed; a tiny slit-sided skirt underneath which she was naked, and very high-heeled boots that had been polished to a gleaming shine – by David of course. He was standing before her, nude but for a leather head harness including a blue ball gag, a slave's collar, and wrist and ankle cuffs; his cock was rigidly erect.

'Hold your hands above your head,' Isabella demanded before squeezing his nipples, tightening fingers and thumbs over them so hard that it made his eyes water.

'You're my whipping boy, David,' she said next, her tone of voice mocking. 'So, what better place for you to be than over the whipping bench.' Isabella told him to bend over the bench and he moved to obey, laying his belly over its top.

The dominatrix picked up a leather whip and began lashing David's back and rear with great energy, sometimes using downward motions of the whip and sometimes upward motions. She paused for a short while and the acute pain David was suffering reduced slightly to a hard insistent throbbing that echoed the throbbing of his erect cock. *Maybe she's about to stop*, he thought.

'What's that I sense you thinking, slave?' Isabella asked. 'You need me to be even more vicious. Is that right? Is that what you want?' David nodded his reply uncertainly. Yet it was true, God knows; there never was anything more true.

Isabella really went for it then, pulled out all the stops. She switched to a cat o'nine tails and used it to whip David mercilessly. On and relentlessly on she punished him, stroke after searing stroke, until the ferocious pain he was suffering caused him to sob in agony beneath his gag.

'Oh dear, I appear to have broken your skin in several places,' Isabella said in a tone of blatantly bogus sympathy as she examined David's severely punished rear. 'You must be in considerable pain, is that so?' He bowed his head in response and continued sobbing beneath his gag.

'No matter,' she announced cheerfully. 'No gain without pain.'

Isabella then allowed David to get up from the whipping bench but immediately pulled him down to a kneeling position again, this time on to the dungeon floor itself. She did this by yanking on the chain to his nipple clamps, causing sharp pain to burn into his flesh.

Next Isabella got on to her knees herself in front of David, saying, 'Let's take this thing off.' She removed his combined head harness and ball gag. She then stood up before him, her legs apart. 'Worship my sex,' she commanded. 'Go on, lick my pussy.'

David had done this very many times before – as a masturbatory fantasy. This was the first time Isabella had ever permitted him to do it for real and he felt both profoundly honoured and immensely excited. He kissed his way sensuously up Isabella's thighs before pushing his tongue into the sticky wetness of her sex. David started to lap at her pussy and it shuddered against his mouth as he did so, just as he'd fantasised so many times that it would.

Isabella then pushed him back, grabbing his shoulders and making him lie on his back on the dungeon floor. She raked her fingers over his smooth, hard body, squeezing his haunches, rubbing his cock.

But there was more, much more to come: the honour of all honours. Because then Isabella straddled him, pressing her groin to his and grabbing his arms and pinning them back above his head. She moved her hips, fitting them around his hardness, finding the spot for her. She pushed down to take him inside her. David let out a short throaty cry, looking up at his magnificent Mistress, wide eyed and exposed and dizzy with lust.

David let himself be taken by the urgency of Isabella's

movements, possessed by her hunger. He felt her grind into him, felt deliciously helpless as she fucked him, her hips jacking and moving fluidly. She gripped his arms more tightly, and pushed her weight forward. He felt as if he was going to climax at any moment.

But there he couldn't have been more wrong. 'You are not to climax,' Isabella said emphatically and then her thrusts became frenzied as she built towards a noisy, juddering orgasm ... and he didn't.

'That will be all for now, slave,' Isabella announced abruptly soon after climaxing. She climbed off David's prone form and looked down on him through half-drawn lids. 'I will be requiring your sexual services many more times than this today. So I won't be allowing you to come until I'm fully sated – and that won't be for some while yet, I can assure you of that.'

'Yes, Mistress,' David replied, thinking frantically: How could she do this to me? His erotic arousal had by this time become agonizing, desperate. His erection, now steely hard, was pulsing fit to explode at any moment.

'Oh, poor slave,' Isabella said. 'Are you absolutely dying to climax?'

'Yes, Mistress,' David replied urgently. 'I really am.'

After a gloating pause Isabella responded. 'Well, you can't,' she said. 'Oh, and by the way, when I do finally allow you to come – *if* I do – it won't be inside me. You will never be allowed to climax inside me, never.' And with that she swept out of the dungeon, leaving David to suffer in silence until her next sadistic visit.

He would have her all to himself again when that happened, though, and that wondrous prospect made his acute sexual frustration bearable to him. No, scratch that. It made it a lot more than bearable. It made it positively blissful in its way – once he had calmed down slightly, that is.

But ignorance is bliss. Little did David know that trouble was just around the corner, big trouble. Her name was Jacqui Walsh. David always blamed himself afterwards for what happened with Jacqui. But he couldn't blame himself for how it started because he wasn't even there.

PART TWO

A BAD GIRL

'In order to know virtue, we must first acquaint ourselves
with vice.'
Marquis de Sade

Chapter Thirty-one

It was just starting to get dark when Isabella got back to her hotel and re-entered its lobby. The dominatrix was feeling a bit flat. It was all something of an anticlimax. Here she was in what surely must be the dreariest town this side of the Downs where she had spent most of the day in one-on-one negotiations with the notoriously awkward owner of a small company that made leather BDSM items of an outstandingly high quality. Isabella's idea had been that she would personally negotiate with the owner on his own territory, so to speak, a deal that would give *La Fetishista* sole distribution rights for all his company's products. The tactic had worked perfectly and, after some predictably hard bargaining with the irksome little man, they'd shaken on the deal. The lawyers could do the rest; the real work had been done.

Isabella knew from the outset that it was going to be an exhausting day and so it had proved to be, but she had covered all the bases when planning for it. She'd considered whether to drive homewards to Brighton at the end of what was bound to be a hard grind of a day or, alternatively, to chill-out for a while, stay the night at what looked to be the best of the small supply of local hotels and return home refreshed first thing the next morning. The latter option had seemed the better one and Isabella had arranged to stay the night at the hotel at the same time that she'd arranged to meet for detailed discussions with the pain-in-the-arse owner of the leather goods company.

She was beginning to think she'd made the wrong decision, though, as she contemplated the hours ahead. Here she was stuck in this grey, anonymous hotel in an equally grey, anonymous town. She thought enviously of her husband, currently living it up in New York with the twins; the contrast was like chalk and cheese. She thought too of David waiting patiently for her at home: naked – definitely; erect or semi-erect – quite probably, knowing him; masturbating – definitely not. He wasn't allowed to masturbate unless she gave her express permission and she had done no such thing.

For a moment Isabella considered changing her plans and going home that night, back to her horny house-slave. But she decided that she couldn't be bothered with the fag of packing all the items she'd unpacked earlier that day and that she certainly didn't feel like driving. No, she'd definitely stay. But what was she to do with her evening? Perhaps that foxy-looking receptionist with the long, dark, curly hair who'd been giving her the eye each time she'd come and gone through the entrance foyer today, could point her in the right direction. She didn't hold out much hope, though, here in a nearly empty hotel in Dullsville on a Tuesday evening. Still, nothing ventured …

'Excuse me, eh, Jacqui,' Isabella said, looking at the name tag on the girl's lapel, which said: Jacqui Walsh – Receptionist. 'What's there to do around here in the evening, can you advise? I don't know the area well and I'm at a bit of a loose end.'

'I could show you, if you'd like. I come off duty in about ten minutes,' the girl replied with a warm smile, the fullness of her lips parting over pearl white teeth. That was more than the standard service industry smile, Isabella thought. It set aglow the young woman's large eyes, which were a deep brown, arched with black brows. She looked extremely attractive. She also seemed familiar somehow, but Isabella couldn't put her finger on it right now. Where had she seen her before?

'That's good of you,' Isabella said with a broad smile, launching her own charm offensive.

'Not at all. It would be my pleasure,' Jacqui replied. 'To tell the truth I'm going to be at a bit of a loose end myself this evening, too, and I'd welcome some company. I live here at the hotel – the flat goes with the job. So, just give me half an hour to have a shower and freshen up and I'll come to your room.

We can take it from there.'

A shower. Yes, what a good idea, Isabella thought. That was just what she needed as well after the day she'd had. 'See you shortly,' she said, starting to move in the direction of the lift.

Isabella entered the bland nothingness of her hotel room, stripped off and made for the shower. She stood under the hot jets of water and sighed as she let them wash over her. The water slipped down over her shoulders, between her breasts, dripping from her nipples, and down her shapely body. She let her mind drift lazily, sensuously, to thoughts about this Jacqui Walsh female. She seemed as if she might have potential, Isabella thought with a tingle of excitement. She was certainly her type physically, a little like a brunette version of Kate with much longer, curlier hair. She definitely looked familiar, too. Now, where had she seen that pretty face before?

Isabella emerged from the shower, towelled herself dry, brushed her hair, and started to consider what to wear. The options were very limited as she'd only packed for the briefest of stays. Her deliberations were interrupted by a tap on the door of her room. She wrapped the towel around herself and opened the door.

'Sorry,' Jacqui said, registering Isabella's state of undress. 'I'm obviously too early.'

'Not a problem,' Isabella replied. 'Come on in.'

'Thanks,' Jacqui said and wandered in, giving Isabella a sexy, full face smile. She really was very attractive indeed, beautiful even, Isabella thought, and what an extraordinarily sensuous mouth she had. And yes, Isabella was sure of it now. She'd definitely seen her before somewhere. But where, for Christ's sake? There were no clues in what she was wearing – a short red cotton T-shirt (no bra, she noticed), skin-tight black jeans and slingback stiletto heels over bare feet.

'I'm sure we've met before,' Isabella said.

'Don't you recognise me, Mistress Isabella?' Jacqui said with a mischievous grin.

That threw Isabella, although she disguised it well. But, no, damn it, she still couldn't place her. It was infuriating. 'How about giving me a clue,' she said.

'Think similar job, different kind of uniform,' Jacqui replied. 'Oh, and a completely different hairstyle. I've only recently changed it.'

'Of course,' Isabella said; suddenly she'd got it. 'You're one of the hostesses at *Club Depravity*. I'm right aren't I?'

'You are indeed,' Jacqui said. 'I wondered when the penny would drop. I kept trying to catch your eye whenever you walked past me in reception today.'

'And I thought it was because you fancied me,' Isabella smiled, raising an eyebrow.

'Who says I don't?' Jacqui replied, the challenge in her gaze unmistakable.

Isabella ignored her response, let it hang in the air. 'Drink?' she asked, picking up two glasses and walking to the fridge.

'Vodka tonic with ice, please,' Jacqui said.

Isabella mixed two of these, handed one glass to Jacqui and raised her own. 'Cheers,' she said and took a sip from her drink, the ice cubes clinking.

Jacqui's hand closed around her glass and she lifted it. 'Cheers,' she said, repeating the toast.

'Now, I'd better get changed,' Isabella said. 'You were going to show me where the action is around here on a Tuesday evening.'

'You're looking at it,' Jacqui replied. The radiant challenge came into her face again, this time full beam, and her big brown eyes shone. She took a sip of her vodka tonic and put it to one side. Jacqui then kicked off her slingbacks before unzipping her tight black jeans. She pulled them down sharply, revealing both that she was naked underneath and that her sex was entirely free of pubic hair. Sitting down on the room's one armchair, she pulled the jeans off completely and dropped them beside her. Next she stood up and removed her top, exposing her bare breasts.

'You like?' she said with a tilt of the head. There was the full-wattage smile once more and the ignited brown eyes. Isabella shrugged and sipped at her drink. What was not to like when you looked at that body? It was soft and full, slim but

176

rounded. Her skin was smooth with a light all-over tan. Isabella looked Jacqui up and down appraisingly and saw before her a lissom young woman with a body in youthful bloom.

She also saw a face betraying all the confidence and arrogance of youth, yes, but something more – a hint of something much darker, and all the more seductive for it. There was a certain slyness there too, Isabella could discern that as well, a sense that this was someone not really to be trusted.

Isabella put her drink down and walked towards Jacqui, allowing her towel to fall to the ground to reveal her own beautiful body. The two naked women stood before one another. For a second neither of them spoke and then the silence was suddenly broken as Isabella, grasping a handful of that long curly hair, slapped Jacqui's face three, four times.

'Oh!' she cried out in shock, her cheeks smarting. Her face turned scarlet and her big eyes welled up with tears.

'What the fuck do you think you're playing at?' Isabella snapped. Her face had become deadly serious, stern and unyielding, her black irises cold pools of anger.

'But, but I thought …' the stunned young woman started to answer. This wasn't the way she'd thought this assignation was going to go at all.

'Thought what, bitch?' Isabella said. 'That because I'm heavily into BDSM I'm a slut like you?'

'I'm really sorry,' Jacqui said in a small voice as tears began to course down her face. 'There's obviously been some misunderstanding.'

'Yeah, on your part,' Isabella sneered, her glare as fierce as ever.

'I can only apologise,' Jacqui said with a sob.

'An apology isn't enough,' Isabella said firmly, sitting down on the edge of the bed. 'Get over my knee this instant.'

Jacqui had no hesitation in obeying and Isabella immediately raised her hand and then brought it down hard with a sudden smack that echoed through the room. The second smack came down on Jacqui's backside just as hard as the first and the searing heat burned her flesh. There was another smack and another, and another, each one landing like an explosion and smarting vividly.

'You love it, bitch, don't you?' Isabella said, before bringing her hand down with another two forceful blows in quick succession.

'Yes, Mistress Isabella,' Jacqui replied, her lips trembling. And it was true because now the burning heat was becoming more diffuse, melting, changing, spreading through her body and connecting deliciously with the growing heat in her sex.

Jacqui arched her back, lifting herself, offering the reddened cheeks of her backside to Isabella's fiery strokes. When the smacks landed now it was almost as if her pussy had been caressed. She was slick with her juice. She was soaking, dribbles of love juice smearing over her thighs. Her clitoris throbbed with pleasure as she lifted herself, opening her thighs so that Isabella's finger tips landed between the lips of her pussy.

Her backside was stinging so much that she writhed with agony and sensation, ached with pain and lust. Jacqui climaxed suddenly, clenching her body tight in that moment of ecstasy as the electric waves of pleasure in her sex surged throughout her body, making it shiver with delight.

The beating stopped. There was silence again. Jacqui's eyes were closed and tears continued to stream down her face. She felt such humiliation, she felt such joy. She hung her head and her luxuriant brown hair fell forward, covering her face with its veil.

Isabella reached over and brushed the hair from Jacqui's face. 'Pleasure me now, bitch,' she said, the harshness of her voice tempered slightly by the sensuousness of her touch. Jacqui knelt down between Isabella's spread thighs. She began to kiss softly, running her lips around Isabella's open sex, which was wet with love juice. She pressed her tongue forward, as stiff and wet as a snake, and it began to work its miracles of delight in Isabella's pussy.

'Play with yourself at the same time,' Isabella said. 'Don't stop licking me and masturbating until I give you permission.' Jacqui pressed two fingers between her pussy lips, rubbing them up and down and into herself. She luxuriated in her own sticky wetness, the heat of her pussy, the pulse of her clitoris.

And all the while, she carried on licking Isabella's sex, probing and flicking with her tongue. She turned her attention to Isabella's swollen clitoral bud, and kissed and sucked and teased her clit until she cried out wordlessly as a powerful orgasm took her. This caused Jacqui to climax again as her fingers pressed hard into the wet heat of her pussy, her body shuddering with waves of delight.

But she knew she couldn't stop until Isabella said she could and Isabella was not about to do that any time soon. Jacqui continued making Isabella and herself come over and over again. She was giving Isabella the ultimate in pleasure as she did the same to herself. The two women climaxed repeatedly, wanting the waves of ecstasy to go on and on until they could do no more.

But all good things must come to an end. 'Stop,' Isabella said eventually, and Jacqui immediately stopped licking her pussy and masturbating. Isabella pulled her up by the hair with both hands and looked directly into her shining eyes. 'It's over now, bitch,' she said. 'Make yourself scarce.'

And that was what Jacqui did ... for the time being. Because it wasn't over as far as Jacqui was concerned. She wasn't going to *allow* it be over.

Chapter Thirty-two

Jacqui gradually, insinuatingly, became a part of Isabella's life after that. In doing so she proved to be determined, devious and more than capable of patiently biding her time. After the entrance doors at *Club Depravity* had been closed and she was free to play, she would always make a beeline for Isabella when she and David were there and ask the dominatrix – oh so respectfully – if she might be allowed to participate in whatever kinky scene she and her slave happened to be engaged in at the time. Every time Isabella and David went to the club when Jacqui wasn't actually on duty she would "happen" to be there anyway and would invariably end up tagging along.

All this required considerable patience and perseverance on Jacqui's part because *Club Depravity* was still only opening its deviant doors on the last Saturday of the month. But her patience eventually paid off because on one of those Saturday nights she ended up going home with Isabella and David. There they engaged in an intense three-way sex session, which left all three of them craving more of the same ...

They were naked on top of Isabella's queen-sized bed, Jacqui between Isabella and David. Isabella smiled seductively at Jacqui before taking the young woman's chin in her hand and turning her face towards David. 'Kiss him,' she said, and she did. Her mouth was warm and wet and she probed his lips with her tongue. Jacqui and David carried on kissing wetly until Isabella told them to stop.

'I'm going to finger-fuck you now, Jacqui,' Isabella then said and brought her hand to the young woman's pussy. She began to make her wet with her fingers, finding her sweet spot, working it, setting the fire raging in her. Jacqui arched her back, pushing the mouth of her vagina further towards her.

Isabella had two fingers inside Jacqui and she began to rub the wall of her vagina with one while turning the other one slightly, trying to push it as far as it would go. Then she began to move both fingers in and out to the rhythm of Jacqui's moans … before switching tack again.

'Eat her pussy now, David,' Isabella ordered, removing her fingers from the wetness of Jacqui's sex.

'Yes, Mistress,' he replied and immediately moved to obey her.

David trailed his lips down Jacqui's body and she spread her legs as wide as possible before putting them around his shoulders. He began to nuzzle her pussy with his lips, searching for her clitoris with his tongue and then sucking it tenderly.

Jacqui looked over at Isabella who was clearly enjoying the show. As the dominatrix watched her house-slave continue to go down on Jacqui, she was working her fingers between her own quivering thighs, masturbating furiously. She tensed, gasped and clamped her thighs around her hand. Her breath came in quick little pants as she climaxed.

Isabella raised her wet fingers to Jacqui's mouth and she licked them, one by one. Then the dominatrix pinched first one then the other of the young woman's nipples with those same fingers, making her shiver and moan at her cruel touch combined with David's mouth as it continued to work tirelessly on her pussy.

'Now fuck her,' Isabella demanded and suddenly David was above Jacqui. She arched against him as he positioned himself between the soft flesh of her thighs. He drove his hard cock into her dripping pussy as she squeezed his muscular backside with her hands. Over and over, David thrust into Jacqui, his cock filling her as her body writhed with pleasure, her legs squeezed tight around him. They could both hear Isabella's soft moans and knew she was watching them and masturbating again.

Jacqui rocked her hips up to meet David's thrusts and with a loud groan she came violently. And so did Isabella. Then David climaxed too. His cock twitched, throbbing inside Jacqui as she squeezed her pussy around him, drawing out everything he had to give – not something Isabella would *ever* have permitted to happen between her and him.

Chapter Thirty-three

Variations on a theme of raunchy threesomes like that – with Isabella ostensibly calling all the shots – started to become a regular event, with one night of passion frequently extending into much of the next day. When Isabella, assisted by David, organised select fetish parties in her dungeon with the likes of Caroline and Matthew and Kate and Tony it became customary to invite Jacqui along too. She started to introduce herself to others on the Brighton fetish scene as Mistress Isabella's slave, and in reality that is what she had become.

How did Isabella respond to all this devious, if less than subtle, manipulation? With apparent equanimity is the answer. She rather liked having a female slave, she said. It reminded her of the "old days" when Kate had been her slave. David was relaxed about the situation too, more relaxed than maybe might have been expected. Anything his Mistress chose to do was all right with him, he reasoned; it had to be that way – that was what his slave contract dictated, apart from anything else. He found that thinking like that as well as continuing to tell himself that "he couldn't have it both ways' helped to keep the green monster of jealousy at bay. Anyhow, Jacqui was undeniably very sexy indeed, a complete turn-on.

What did Isabella's fellow dommes Caroline and Kate think of Jacqui? Caroline viewed her with relative indifference, couldn't really have cared less about her one way or the other. As for Kate, she definitely wasn't a fan of the young interloper but for reasons she would have found it hard to articulate. It was essentially a gut feeling, borne maybe from some special insight she'd gained from having once been Isabella's slave herself. Personally, she wouldn't have trusted Jacqui as far as she could have thrown her, suspected, in fact, that she had it in mind to try and usurp David's hard-earned position as Isabella's house-slave. But she had no proof. It was just that gut feeling again. So she kept her own counsel and hoped for the best.

But Isabella remained blind – or seemingly blind – to any ulterior motives her doting young acolyte may have had. When Jacqui changed her job and no longer had the service flat that had gone with her receptionist post with the hotel it didn't take more than a couple of heavy hints on her part for Isabella to respond, suggesting that she live with her for a while until she'd sorted out her accommodation difficulties. She had plenty of spare rooms, the dominatrix assured her. Isabella made it clear, however, that Jacqui would be bound by the same nudity rules as those that applied to David around the property. The smitten slave had no hesitation in agreeing. Isabella also added a further instruction that turned out to be superfluous. She told Jacqui that as her slave she was forbidden to ever wear underwear whenever she was out and about. She replied that she never did anyway.

Jacqui adored Isabella's dungeon, that couldn't have been clearer. 'It's got absolutely everything,' she enthused virtually every time she entered it. Jacqui really loved playing there with Isabella and David too, found every experience there tremendously thrilling. It was deeply addictive to her, like some powerful drug she couldn't get enough of …

Isabella had securely strapped David on his back to the St. Andrews cross and had put a black leather hood over his head. Apart from the hood, which had open eye, nose and mouth holes, David was entirely naked. His cock was rock-hard, a rivulet of precome trailing from its swollen head.

Jacqui was kneeling submissively at Isabella's feet, both women wearing nothing at all. The dominatrix told Jacqui to stand up, and led her over to the horizontal torture chair. 'Lie on it face up with your arms and legs spread out,' she told her before securing her wrists and ankles to the chair by its strap attachments.

Isabella went on to use the leather tip of a riding crop to beat Jacqui's clit and pussy. She did this more sensuously than sadistically, and by the time she had finished the young slave was groaning with desire. Threads of love juice were dripping from her labia, making the leather surface of the torture chair beneath her wet.

Next the dominatrix freed Jacqui's arms and legs and released her from the horizontal torture chair. She took her over to the horse, positioning her on her front lengthwise over it and securing her wrists and ankles to either side of its base by means of the leather straps there. She proceeded to attach clamps to the lips of her sex. This was intensely painful to Jacqui, causing her beautiful face to grimace and her pussy and anus to pulse uncontrollably.

Isabella was starting to really get into her sadistic stride now. She took hold of a heavy leather flogger and immediately set to work with it on Jacqui's backside. The cruel implement hissed noisily when she swung it through the air before landing with a sharp crack on its fleshy target. She beat Jacqui with it remorselessly until her rear was covered with angry welts and she was crying out in pain. 'Too much noise, slave,' Isabella announced, putting a red ball gag into her mouth and buckling it firmly into place behind her head.

Isabella next lit several red candles and proceeded to drizzle molten wax onto Jacqui's already heavily punished backside. This caused the young slave to shudder violently, her wrists and ankles straining against the leather straps that held them tightly in place. At the same time the ball gag muffled her agonized cries of pain.

Eventually Isabella detached Jacqui from the horse, carefully removing the clamps from her labia, but leaving her gagged with the red ball gag. She also released David from the wall-mounted cross.

Isabella then led David and Jacqui over to one of the spreader bars that hung by chains from the dungeon ceiling. The spreader bar had two manacle attachments at each end and she stood the gagged slaves together face to face and manacled their wrists to either end.

Isabella went on to take hold of David's throbbing erection and hold it at the entrance to Jacqui's tight wet pussy. 'Push your cock inside her, slave,' she ordered. As David entered Jacqui he felt her body tremble and she groaned with desire beneath the red ball gag, making him stiffen even further inside her.

Isabella removed Jacqui's ball gag and covered her eyes instead using a blindfold of soft red leather. She also clipped the blindfold attachment of David's hood into place. 'When you beg for my mercy, slaves, as you most surely will,' she told the blindfolded slaves, 'you have my permission to come.'

The dominatrix picked up two leather-covered swagger canes, one in her left hand and the other in her right, and gave them a couple of experimental swishes through the air. The ambidextrous domme went on to cane David and Jacqui simultaneously and with increasing ferocity, each swipe more agonizing than the last.

For a long time the dungeon resounded with the double swish and crack of two swagger canes striking two punished backsides. Isabella caned their rears with ever harder strokes until they were criss-crossed with clear stripes. Throughout this ferocious beating, Jacqui's pussy clenched in spasms around David's stiffness, which was steely-hard inside her, and her body quivered against his.

At last neither of them could hold out any longer. Together David and Jacqui cried out desperately for mercy. At the same time the extreme pleasure-pain they were experiencing tightened and then erupted through them in orgasms that sent them off into the stratosphere. The experience lingered in their memories long after they'd fallen back down to earth.

Chapter Thirty-four

David and Jacqui's next session in the dungeon ended up being even more memorable for both of them than that ... but for all the wrong reasons. The best that could be said of it was that it started extremely well.

Isabella was as totally, utterly naked as her two slaves. She entered the dungeon with them, and threw herself back on to the leather-covered bondage table, lifting and opening her legs wide. 'I feel so fucking horny it's unbelievable,' she announced. 'Service me, slaves. You, Jacqui, lick and finger my pussy. David, pleasure my anus.'

The two slaves instantly obeyed. Jacqui pressed her face into Isabella's sex, which was already gleaming with wetness. At the same time, David planted a kiss between the cheeks of her backside, touching his lips to her anus. He pushed his tongue into her anal hole, pushing against the rim of muscles and going into her body. Meanwhile Jacqui licked deep and hard into Isabella's pussy while stroking her clit with her fingers. Isabella opened herself further, lifting her pussy to Jacqui's welcome attentions.

Jacqui's fingers went deep into Isabella's sex, penetrating hard and fast. She concentrated on Isabella's clit with her mouth, teasing it with her tongue so that Isabella writhed with pleasure. All the while David was licking her anus hard. The sensations were exquisite. It felt delicious; spasms of electricity pulsed through her body and she shivered with pleasure. A shuddering groan escaped her and moments later she climaxed powerfully.

'That was great – just what I needed,' Isabella said,

climbing down from the bondage table, and suddenly all business. 'Now, I'm going to park you two slaves here for a few hours while I get on with some work. I've got a board meeting tomorrow morning and I want to be properly prepared for it.' She told them to kneel back to back. 'You are not allowed to talk or move your positions until I return,' Isabella said and, with that instruction resounding in their ears, she promptly turned tail and left.

It was extremely quiet in the dungeon, the silence so thick that it was almost audible, and time hung heavily for the two slaves. But neither of them moved much more than a muscle for what seemed like an eternity. But how long had they actually been there? There was no clock in the dungeon to tell them. Time continued to pass but had lost its usual dimensions. Had they been there twenty minutes, three-quarters of an hour, over an hour? It was impossible to know. David did what he always did after a while in this sort of situation – he disappeared into his own subspace, fundamentally content to do whatever his Mistress instructed, no matter how seemingly unreasonable her requirements might be.

Jacqui went inside her head as well, letting her mind roam back to when she'd been a sexually adventurous undergraduate. Actually Jacqui had dropped out of university after not much more than a year. She'd found that she just couldn't settle, which was the story of her life in many ways. But she didn't dwell on that aspect while she knelt waiting there in the dungeon. What she dwelled on instead was the most memorable erotic experience she'd had when she'd been at university. It was one that had almost not happened at all because she'd left things to the eleventh hour, and even then they hadn't exactly gone to plan. She saw it all now as clearly as a movie rolling before her eyes ...

Jacqui was running out of time. Right from the start there had been a strong spark of mutual attraction between her and Anne, the woman she was temporarily lodging with while her rooms in the university hall of residence were being renovated. Jacqui had firmly resolved to fully ignite that spark before leaving

Anne's home. However she was due to move back to the hall of residence the next morning and had already packed most of the few things she had with her at Anne's place. So it was now or never.

It was easy to understand why Jacqui was so attracted to Anne, an agelessly beautiful woman with honey-blonde hair and a captivating smile. Her eyes were blue and green, bright and sensual, and her figure was to-die-for. Jacqui could tell Anne was lonely, though. She had a husband she clearly adored but he made his living as a musician and was constantly on the road.

Jacqui seriously had the hots for Anne who had an air of control about her that really turned the young woman on. She had spent virtually every night since moving into Anne's home pleasuring herself while fantasising about having steamy sex with her. Jacqui had found herself increasingly yearning for the real thing though and had finally determined to make that happen before she moved out. But she was cutting it very fine. It had to be today or not at all.

Jacqui's first manoeuvre on that now-or-never day was to go into her bedroom in the mid-afternoon, strip naked and lie on top of the bed masturbating, having first "accidentally" left her bedroom door half open. When Anne walked by her bedroom as Jacqui had known she eventually would, she couldn't help but look her way. Seeing that Jacqui was stark naked and masturbating furiously, Anne averted her gaze straight away and quietly shut the door.

It was enough, Jacqui was sure of it. As she continued vigorously masturbating, her pussy now dripping with wetness, she kept replaying that moment. She could see again Anne's blue-green eyes flashing over her and widening with excitement as she took in what she was doing to herself with her busy fingers. In that short moment Anne had registered unmistakable sexual desire before regaining her composure, averting her gaze and silently shutting Jacqui's bedroom door.

The thought of what she'd just orchestrated was incredibly arousing to Jacqui. She brought herself to orgasm, gasping and moaning, all the time thinking of the look of desire she'd seen on Anne's face. Jacqui then showered, brushed her hair, applied a little makeup and slipped her long, pearl-coloured silk robe on over her naked form. It was time to take things to the next stage, which she knew she needed to do quickly. She had to strike while the iron was hot. She adjusted her robe to ensure it was loose at the top, the ripeness of her breasts partly exposed, and pressed on with her mission to seduce the lovely Anne.

When Jacqui padded bare footed into the living room she found her sitting on the couch, leafing through a glossy magazine. Anne looked up and gave Jacqui a pleasant smile that gave nothing away. There was not even a glint in the eye to say that she'd been affected by what she'd seen her doing, nothing to acknowledge the desire that Jacqui was now sure she felt for her.

'Anything I can do for you?' Jacqui asked meaningfully.

'You could get dressed,' Anne suggested, barely looking up from her magazine. It was not an encouraging response.

Jacqui however was undeterred. She was determined, come what may, to have sex with Anne before the day was out. 'I'll go and put some clothes on,' she said.

'Fine,' Anne replied, flicking on to the next page of the magazine. She appeared to be indifference personified but she couldn't fool Jacqui. She'd seen that look in Anne's eyes when she'd been outside her bedroom and caught sight of her pleasuring herself so energetically.

When Jacqui returned to the living room she was still bare footed but was otherwise dressed...kind of. She had on a singlet that was black and very tight, her beautiful breasts pressed against the thin cotton, her erect nipples protruding. She was also wearing an extremely tight pair of soft black leather shorts. They were cut very high indeed, exposing smooth bare thighs, the cleft of her sex and much of the curve of her backside. Jacqui felt very aroused by the shameless way she was exposing her body to Anne. 'I must have put on weight recently,' she said giving her a wicked grin. 'I could barely squeeze into these shorts.'

Jacqui, who was naturally slim but well rounded, had

certainly put on some weight lately. However this was only in the sense that she'd regained the pounds she'd lost a few months ago when she'd dieted for a while with unduly excessive zeal. She'd bought the tight leather shorts when her weight had been at its lowest. They'd looked incredibly sexy and provocative then. They looked more than that now: they looked positively obscene.

Anne put her magazine onto the coffee table. 'I can imagine you had difficulty squeezing into your shorts,' she said, hardly taking her eyes off her this time. 'I'm surprised you can even move in them.'

'Oh, I can do that all right,' Jacqui said. She did a seductive little walk, padding back and forth in front of her and wiggling her hips sexily as she moved.

Nothing could disguise the desire she saw in Anne's eyes as she flaunted herself in front of her. Jacqui was wearing no underwear, as was her wont even then, and the thin strip of black leather was pulled up tight between her pussy lips, rubbing against the wetness of her sex. It aroused her even more, making her nipples poke even more insistently against the scanty black cotton top.

'I think you've made your point – or should I say points,' Anne smiled, eyeing her rigidly erect nipples as they strained against the tight material of her singlet. Rising gracefully to her feet, she stood in front of Jacqui. She then reached out for her, took her by the waist and pulled her close. The two women looked at each other for a long moment and then Anne put her lips to Jacqui's and kissed her hard. 'This is what you want, isn't it,' she whispered.

'Yes,' Jacqui said breathlessly. 'And a lot more besides.'

'You want to go all the way?'

'I'd *love* to go all the way,' Jacqui replied, still breathless.

'Even though you know that I'm a happily married woman?'

'That just makes you all the more appealing to me,' Jacqui said, 'all the more tempting.'

'And that makes you a bad girl, doesn't it.' Anne's eyes were shining brightly.

'That makes me a bad girl,' Jacqui agreed.

'Let's sit together on the couch and take things from there,' Anne suggested huskily.

'Yes let's,' Jacqui replied, and they sat down side by side. Things were really going Jacqui's way, she thought. She felt in control of the situation.

Then all of a sudden she didn't. 'As far as I'm concerned bad girls like you need to be punished,' Anne said, her voice suddenly cold. She took Jacqui firmly by the hands and pulled her across her lap. Jacqui turned and looked over her shoulder at Anne, catching the gleam of determination in her eye. Jacqui may not have been in control any more but she as sure as hell knew what was coming next and it made her shiver with excitement. She was about to get rather more than she'd planned for today – and that was just fine by her.

Jacqui cried out when the first stinging blow came down, the flat of Anne's hand slapping firmly down on her rear cheeks. It was an explosion of pain, a raw livid sensation that turned her skin red. Then the second stroke came down and it was as sharp as the first, the sound reverberating around the room. Anne held Jacqui down, keeping her in place across her lap. She spanked her four more times in quick succession. The pain escalated with each blow, a fire building on her flesh. But those few blows were only the beginning. The spanking went on and on and on. Anne simply did not let up and the pain burned hotly on Jacqui's backside, sinking ever deeper. But with the pain came the pleasure and throughout the beating Jacqui could feel its heat build up in her sex, which rubbed excitingly against the thin strip of leather pressing tightly against it.

At last the thrashing stopped and Jacqui twisted round to see the curves of her cruelly spanked backside. They were dark red against the black of the ultra-brief leather shorts, the imprint of Anne's fingers on her flesh merging into a deep flush of pain. Jacqui tried to get up but Anne kept her in place. She began to run her hand over the soreness of her rear, feeling the burning heat that she had inflicted on her skin. Jacqui sighed as Anne went on to stroke her fingers between her thighs. She pushed the leather deeper between her pussy lips, making her shudder with desire.

Jacqui sighed again and shuddered even more as Anne's fingers pressed harder against the wet material. She arched her back, on the verge of orgasm as Anne pressed her fingers harder still against the love juice-soaked leather. Then she stopped, pushing Jacqui off her lap. 'Bend over the edge of the couch and wait,' she ordered, getting to her feet.

Jacqui was soon in position, breathing heavily with sexual arousal. She closed her eyes, wondering excitedly what form of chastisement Anne was going to subject her to next. She also wondered, as she listened to her leaving the room, how long she'd make her wait for it. Anne was not gone long. Jacqui's eyes flew open and she cried out loudly as the crop came down with a swish followed swiftly by a snap of leather on flesh. 'I gave up riding years ago,' Anne said. 'But I hung on to this. I always knew it would come in handy one day.' Jacqui let out another loud cry of pain as Anne brought the crop down again, striking another line of fire across her backside. Then a further harsh stroke landed across her rear cheeks. It was followed by another viciously harsh stroke, and then another ...

Jacqui lost count of the number of times Anne used the riding crop on her, but when the beating was finally over and she was allowed to stand up, her rear was criss-crossed with red lines and her flesh was quivering and burning with both pain and pleasure.

Jacqui suddenly became conscious of the passage of time. The light outside the window had faded and the colours in the room had dimmed and were tinged with shadows. It was evident that afternoon had morphed into evening during the course of her prolonged punishment. Now for what she'd actually planned for, Jacqui said to herself with an inward smile. Now for some pure, correction *impure* sex with Anne.

But Anne had other ideas altogether. 'That's all you're getting out of me,' she said with grim finality, her eyes hard. 'I want you to go to your bedroom now, shut the door, strip off your little fuck-me outfit and spend the rest of your time under this roof playing with yourself – like you were doing this afternoon for my benefit.' She went on, 'I want you to leave at daybreak and never return. You might have been determined to seduce me today, Jacqui, but I was even more determined that you wouldn't. I told you I'm a happily married woman. I'm also monogamous, and that's the way I'm going to stay.'

Jacqui did as she'd been told, climaxing time and again as she masturbated deliriously for hours on end, her skin marked deeply by the heavy chastisement Anne had inflicted on her.

The pain Jacqui was still suffering as a result of her earlier beatings and the knowledge of what had caused that pain in the first place made her epic masturbation session and the multiple orgasms that went with it a hundred times more intense.

Jacqui's night of onanistic excess did come to an end, though. It *had* to come to an end because Anne had been very specific in her instructions. There was nothing else for it, nothing that could be done, it was all over.

Jacqui left Anne's home by dawn's early light, just as instructed, closing the front door behind her as quietly as Anne had closed her bedroom door the day before.

Chapter Thirty-five

'David,' Jacqui whispered, breaking the silence in the dungeon.

She got no answer. Isabella had been quite clear that they were not to speak or move from the positions in which she had left them and David was not about to disobey her.

'David,' Jacqui repeated.

There was still no answer.

'David, playing with Mistress got me all sexed-up. I know it did the same to you. I noticed that you had a huge hard-on when you were licking her anus.'

Silence.

'David,' Jacqui persisted. 'I still feel incredibly horny. I've been having some really sexy thoughts – horny memories – while I've been kneeling here back to back with you.'

No reply.

'My pussy's dripping, I can tell you,' Jacqui continued. 'So I'm going to play with myself, can't resist it.'

David still gave no answer but his cock swelled anew as he heard what he heard next. It was the wet sound of Jacqui's agile fingers working rhythmically in and out of her pussy and her accompanying moans of pleasure, which he was sure she was exaggerating to increase his lustful discomfort.

'David,' she said, and he felt her naked breasts rub against his shoulders, her breath hot against his neck. 'Yes, that's right, I've shifted position. Naughty, aren't I? Want to be naughty, too?'

David gave no answer.

'Let me see if you want to be naughty,' Jacqui said, reaching round to the front of him and grasping hold of his cock, which was now massively erect. 'I knew you did, and here's my proof.' She began to masturbate him, her fingers pulling on the length of his erection, rubbing ever harder.

'David,' she breathed, letting go of his throbbing shaft. 'I so much want to suck that big cock of yours.' She crawled to the front of him and pressed her mouth to the head of his cock, savouring the feel of it against the softness of her lips. She traced her tongue under it. She closed her mouth around it, sucking on it. Then Jacqui began to work her mouth up and down David's erection until he was panting with desire as her pace grew faster and faster. And then she stopped, removing her lips from his shaft.

'David,' Jacqui purred, turning round and getting on to all fours in front of him. She looked back into his guilty, anguished face. 'I'd just love it if you'd fuck me in the arse,' she said, putting her hands behind her and parting the cheeks of her backside. 'I've been looking forward to it all day. Got my arsehole all prepared, lubed up and everything, in readiness for your *great – big – cock*.'

David didn't say anything, didn't move. But, my God, the enticement of Jacqui's seductive words and that anus pulsing and twitching eagerly, hungrily, wantonly.

'Come on, David, you know you want to,' Jacqui cajoled, placing her hands back on the floor in front of her and parting her thighs a little further with a seductive wiggle of her backside. 'Think how it would feel plunging your stiff cock into my tight arsehole and fucking me hard until we both come.'

Suddenly David's resolve deserted him. He couldn't hold out any longer against this most persistent, most voracious of temptresses. He crawled forward and thrust his rampant cock into Jacqui's anal hole, causing her to utter a loud moan of pleasure. David buggered her powerfully, faster and faster, each thrust going deeper into her anus until she screamed out her climax. David called out, too, a wordless explosion of lust as he pumped squirts of hot semen into Jacqui's anal hole.

At that moment the door of the dungeon burst open with a heavy crash and Isabella stormed in. 'What the hell is going on here?' she said with raised voice, her dark eyes blazing. 'I told you two not to move position or speak and what do I come in here to discover? I find you, David, fucking Jacqui in the arse. You climaxed, as well, didn't you, you bastard. The evidence is before my eyes.' David had withdrawn his cock and a gentle dribble of jism was beginning to run slowly out of Jacqui's anus and down her thighs.

'Yes, Mistress,' David replied shamefacedly.

'Lick that up,' Isabella said pointing to the come leaking down Jacqui's thighs.

'Yes, Mistress.' He got on with his task straight away, his tongue working fast.

'Now, lick all your semen from out of her arsehole and swallow it down,' she demanded and David, again, complied immediately. He sucked and slurped at Jacqui's gaping anus, gulping down his own come greedily until Isabella told him to stop.

'You're both a couple of disobedient fuckers, there can be no denying that,' Isabella said. 'But what I really want to know is which of you started all this?'

'David did, Mistress,' Jacqui replied almost before Isabella had finished speaking.

'Is that true, David?' Isabella asked.

David was silent, momentarily dumbstruck by Jacqui's outrageous duplicity. He opened his mouth to speak, but nothing came out.

'Well?' Isabella snapped. 'Is what Jacqui has just said true?'

He shook his head vigorously. 'No, Mistress.'

'One of you is lying,' Isabella said, taking hold of a heavy leather flogger, 'and I intend to find out which one it is. I'm going to beat the shit out of both of you until I get at the truth. You first, Jacqui, over the whipping bench with you.'

'Yes, Mistress,' she said, getting into position.

'Now, I'll ask you again – who started it?'

'David, Mistress.'

Isabella began to whip Jacqui with considerable ferocity. The lashes struck her backside in a regular harsh rhythm, and each time the whip cracked against her skin, she cried out in pain. Isabella began to strike more quickly, inflicting ever more excruciating pain on her, and Jacqui's cries came faster and faster. Pain soared through her and she began to sob, the tears forming in the corner of her eyes and rolling down her cheeks in a constant flow. Tremors ran through her body too and her backside was crimson from its punishment.

Isabella stopped whipping Jacqui and asked again who had started it.

'David, Mistress,' she sobbed.

'Get back on to your knees, bitch.'

'Yes, Mistress.'

'Your turn now, David,' Isabella said and he got up from his kneeling position in order to change places with Jacqui. 'Who started it?'

'Jacqui, Mistress,' he said, trying desperately to catch Isabella's eye but she determinedly avoided returning his gaze. He bent over the whipping bench, one extremely worried slave.

Isabella thrashed him as ferociously as she had flogged Jacqui, whipping him over and over until the sharp pain burned like fire into his flesh and his aching backside was thoroughly striped with the marks of the flogger. The pain was excruciating but still she went on. David gasped and sobbed with the agony of trying to bear it. The only way he could cope with the intense pain was to block everything else out. He thought of nothing, imagined nothing, the vicious strokes that burned on his backside his only reality.

Isabella stopped whipping David and asked him again who had started it.

'Jacqui, Mistress,' he said, his face streaked with tears. She told him to get back on to his knees next to Jacqui.

'Well, I'm loathe to admit it, but torture isn't always the answer,' Isabella said, looking contemptuously from one slave to the other. 'I'm going to have to make a judgement call on this one and decide which one of you two disobedient slaves is also lying.' There was a long silence, heavy with tension.

'David,' Isabella said, gazing at him with all the warmth of a rattle snake. 'Crawl into the cage.' He obeyed and Isabella immediately locked him in and told Jacqui to get up from her knees. She walked with her from the dungeon, switching off its lights before shutting the door and, for good measure, locking it as well. David was left imprisoned in the cage and the dungeon in darkness and despair.

'I was going to watch a pornographic film I have that's a bit special,' Isabella said to Jacqui as they entered the living room together. 'Care to join me?'

'Yes, Mistress,' Jacqui said, her expression that of the proverbial cat that had got the cream. 'Can we masturbate each other while we watch?'

'You never know.'

The mahogany cabinet that housed the television was open and Isabella picked up the remote control. She and Jacqui then sat down together on the leather couch opposite the screen. Isabella wound the tape that was already in the machine back to the beginning. There were no credits, just some fizzing on the screen. There was a small glitch on the tape, giving the impression that it had not been professionally made. Isabella fast forwarded and pressed to play. The picture had been taken from one angle only and the two people in it obviously did not know they were being filmed.

Those two people were David and Jacqui. And Jacqui was the one giving the star performance: Jacqui lavishly playing with her wet pussy, Jacqui turning round and masturbating David as she whispered provocatively in his ear and rubbed her breasts against his shoulders, Jacqui crawling in front of David and sucking his cock, Jacqui opening the cheeks of her backside and inviting David to sodomize her ...

Isabella stopped the tape.

'You're always saying that my dungeon's got absolutely everything,' she said, turning to face Jacqui. 'That's true. And that includes a well hidden CCTV camera. It's extremely rare for me to use it but today I made an exception and I'm very glad I did.'

'I don't know what to say,' Jacqui said, not meeting her eye and looking extremely shamefaced.

'Don't say anything,' Isabella replied, curling her lip with distaste. 'Go and pack your bags right now and get out of this house.'

'But, where will I go?' Jacqui said, her voice pleading.

'Don't know. Don't care,' Isabella hissed sharply. 'All I know is that I don't ever want to see your lying face again.'

Chapter Thirty-six

Jacqui gave up being a hostess at *Club Depravity* immediately after that and disappeared off the radar. 'I never did trust her,' Kate said to Isabella the next time they met.

'Neither did I, not for a single moment,' Isabella replied. 'I wasn't born yesterday, you know. I was merely toying with the devious little bitch. She thought she was manipulating me and yet it was the other way round all along.'

Kate laughed quietly. 'I might have known it,' she said.

The two dommes were having this conversation in Isabella's dungeon and were both gloriously naked except for identical black leather and diamante chokers and shiny high heeled boots. David and Tony were in the dungeon too and were in bondage.

David was on his knees inside the steel cage in which he'd been left incarcerated when he'd *thought* the treacherous Jacqui had managed to fool his Mistress – more fool him for having thought that, he'd told himself afterwards. On this occasion his wrists were handcuffed to one of its bars, he was wearing only a black leather hood with open eye, nose and mouth holes, and there was a metal cock ring at the base of his erect shaft.

Tony was standing with his back to the wall-mounted cross, his arms outstretched. His wrist cuffs were attached by metal trigger clips to chains attached to either end of the horizontal section of the cross and his ankle cuffs were attached together by another trigger clip. He was naked apart from a metal slave's collar and a black leather cock corset that tightly encased his erection.

'No, I never trusted Jacqui – not one little bit,' Isabella went on. 'And while we're on the subject of trust,' she added, 'do you want to play a little game that's all about that very subject?'

'Sure,' Kate said. 'What did you have in mind?'

'We'll each in turn say something we want one of our two slaves here to do or have done to them,' Isabella said. 'Whatever one of us says, the other must allow, come what may. Why? Because we trust each other, simple as that. Want to play my game?'

'I certainly do,' Kate said, her violet eyes gleaming.

'Then let's begin,' Isabella said.

'Would you like to go first?' Kate asked, deferring to her former Mistress as always.

'OK,' Isabella said and reflected for a moment. 'Let's start the proceedings gently. I would like your slave to worship my feet.'

'All right, why don't you sit down and I'll bring Tony to you,' Kate said. She then strode over to the cross, detached Tony from it and led him, crawling, to kneel at Isabella's feet. He bent his head low and pressed his lips against the toe of the boot Isabella presented to him. He slid his tongue along the pure leather, his lips caressing the instep and then sucking on the high, pointed heel. She presented her other boot to his lips and he did the same, soon lost in the action.

'That's enough,' Isabella said eventually, pulling her boot away from Tony's lips. 'Your turn to decide now, Kate. My guess would be that you'll want to go to the opposite extreme.'

'And you'd be right,' Kate said, taking her cue. 'I'd like Tony to go over and select the whip of yours that he thinks he'd find the most painful. He will do this in the sure and certain knowledge that you are about to use it on him with the utmost ferocity.' Both Isabella and Tony got to their feet, Tony to collect the whip that he feared the most – a vicious flogger of braided red and black leather – and Isabella to use it on him as soon as he had handed it to her.

'Thank you, Tony,' Isabella said with a slight sideways nod of the head as she took hold of the braided flogger. 'See how polite I am?'

'Yes, Mistress,' he replied, trembling noticeably.

'I want you to return the compliment and be equally courteous,' she told him. 'You must thank me every time you feel the lash of this nasty whip, counting out the strokes each time you receive them. Understood?'

'Yes, Mistress.' His voice was unsteady.

'Good,' she said. 'Now, get on to your hands and knees.' As soon as Tony was in position Isabella brought the braided flogger down on his backside with a blow that was exceptionally stinging and sharp.

'One, Mistress, thank you,' he gasped. She whipped him again and there was another sharp flash of pain.

'Two, Mistress, thank you.' And again and again and on and on, each strike a hard explosion of sound, until the pain tore at his body and he was sobbing out his thanks piteously, tears cascading down his face. Isabella put the braided flogger to one side when the sobbing slave had counted all the way up to fifty. She looked over at Kate.

'Your choice this time,' Kate said. 'It's your turn to decide.'

'I'd like you to clamp Tony's nipples,' Isabella said after a moment's deliberation.

Kate took hold of a set of clover clamps, walked over to her slave, got him to kneel upright and attached them to his chest. Tony cringed with pain as the clamps pinched into his nipples. Kate then pulled them hard and he cried out. His nipples throbbed painfully, sending spasms of sensation directly to his shaft which pulsed within the tightness of his leather cock corset.

'Now you choose,' Isabella said. 'You make the decision.'

Kate picked out a double dildo strap-on and handed it to Isabella along with a bottle of lubricant. 'I'd like you to fuck my slave in the arse,' she said.

'It would be my pleasure,' said Isabella, getting into the strap-on harness and easing the internal dildo into her wet pussy. 'My pleasure indeed.' She pressed the internal dildo hard so that it nudged exquisitely against her clitoris, and she let out a moan of pleasure as she did so. The other end extended from her pubis, a thick, erect cock that was identical to the one she had just inserted into herself. She tightened the straps of the harness, testing the dildo that jutted out from her body and delighting in the feeling that it caused as it pushed against the one inside her that was its mirror image.

Isabella liberally coated the dildo jutting from her crotch with lubricant. 'Adopt the position to be penetrated, slave,' she ordered. Tony obediently leant forward and then reached back with both arms and held the cheeks of his backside apart, presenting his anus to Isabella. She gently worked the thickness of the dildo in and out of the rosebud opening a few times, pushing it in a little further with each thrust and stretching Tony's sphincter. He suddenly felt the dildo spasm right into him until his anal ring was tight against its base. He put his hands on to the ground and Isabella began to fuck him, slowly at first and then building increasingly in intensity.

'My turn to choose now,' Isabella said as she continued to sodomize Tony. 'I'd like you to release David from the cage, bring him to the centre of the dungeon on all fours and use a riding crop on him just as hard as I whipped your slave – harder if it pleases you.'

'It most definitely does please me,' Kate replied with a sadistic laugh as she strode over to the cage. She bent forward to remove the handcuffs from David's wrists that had been shackling him to the cage, which she then opened. Kate let him crawl out and then took hold of a riding crop.

She weighed the implement in her hand and then began. The first swish of the crop whistled down and landed hard across David's backside. He gave a cry of pain through the mouth hole of the leather hood and a red stripe appeared across his flesh. There was another whistle of the crop, another flash of pain and a further stripe. Soon David lost count as stroke after stroke fell across his rear, slicing red heat through his body. Each stroke made him jump and shudder and cry out. Sometimes Kate brought the crop down in rapid succession, other times her strokes were drawn out, making him wait, in tense anticipation for ages. And then she stopped altogether, putting the crop to one side.

'Your call,' Isabella said, when she saw that Kate had finished.

'I'd like to give his genitals a good thrashing now,' replied Kate.

'Then, do it.'

Kate went to select a small but vicious flogger that she knew from experience was perfect for cock and ball torture and told David to lie on the dungeon floor on his back. Despite, or more accurately because of the severity of his recent punishment and the certainty of more to come, David was extremely aroused. When he lay on his back his erection reared in the air, straining against the metal cock ring that now gripped its base like a tourniquet. Kate knelt beside him and got to work. The first stroke of the vicious little flogger brought a white flash of pain as did the second and third. By the tenth agonizing stroke David's flesh was burning deep and the pain was almost unbearable, yet still it did nothing to diminish his sexual excitement, quite the reverse. He was on fire with lust. She stopped anyway.

'What now?' Kate said, getting to her feet.

'I'd like him to crawl over to your slave,' Isabella said, not even breaking stride as she continued to sodomize Tony. 'I want him to get on to his back facing me, this time with his hard, punished cock right in Tony's face.'

'Then what?'

'I would like Tony to suck him off and swallow all the come he ejaculates,' Isabella replied. 'This game won't be over until Tony has sucked David completely dry, which I absolutely *insist* that he does. Are you happy with that?'

'I couldn't be happier,' Kate replied gleefully.

David got into position. With Isabella still ramming her strap-on into Tony's anus, he opened his mouth and closed his lips around David's aching cock, circling his tongue around its swollen glans. He held him in his mouth, sucking more and more greedily, energetically deep-throating him all the way down to his tight cock ring.

Isabella, still sodomizing Tony as hard as ever, looked over at Kate. 'What would you like now?' she asked. 'Want to join this daisy chain by any chance?'

'That's exactly what I want,' Kate replied, her violet eyes

shining more brightly than ever. 'I'd like to straddle your slave's hooded face and have him lick my pussy.'

'Then do it, my dear,' Isabella replied.

Kate duly squatted down over David's face, settling her dripping thighs over his mouth. She opened her pussy lips with her fingers so that David's hot tongue could poke through the mouth hole of his leather hood and enter her. He pressed his tongue into her pussy and she moaned with pleasure.

Isabella carried on energetically buggering Tony as he sucked David's hard cock with equal energy. She also reached down between Tony's legs and began firmly stroking his leather-encased erection, which was now dribbling precome constantly.

The four of them fucked and sucked and licked and stroked with increasing fervour. They were all locked together, giving each other ever more intense pleasure until they each in turn tumbled over into orgasms that racked their bodies with spasms of delight.

First Kate, pushing her sex down hard onto David's mouth, climaxed with an animal-like moan. This was swiftly followed by Isabella who shuddered deliriously at the exquisite sensations she was receiving from her internal dildo as she fucked Tony in the arse with the strap-on and brought him off at the same time with her hand. As waves of come spilled from Tony's trussed-up tumescence onto the dungeon floor he could feel David's cock in his mouth swell and pulse as he reached his own peak, tensing his body and then yielding to the ecstasy of release. He uttered a muffled cry of pleasure from beneath Kate's quivering thighs and climaxed powerfully, his cock flooding streams of come into Tony's mouth in an orgasm that went on and on.

David filled Tony's mouth as he emptied one thick spurt of hot come after another over his tongue and into the back of his throat. Tony sucked and sucked at this deluge, gulping down the come over and over until David at long last stopped ejaculating.

Kate, still buzzing and tingling from the huge climax she had just enjoyed courtesy of the slave on whose leather-hooded face she continued to sit, looked at Isabella and Tony. Isabella had finally stopped thrusting into Tony's rear and had withdrawn the dildo from his anus, but he continued to hold David's spent cock in his mouth just in case he produced any residual jism he would have to swallow. He had to suck him completely dry – Isabella had been insistent about that.

Isabella's game, which she'd said was all about trust, was almost over and it had been a good one in Kate's view. It had pushed limits, pushed boundaries right to the very max but had not crossed them. That of course had been the whole point, Kate said to herself. Trust was the name of the game.

Chapter Thirty-seven

Dear Mistress Isabella,

I just wanted to write to say how extremely sorry I am for the despicable way I behaved, particularly towards David, when I had the immense privilege of being your slave.

I blew it completely because I was crazy in love with you ... and also because I'm a manipulative, deceitful bitch – I hate myself for it.

Please forgive me.

Jacqui

The letter did not show an address, phone number or e-mail address for Jacqui, and had been hand delivered some time in the night. It was marked for Isabella's personal attention, although she showed it to David anyway. She presented it to him, saying offhandedly, 'You're mentioned in this missive, so you might as well read it.'

'What do you think?' Isabella asked when he'd done this. 'Sincere or what?'

'Difficult to say, Mistress,' David replied, complimented to be asked his opinion by Isabella for once. 'A tigress doesn't ... '

'... change her stripes,' Isabella said, finishing his sentence. 'No, that's true. Although I must say that the idea of giving her some new ones has its attractions from my point of view.'

'I see, Mistress.'

'But what do you think, slave?' Isabella went on. 'Have you got any particular concerns about her coming back into the fold?'

There, she'd done it again: paid David the compliment of

actually asking him for his opinion. Great – or it would have been if he'd gone on to give her a properly considered reply. But David didn't do that and, my God, how he would come to bitterly regret that fact.

'No, I don't have any particular concerns, Mistress,' he said, the reply tripping glibly off his tongue. 'Just one thing, though – how shall we find Jacqui?'

'I don't think we need to worry about that,' Isabella said, giving him a sidelong look, a sardonic little smile twitching at the corner of her mouth. 'I'm sure she'll find us.'

Twilight was just shifting into night as they drove up to the large, vine-covered house where the fetish party was taking place. The house was located right on the furthest outskirts of Brighton, well beyond the urban sprawl. It nestled in a fold of the South Downs, hidden from the road by tall trees. The place was quite crowded by the time Isabella and David arrived. Even so, the party was not yet in full swing and the murmur of voices was louder than the sounds of the music that drifted from the open door to welcome them.

They entered the house and were greeted by their hosts, a long-standing male-Dom couple called Master Clive and slave Suzie that Isabella and David knew from *Club Depravity*. They directed them to the changing area where they got into their fetish wear. Isabella squeezed into a skin-tight leather cat suit with some assistance from David, who also helped her on with a pair of tall boots with very high heels. He then put on the infinitesimal outfit she had selected for him, which consisted of only a tiny leather g-string on top of the tight metal genital ring he was already wearing at her insistence. They made their way into the big main lounge and picked up a couple of drinks.

The party was warming up very nicely, the buzz of conversation punctuated by the occasional sound of laughter. People were enjoying a chat and a drink, admiring one another's sexy outfits, and generally getting in a great mood for what was to follow. David let his eyes scan the room. He recognised some familiar faces from the various occasions he'd attended *Club Depravity* with Isabella, although there was nobody there from her immediate entourage. His gaze was drawn away from the other party guests for a moment to an erotic film that was playing silently against one wall. It was nothing too heavy, in fact rather beautiful: scenes of fetish passion and sensuality in the broad daylight in a sunlit wooded area somewhere.

David looked back at the other party guests. It was already clear that this was going to be a good night. Small groups of people were clustered together, absorbed in conversation but there seemed to be quite a bit of movement from group to group. It would not be long now before one couple or another started to use one of the various items of high quality dungeon equipment positioned around the large room they were in and the even larger one beyond it, which was devoted entirely to BDSM play.

Isabella and David continued to stand together and sip their drinks, the ice clattering in their glasses. They saw Jacqui before she saw them, apparently. They watched her crossing the room in their general direction, walking with rhythmic strides that snapped her high heels down hard on the polished floor as if to announce her presence. She stopped a short distance away from them next to a black leather couch, which was situated under a large, rectangular window. Pulling its curtains slightly apart, Jacqui flicked her long curly hair and gazed pensively out into the darkness. She looked not only suitably flamboyant but gorgeous too, dressed as she was all in black leather in an extremely short skirt, high heeled shoes and a corset that cinched her waist and pushed her breasts up enticingly.

Jacqui turned round and saw Isabella and David for the first time, or so she would have had them believe. 'Oh, hi Mistress Isabella, David,' she said, her brown eyes glittering. 'What a surprise to meet you here.' They watched a look rise into her face that communicated surprise and delight as well as embarrassment and contrition too, as she bit her lip softly. You had to hand it to Jacqui. It was a well nigh faultless performance.

To cut a long story short, Jacqui launched into a total charm offensive that evening, which David thought was more of a *smarm* offensive. She hung like a limpet on every word Isabella uttered, grovelled unashamedly to her, and did everything the dominatrix told her to do in an instant. This included stripping completely naked and crawling around the floor at her feet. It also included allowing herself to be punished most cruelly by the dominatrix – while David looked on, feeling like the invisible man for most of the time ...

The room devoted exclusively to BDSM play had quickly become a hive of kinky activity as the evening progressed. There was strap-on action and girl-girl action and girl-boy-girl action. There was needle play and wax play and rope play. And there was Jacqui, buck naked and on her knees beneath Isabella who was about to give the young woman her undivided attention.

'Kiss my boots, slave,' the dominatrix ordered and Jacqui immediately dipped her head, pressing her lips to the shiny leather of the boots.

'Now suck this heel,' Isabella commanded, and that's what Jacqui did. Bringing her mouth to the heel, she sucked the hard, shiny dagger in and out of her mouth. When Isabella finally pulled the boot away from Jacqui, its heel was wet with her saliva, the smear of her lips on the black leather.

Telling David to follow them, Isabella next walked Jacqui over to a metal spreader bar that hung by two chains from the room's ceiling. A naked, multi-pierced young black woman with very short hair and a stunning figure had just been freed from the spreader bar by her Master who had virtually covered her body with hot white candle wax while she'd been manacled to it.

Isabella told Jacqui to raise her arms and David to attach her wrists to the manacle attachments at either end of the bar before standing back. The dominatrix then took hold of a leather flogger and wasted no time in putting it to use.

'Aah!' Jacqui cried as the first red-hot strike from the flogger landed across the middle of her backside. She gave another gasp of pain as Isabella's next stroke planted a second line of fire across her rear. And so it went on. The beating continued unremittingly, causing the cheeks of Jacqui's backside to smart with a fire that made her squirm and gasp in pain.

Isabella then got David to release Jacqui from the spreader bar and told both of them to come with her. She walked them over to a single chain with manacle attachments, which hung down to around waist height from the ceiling hook to which it was attached. It was about the only piece of equipment in the room not in use by this stage, the fetish party now being in full swing.

Immediately to their right a naked man wearing a blindfold and a gag had been strapped on his front over a whipping bench by a rubber-clad dominatrix who had left him there on his own for the time being. The man's backside had already been whipped a livid red, the black base of a vibrating butt plug protruded from his anus, and numerous metal pegs were attached to his genitals.

Isabella told David to secure Jacqui's wrists behind her back to the manacle attachments at the end of the chain. While he was doing that Isabella took hold of a red ball gag and a set of clover clamps. She put the gag into Jacqui's mouth and buckled it into place behind her head.

'I'm now going to give you a serious beating,' Isabella informed Jacqui as if the flogging she'd already received from her had been no more than a trifle. 'I'll place these into your right hand,' she added, showing her the clover clamps. 'If the pain gets too much for you, drop the clamps.' Jacqui nodded her head in obedient response as she felt the item being placed behind her into her hand.

Isabella went on to beat Jacqui's backside with a leather tawse. Harsh stroke followed harsh stroke in quick succession and agonized moan followed agonized moan from beneath Jacqui's gag. Isabella rained increasingly heavy blows on Jacqui's backside, beating her with ever more ferocity until her rear blazed like a red-hot furnace.

Eventually the searing sensations of pain became too excruciating for the slave and she had to drop the clamps she had in her hand. These clattered to the ground, their links making a pool of silver on the hardwood floor. Isabella stopped beating her immediately. She unbuckled and removed the ball gag Jacqui had been wearing and masturbated her hard to an orgasm of great intensity. Jacqui's breath came in quick little pants and her whole body was shaking and shivering as she climaxed, making the chain behind her strain against the ceiling hook that held it firmly in place.

Chapter Thirty-eight

Jacqui was still hyperventilating when she was released from the chain. She said that she needed a couple of stiff drinks to get over the whole experience. At the end of the evening, Jacqui said she thought she might be over the drink driving limit. Could she perhaps sleep at Isabella's house, she wondered – *quelle surprise!* The dominatrix agreed and took her to bed with her that night, sending David, the invisible man, off to his own quarters until morning. There was no raunchy threesome for him this time round. What there was instead was a raunchy twosome for Isabella and Jacqui – with a wickedly exciting twist of something extra …

Isabella turned on to her stomach on the bed. She and Jacqui were naked, their beautiful bodies bathed in the soft glow of the bedside light. 'Finger-fuck me and lick my arsehole, slave,' Isabella ordered, opening her legs. She could feel her pussy go nice and wet as she said the words.

Jacqui knelt between her spread legs, looking down at her beautiful backside and the slit of her sex. 'Your word is my command, Mistress,' she whispered as she plunged her fingers into Isabella's pussy, making her groan with desire. She began pushing her fingers in and out of her, fast and hard.

Then Jacqui brought her mouth to Isabella's rear cheeks and pressed her lips to her anus, licking her until she trembled with desire. And all the time her tongue was flick-flick-flicking over Isabella's anus she carried on masturbating her, making her clitoris pulse with a moist insistent throb until a powerful orgasm washed over her.

Finally Isabella's orgasm subsided and she told Jacqui to

shift position and lie next to her. She rolled over then herself, revealing her naked breasts and erect nipples and the copious wetness between her thighs. 'Your turn now, slave,' she said.

Jacqui's eyes were shiny and her breathing shallow as Isabella pulled her down into her arms. She pressed her lips to hers and kissed her hard as she rolled on top of her. Isabella then put her lips to Jacqui's throat and licked a gentle trail down to her sex and began kissing her there. Her pussy was as wet and gleaming as her own and Isabella subjected it to a persistent licking, making it wetter still. Jacqui groaned deeply and ran her hands up over her stiff nipples and pinched them as Isabella licked deep inside her vagina, which was now sopping wet. She cried out in total abandon when she licked her to a blissful orgasm.

Then Isabella slithered back up the bed. 'You've made me incredibly wet, Mistress,' Jacqui told her huskily.

'I know,' Isabella replied. 'Wet enough to fuck you with my fist, which is what I'm going to do now.'

Jacqui remained on her back, her body arching towards Isabella. She was slack-mouthed and her eyes were glazed with lust, her pupils dilated. She opened her legs wide apart. Her pussy was wet and sticky, dripping with liquid.

Isabella then put a hand down on her and started to rub, started to grind her fingers against her clitoral bud. She put two fingers into the slickness of her pussy, feeling the soft wetness of her insides. And Jacqui thrust her hips lasciviously against her probing fingers. They were really working Jacqui's pussy now and Isabella twisted a third one in. She drove all three of them deep inside her, plunging hard into her wet, wet sex. Jacqui was tight around her fingers as Isabella snaked her hand down to rub her stiff shiny clitoris again, this time with her thumb, and simultaneously she inserted a fourth finger into her vagina.

She forged deep into her sopping wetness several times before she inserted her thumb. She had her whole hand inside Jacqui's sex now, plunged into the hot oozing wetness of her. Jacqui was in a delirium of lust. Her breath was coming quicker and quicker. Her sex was soaking, drenched. Isabella's hand was drenched too as she pushed and pushed until Jacqui climaxed, shaking and moaning. Her face screwed up as her orgasm reached its peak and she cried out loudly. Isabella removed her hand. Her palm and wrist were soaked. The bedspread was wet with juice.

'That was awesome, Mistress,' Jacqui said. 'The whole evening was – thanks to you. What extraordinary luck it was that I bumped into you.' Yeah right, Isabella smiled to herself. Believe that last statement of Jacqui's and you'd believe anything.

Chapter Thirty-nine

That night spent by Jacqui under Isabella's roof turned into a week during which she informed Isabella that she was currently between jobs, had been sleeping on a friend's couch. Could she, maybe ... blah, blah, blah.

So, the week turned into a month, turned into a second month. Jacqui was over the moon, thought she'd died and gone to heaven. David just wished she'd go to hell. Except, well, that was only half the truth. It was also a fact that, not to put too fine a point on it, she turned him on considerably, made him quite incredibly horny.

David couldn't help himself – despite Jacqui's transparent deviousness, despite the fact that she had once shown herself all to willing to hang him out to dry when it had suited her purposes, he really liked having the randy little madam around. And he loved it when he and she were disciplined together by Isabella. It was intoxicating, it was extreme ...

Isabella was standing in the middle of the dungeon, looking exquisite in a miniscule chain mail bikini and pointed leather shoes with sharp stiletto heels. She was admiring her efforts so far:

A naked Jacqui, her eyes wide and glassy, lay on her back on the black leather-covered bondage table. Isabella had clipped the chains at the four corners of the table to the red leather wrist and ankle cuffs Jacqui had on. This had had the effect of spreading her arms and legs widely apart. Jacqui's bald pussy was completely exposed. It was moist and silky, dripping with liquid, and her clit was twitching.

David was also naked and in bondage. Isabella had beaten

him thoroughly already and now had him strapped tightly into the upright torture chair. The dominatrix had gagged him with a soft black leather gag and attached clover clamps to his nipples. His cock was rigidly erect.

Isabella strode towards the leather-covered bondage table to which she had Jacqui spread eagled. The domme's shapely thighs quivered and rubbed together provocatively as she moved and her stiletto heeled shoes click-clicked against the dungeon floor.

It was Jacqui's turn to be disciplined now and the young slave knew it. She could feel her heart thumping and her pussy began to tighten moistly, her clit to twitch still more. Her breath was coming fast and furious.

Isabella didn't start Jacqui's discipline with anything even approaching a warm up. Instead she began whipping her breasts hard with a heavy leather flogger, marking the two fleshy orbs with vivid lines that were a fierce red in colour. She then switched disciplinary implements and started beating Jacqui's pussy with a small but vicious leather flogger. It hurt like the devil, that flogger, each harsh strike causing Jacqui to jump and shudder in her bonds. Her eyes started to brim with tears, pain and fear colliding in her punished body.

The dominatrix stopped beating Jacqui all of a sudden. 'This nasty little flogger works even better on a man's genitals,' she announced as she strode away from Jacqui and returned her attention to David who remained gagged and tightly strapped to the upright torture chair. The hard flesh of his erection was now smeared copiously with precome fluid, which had worked itself from its glans.

Isabella used the vicious little flogger to whip David's shaft ferociously hard. It reared up even higher in response, angrily purple and veiny. David jerked against his restraints at the indescribably sharp pain he was experiencing, but still Isabella kept on beating his aching erection. Eventually the desperate look in David's eyes told her that the pain was becoming too much for him to bear and she stopped whipping him. She released him from the torture chair and removed his nipple clamps and gag.

The dominatrix then released Jacqui from the bondage table. She led her and David to a part of the dungeon where four chains hung from the ceiling to about four feet from the ground.

Isabella placed the two slaves standing back to back either side of the chains, and took hold of a box of red pegs. She used all of these, attaching them painfully to their nipples, Jacqui's pussy lips, David's scrotum and one to the small flap of skin just under the head of his engorged cock.

Isabella then blindfolded them both and told them to turn round. She clipped their wrist cuffs to the end of a chain each and then winched the chains up so that their arms were outstretched above their heads. Finally she manacled Jacqui's ankles to either end of a wooden hobble bar and attached David's ankles to another hobble bar in the same way.

'Now for some more torture,' announced the dominatrix, her voice harsh. She selected a rattan cane for the purpose and went on to thrash their backsides with it, alternating four stripes per slave. She sliced the cruel implement through the air in one quick swipe after another. The blows of the cane cracked hard each time against their flesh and made them wince and squeal and buck within their bonds.

Isabella steadily increased the severity of her caning until they were both shuddering violently in agonized ecstasy … and then she stopped abruptly, dropping the rattan cane to the floor where it landed with a clatter. The dominatrix marched away from the two slaves to the door of the dungeon, opened it and left.

Jacqui lifted her lips to David. She kissed him on the mouth, her warm lips pressing hard against his. David felt the tip of her tongue probe his lips. Jacqui moved her mouth away for a fraction, and then brought it back. She kissed his open mouth again, this time pushing her tongue into his, sliding it over and over.

Jacqui felt horny beyond belief, the heat of desire sweeping through her body. Her clit was buzzing, burning as if David's thick long cock was already thrusting away inside her. She was ripe, ready. David felt ready too, more than ready.

The two blindfolded slaves would have loved to have fucked then, *loved* to. They imagined fucking, imagined doing it again and again with amazing intensity. But their bondage – the taut chains, the hobble bars, the pegs attached to their genitals – made anything like that a physical impossibility.

David and Jacqui did the only thing they could do. They continued to kiss deeply, David letting Jacqui explore his mouth still more with her hard wet tongue. They kissed for a very long time. They kissed and kissed and kissed. Jacqui's lips were soft and her tongue voluptuous. David abandoned himself to that lengthy kiss, surrendered to it, his senses exploding. It felt so right to him. It felt too right. It felt so right it was wrong.

Chapter Forty

Looking back, David knew he would have acted very differently if he could have had his time over again. But we are all blessed with 20-20 vision when it comes to viewing events in hindsight. David didn't have perfect vision at the time. In fact, he couldn't see a damn thing. And he wasn't even blindfolded on this occasion, neither of them were.

Isabella had arranged to meet up with Kate for dinner and decided to "park" Jacqui and David in her absence. She chose to take the pair of them, both naked as usual, down to the dungeon and lock them inside its metal cage. She left them there where she had positioned them, kneeling side by side and about a foot apart. 'You can talk as much as you like but no touching,' she ordered, adding, 'I won't bother to monitor you with the CCTV this time. There'd be no point.' They had both begun to ponder what might have been the significance of that last remark when everything suddenly went pitch black as the lights zapped off, and Isabella slammed shut the dungeon door behind her departing form.

David felt as if he was in a darkened cinema waiting for the big film to start, and it was an erotic film. He could smell the sensual, musky scent of Jacqui's perfume. And then her soft, warm breath was by his ear. Her mouth was so close he thought she was going to kiss him. He very much hoped she wouldn't try anything like that, delicious though the prospect was, and indeed she didn't. She whispered to him instead but what she said was indistinct, he didn't catch it.

'What was that?' he said.

'Mistress said we can talk,' she said. It looked as if Jacqui was going to behave herself this time, but you never knew with her.

The darkness around them was thick and close.

'What do you want to talk about?' David asked.

'All sorts of things,' she said.

'Like what?'

'Well, let's see … I understand that Mistress required you to sign some kind of slave contract when you first moved in with her to be her house-slave,' Jacqui said. 'Is that right?'

'Yes it is,' David confirmed. 'I didn't have any reservations at all about signing it.'

'No?' Jacqui sounded sceptical.

'No, honestly,' David insisted.

'What, signing over your independence completely to another person?'

'That's right,' David replied. 'As far as I'm concerned, as Mistress's house-slave, contract or no contract, I exist only for her pleasure. I was only too happy, honoured even, to sign a document committing myself to unconditional devotion to Mistress and to live by the rules she wanted to set for me.'

'I can relate to that, the way you explain it,' Jacqui said, sounding convinced. 'I'd have signed it too, I reckon, if the opportunity had ever arisen.'

There was silence for a while in the darkness, and then Jacqui spoke again. 'Our world is a strange one, don't you think, David.' Her tone of voice was reflective.

'How do you mean?'

'Well, it's fantasy and reality all mixed together, isn't it. Everything is topsy-turvy. You know, pleasure is pain, bondage is release, submission is freedom.'

'It is strange, but wonderful too,' David said. 'To my way of thinking a life of subservience to Mistress is a perfect life. I find liberation and happiness in my enslavement to her and worship her completely. I know that when I break one of her rules she will beat me, but, then, I like being punished physically.'

'You just can't lose!'

'I wouldn't say that exactly,' David said, smiling into the darkness. It was a smile he would all too soon be wearing on the other side of his face.

'What made you the way you are, do you think?' Jacqui asked. 'Was it how you were brought up, maybe, or some incident in your childhood or adolescence? Were you by any chance brought up as a Catholic?'

'Why bring the Catholic church into it?'

'Well, you know what they say,' Jacqui replied. 'Catholicism and filthy sex go together like salt beef and rye!'

David laughed. Oh what fun he and Jacqui were having – for now. 'No, I wasn't brought up a Catholic, wasn't brought up with any religion, actually.'

'What sort of relationship did you have with your mother?'

'Was I a mother's boy, you mean?'

'Well … yeah.'

'Not in the traditional sense. I ...'

'Did she ever beat you?' Jacqui interrupted.

'Ah, the cross-examination continues,' David said. 'Yes, she did used to beat me – constantly, if you must know.'

'Ah ha!'

'How about you?' David asked quickly, anxious to deflect the conversation away from himself when it came to this particular sensitive subject. 'Are there any Freudian skeletons hanging in your closet?'

'There certainly are,' Jacqui said. 'I can trace my masochism back directly to my upbringing.'

'Tell me about it,' David said. 'Paint me the picture.' And Jacqui did, kneeling there side by side with him inside the locked cage in the bitumen-blackness of the dungeon.

'My mother was brought up by parents who were extremely religious. And yes, before you ask, David, they were Catholics. They were also what you might call old-fashioned disciplinarians. My mother's motto was 'Spare the rod and spoil the child'. She used to insist that it never did her any harm and she imposed a similarly strict disciplinary regime on me. Whenever I was the slightest bit naughty, she used to spank me hard on my bare bottom with the flat of her hand. Later, she progressed to using a wooden paddle and the stinging sensations I felt after a really heavy correction – and

223

they usually were just that – caused me to masturbate. Mother started using a cane on me not long after that and these sessions invariably left me with a warm, tingling feeling even though they were always very painful and left bruises that took several days to fade. During those days I couldn't keep my hands from out of my pants, I masturbated so much. I found myself deliberately being naughty more and more just so she would beat me and I'd get those delicious sensations again. Sound familiar, David?'

It sounded very familiar, uncomfortably so. 'Yes it does rather,' he replied flatly, careful not to let any emotion slip out.

Jacqui went on, 'Once, mother caught me masturbating after one of her beatings and punished me for it by caning me so hard that I climaxed during my punishment. I became an even more persistent masturbator after that, fantasising all the while about being caned. It was a vicious circle.

'After masturbation I discovered fucking – with men and women alike – but by then, thanks to my upbringing, I was already much too perverted to put up with a vanilla sex life. I developed a tremendous craving for something that would take the place of mother's frequent beatings and I'd often resort in desperation to self flagellation while masturbating – particularly after I met a woman called Anne while I was at university, but that's another story. All that self abuse – in both senses of the term – wasn't anything like enough for me, though. It did not take long for my deep masochistic cravings to lead me to S&M sex clubs like *Club Depravity* and extreme fetish parties like the one where we got reacquainted so memorably a few months ago.

'So, I have come a long way as a pervert in my young life but I trace the roots of it all to my upbringing. I still associate being bad – wilful, deceitful, treacherous, whatever – with the pleasure of being punished for it, with the pleasure of pain. And the person who's dishing out the pain simply has to be female, echoes of my dear but not so sainted mother, I have no doubt. I don't blame her for what she did to me, though, what she *made* me. I really like being a pain-slut. Words cannot express how much I do.'

'Me too,' David said. He had become turned-on despite himself by Jacqui's vivid account, which resonated strongly with some of his earlier experiences in ways he preferred not to think about directly. He made sure that he kept the conversation in the hear-and-now by going swiftly on to say, 'I love to be disciplined by Mistress. Being submissive to her is my whole life.'

'When are your happiest, horniest times?' Jacqui asked, a throaty catch in her voice.

'Let me think now,' David said, uncomfortably aware of the further stirrings in his loins as his imagination got to work. 'I guess it's when I'm on my knees and licking Mistress's pussy, tonguing her to orgasm while my punished rear glows from the most recent beating she has given me. I love to kiss and lick her feet, to use my tongue to explore her anus, to do anything at all that Mistress tells me to, no matter how perverted.'

'That makes two of us,' Jacqui said. Her voice had become hoarse with excitement. 'I love being available to Mistress, submitting to her every erotic and sadistic whim, giving myself completely to her. I love it when she orders me about, love it almost as much as when she beats me hard or fucks me senseless with one of her strap-ons.'

'Me too,' said David, who was getting as sexually excited as his young companion by all this hot talk. 'Her orders always make me horny, I don't really know why, but there we are, they do.'

'How do you feel about always having to call her "Mistress"?'

'I love it. Each time I call her "Mistress" I feel a definite erotic thrill. Real weirdo, aren't I?'

'*Moi aussi*,' Jacqui said. 'Weirdoes of the world unite, that's what I say. You have nothing to lose but your liberty!'

There was silence for a lengthy moment and it was replete with sexual tension. Then Jacqui whispered in David's ear, 'All this talk of submission and punishment has made me feel incredibly horny.'

'Now don't start all that again,' David warned. 'Remember the last time.'

'When Mistress used the hidden CCTV camera on us, you mean.'

'Exactly.'

'There's no CCTV camera this time, is there?'

No answer.

'Well, is there?' Jacqui whispered hotly in his ear again. 'You heard what she said.'

'I did, but …'

'I'll bet you're feeling just as horny as I am, David,' she said and she'd certainly got that dead right. It was the proximity of her more than anything else that was doing it now. It was overwhelming his senses.

'No, I'm fine,' he lied, his heart racing. He could smell her, almost taste her.

'So, if I were to reach out for your cock in a moment I wouldn't find it rock-hard?'

'No Jacqui, don't …' But David was done for and he knew it. She took hold of his shaft, which was indeed rigidly erect. It throbbed and flexed in her hand. She smeared her fingers with the tears that cried from its tip and began to stroke it. The more Jacqui stroked David's cock, the faster she went, her hand going up and down in the precome wetness that now thoroughly coated it.

'Do you want me to suck you off?' she asked.

'Y … yes,' he stammered.

'Then say it, say the words.'

'I want you to suck me off,' David said. Jacqui opened her lips and took his cock deep into her mouth. Her tongue licked its thickness, her lips kissing and rubbing against it so that it pulsed and strained against her mouth.

'B … but what if Mistress finds out?' David just about managed to stammer out, given his ever more feverish state of excitement. Jacqui stopped what she was doing, removing her mouth from his erection.

'I won't say anything if you don't, I swear on my life,' she said, adding, 'Also I'll swallow the evidence. Mistress will never be any the wiser. Trust me. You *do* trust me don't you, David?'

'Yes,' he gasped.

'Say it, then.'

'I trust you,' David, the idiot, replied, his cock now entirely doing his thinking for him.

It had been as black as pitch in the dungeon for several hours when all of a sudden the door opened and Isabella entered, flicking on the light. She looked in the direction of the padlocked cage and saw her two slaves kneeling as she had left them, about a foot apart. They both blinked in the abrupt glare of the light, trying to adjust their eyes, before adopting the most innocent expressions imaginable. David's face was as bland as could be and Jacqui looked as if butter – or anything else – wouldn't melt in her mouth.

'I hope you two have had a nice chat,' Isabella said, her own face expressionless. 'Have you?'

'Yes, Mistress,' they replied in unison.

'Glad to hear it,' Isabella said. Her gaze had suddenly developed a hard edge. 'I look forward with eager anticipation to listening to the tape recording I made of your conversation.'

David tried his best to keep any emotion from showing on his face but inside he was in a total panic. Shit! Shit! Shit! Shit! Shit! he cursed to himself. And well might he have done because there was no doubt about it: the shit had undeniably, irrefutably hit the fan now. Why, oh why had he done it? Why had he trusted Jacqui of all people, for God's sake? She had been the instigator, the one who had been doing all the seducing, the real culprit. Mistress would see that when she played the tape back, surely, wouldn't she? *Wouldn't she?*

Chapter Forty-one

Isabella had listened to the tape. The inquisition was about to begin. Her two naked slaves stood before her in the dungeon as she strode from side to side, her arms clasped behind her. She was holding something silver in one hand but neither of them could see what it was.

'Did you really think you'd get away with it a second time, David?' Isabella asked.

'Mistress?' he said, barely able to meet her gaze. His heart was beating double time.

'You know what I'm talking about,' Isabella said, glaring at him so hard that she seemed to be trying to cook him with her eyes. 'Allowing Jacqui to behave exactly according to type and letting her get all the blame for it. You've done it once before. Thought you had a winning formula, did you, eh?'

'No, Mistress. You see I ...' But before David had a chance to say any more, Isabella slapped him hard across the face, causing a dark flush to stain his cheek. In slapping him she also caught his upper lip, which immediately began to swell. Blood mingled with his saliva.

'Shut your lying mouth, David,' Isabella barked. She turned her hard stare towards Jacqui who looked positively terrified, no acting this time. 'You have always aspired to be my house-slave, haven't you, Jacqui,' Isabella said. It was a statement, not a question.

'Yes, Mistress.'

'Consider yourself duly appointed,' Isabella said curtly and switched the hard glare of her gaze back to David. 'As for you, you *fucking worm*, let me give you some idea of what's going to happen to you. First, and let me emphasise, this is just for starters – to soften you up before your real punishment begins – you are to remain in solitary confinement in this dungeon for as long as I consider it appropriate. There are perfectly adequate toilet and washing facilities here already, needless to say, so you can shower and shave and the like. As far as subsistence is concerned, Jacqui – who is not allowed to speak to you from now on, incidentally, *ever again* – will deliver two bowls to you each morning, one containing drinking water, the other some scraps for you to eat. That will keep body and soul together for you, just about, and even that's more than you deserve because you're the lowest of the fucking low. Do you agree with that assessment?'

'Yes, Mistress,' David replied. He certainly did agree. He was conscious that he'd begun trembling, couldn't stop.

'A couple of other matters,' Isabella said, her mouth twisted with disgust. 'When I first took you into my home you signed a slave contract that required you, among other things, to always do what I tell you without fail. You have blatantly disregarded that, which is utterly inexcusable, is it not?'

'Yes, Mistress,' he replied, his body quaking like an aspen now.

'That slave contract agreement is no longer worth the paper it is written on because of what you have done.'

'M … m … mistress…'

'You are also under a standing instruction not to masturbate unless you have my express permission,' Isabella went on, her dark eyes glinting savagely. 'That's right, isn't it?'

'Yes, Mistress.'

'For painfully obvious reasons I can no longer trust you to comply with that instruction. From now on I shall require you to wear this.'

Isabella produced the mysterious silver object she was holding from behind her back. It was a chastity device constructed of lightweight aluminium and she immediately proceeded to enclose David's cock and balls with it. The device had a key closure, which she locked, and a drainage hole that David was going to have to rapidly get accustomed to using. The device was actually fairly comfortable but David knew that would drastically change if he started to get a hard-on. And, face it, he was always getting hard-ons. David started to anticipate the searing pain in his groin he was going to suffer, the appalling pressure he would be feeling there.

'It was Mistress Kate's idea,' Isabella said. 'She gave it to me as a gift this evening when we met for dinner. She's never trusted Jacqui and thought you might be safer from temptation if you wore a chastity device. Too late, wasn't she, slave?'

'Yes, Mistress,' David replied miserably. A torrent of guilt and shame and fear flooded through him.

'And don't think you're going to get off lightly, Jacqui,' Isabella said, turning to her new house-slave and giving her the most scathing of glares. 'I intend to give some concentrated attention to thrashing that devious, deceitful nature of yours right out of you. I don't hold out much, if any hope, of being successful, I'm afraid to say, given that it's a virtually impossible task. But I'll have a damn good try. Believe me, I am going to be an outstandingly harsh task Mistress.'

Jacqui believed her all right.

By the time Isabella had locked him in the dungeon, David was in a dreadful state: consumed with both profound remorse for what he'd done and infinite fear for his future. He was acutely aware from what Isabella had said that his solitary confinement was just the start, a taster of whatever punishment she had in mind for him after that. He remained thoroughly miserable for the entirety of his imprisonment, which went on and on. Days passed, weeks passed.

Even the darkest cloud has a silver lining, though, and the dreaded painful erections he had anticipated as a result of wearing the chastity device never materialised. But that was because David was too genuinely distressed and afraid to ever become erect. A combination of hopelessness, shame and fearful anticipation battled for possession of his head, blurring everything. He felt truly wretched the whole time he was incarcerated and terrified of what the future might hold for him.

During that time the only company David had, if you can

call it that, came in two forms. The first was Jacqui's silent delivery early each morning of his meagre rations for the day – neither of the slaves could bring themselves to look the other one in the eye. Second were the occasions every day when Isabella came into the dungeon to punish her new house-slave. These sessions always started with the same routine. Isabella would unlock David's chastity device and give him a few moments to clean both the device and his genitals. She would then lock the chastity device back into place and tell David to kneel in the corner of the dungeon with his face to the wall and his eyes closed firmly shut. He saw nothing from that stage on, of course, but what he heard made his blood run cold.

He heard Jacqui's pitiful sobs as she counted out each hard slap that Isabella gave to her face – all thirty of them, no less. He heard the sound of Isabella's most savage flogger swishing through the air constantly, sounding like a nest of angry snakes, and Jacqui's agonized screams that seemed to be being torn from the very core of her being as her backside was whipped what must have been red raw. He heard her squeal and beg for mercy as Isabella attached excruciatingly painful weighted metal clamps to her breasts and labia. He heard her anguished yelps and shivering moans as Isabella poured red-hot molten wax on her body. He heard with a sensation of mounting nausea the sound of Jacqui's frequent gagging as, on Isabella's insistence, she deep throated the strap-on dildo with which she had just finished fucking her ferociously hard. He could imagine the engorged tip prodding against the back of her throat, causing it to spasm horribly. He knew what Isabella was doing this time and all the other times. She was pushing Jacqui over and over again not up to her limit but beyond that limit – frequently way beyond – and it was an awful thing to have to listen to, but listen to it he had to ... And there it was again – that dreadful gagging noise. David began to weep silently, tears of mortification dripping from his eyes.

When he was back on his own he could not stop thinking about what he'd heard. The nights were the worst. He endeavoured to get to sleep in the only place that felt remotely comfortable for that purpose, which was the leather-covered bondage table, and tried desperately to empty his mind. It didn't work at all. The screen kept filling up with mental images of those hideous scenes he had listened to, the ones of Jacqui's extreme torment and humiliation. They played through his mind in an uninterruptible loop like some obscene and endless horror film. All of this could so easily have been avoided, David was painfully aware, if he hadn't proved himself to be such a weak, disobedient, deceitful bastard, such a pathetically useless slave to his Mistress. He suffered paroxysms of remorse.

David knew exactly where he'd gone wrong – that wonderful thing called hindsight again. He should never have disobeyed Isabella, that went without saying. But more than that, he should have given far more serious thought to the implications of the slave contract before signing it so readily when Isabella had first decided to take him into her home as her house-slave, having told him that he'd proved himself a good and loyal slave.

His attitude had essentially been that if his Mistress wanted him to sign such an agreement, it was fine by him, just like anything else she wanted him to do. But that had been to entirely miss the point of such an important document. He should have studied it very carefully first. Once he had given it the consideration it deserved and had signed it, as frankly there was no doubt he would have done, he should have stuck to its conditions come what may like super-glue.

By allowing himself to be seduced by Jacqui – not once but twice, for crying out loud – he'd ended up making a complete travesty of the slave contract, Isabella had said as much. By doing such a thing he thoroughly deserved the dire consequences that he was now suffering and would be certain to be suffering in the future.

Also, David told himself ruefully, when his Mistress had paid him the compliment of asking him his opinion for once – asking him whether he had any concerns about Jacqui coming back into the fold, as she'd put it – it might have helped if he'd given more than a nanosecond of consideration to the question before giving her his glib response. How profoundly he regretted that he hadn't done that now that it was too late.

There was another thing, as well. He'd baulked at the accusation that Isabella had levelled at him at first, but hadn't she been absolutely right? At a subconscious level, at least, hadn't he allowed Jacqui to seduce him, thinking that because it was her he could somehow abrogate responsibility for his own actions? Once again he'd revealed himself to be all too susceptible to Jacqui's blandishments when she went into full seduction mode and in his heart of hearts he'd always known he would respond in the way he'd ended up doing. And then he'd gone and added insult to injury by trying to deceive Isabella about what had happened; it was absolutely outrageous.

When Isabella had been subjecting him to all those tests and challenges before granting him the ultimate prize by making him her house-slave, she'd essentially been testing his capacity for punishment, humiliation and perversion. She hadn't found him wanting. When she'd actually put temptation in his way in the person of Jacqui, doing so on two separate occasions, he'd succumbed to it with remarkable ease both times like the cock-happy son of a bitch he'd proved himself to be. He was extremely sorry for all this, more sorry than he could ever say.

David was extremely sorry for Jacqui too. He was sorry for her for what she was having to go through in the dungeon. He was sorry for her, full stop, although he knew that the pity he felt for her was to some extent a form of self-pity. Part of a poem by Philip Larkin kept flashing through his mind: '*They fuck you up, your mum and dad. They do not mean to but they do.*' Jacqui's sadistic mother had herself had parents who'd been strict disciplinarians, never "sparing the rod". They no doubt hadn't meant to but they had managed to fuck up their daughter, and she in turn had fucked up her own daughter, fucked her up big time. The constant heavy beatings she had given the young Jacqui had created someone whose responses were Pavlovian in their predictability. Jacqui behaved badly in order that she might be punished, in order that she might feel pain, in order that she might feel pleasure.

But David knew that he was not so very different from her

himself when it came to the crunch. Everything he'd been through with his mother – everything she'd done to him – had left him well and truly fucked up. That was an irrefutable fact. The "good boy" he'd turned himself into after her tragic death had been damaged goods, a broken person, thanks to her sadism towards him. And hadn't he, after all these years merely regressed, reverting to type at long last so that he might be punished like Jacqui – thoroughly beaten and chastised for being "bad"?

Well, both he and Jacqui had clearly bitten off way more than they could chew this time. He was now utterly miserable and deeply afraid for his future and Jacqui simply could not have been having a tougher time in the dungeon. Maybe, David speculated, she was faring better as Isabella's house-slave. He could not have been more wrong ...

Isabella found fault with everything Jacqui did. If she produced a meal for her, it was more often than not dismissed as being worse than the scraps she was providing for David. The meat was always overcooked or under cooked, there was too much seasoning or too little, and the contents of the plate ended up being unceremoniously binned by the disgruntled diner. Isabella pushed Jacqui to the floor when, as was invariably the case, her boot and shoe maintenance fell short of the extremely high standard the dominatrix required. If Jacqui drew her a bath, the temperature of the water was always wrong, something Isabella would demonstrate to her by grasping her by the hair and dunking her face below the surface until she thought she might drown. The kitchen floor was never clean enough for Isabella, no matter how many times Jacqui scrubbed it on her hands and knees, although admittedly the sight of her doing so was undeniably a pleasing one, her heavily punished rear, pouting anus and shaven pussy prominently on display. Jacqui's attempts at maintaining the secluded rear garden, which Isabella made her do while it was raining, were regarded by the dominatrix as so feeble that she felt duty bound to push the naked slave into the wet mud and then turn a hose of freezing water onto her.

But it was vanity that did for Jacqui in the end. 'How can you hope to be an even half-way effective house-slave to me with all that long curly hair falling over your face?' Isabella announced one evening, after she'd given Jacqui a particularly miserable time over what she deemed to be the very poor quality of her housework. 'When you present yourself to me tomorrow morning I want you to have cut it all off, every last strand. I want your head completely shaved so it matches your pussy. I want you as bald as an egg.'

That was a humiliation too far for Jacqui. She could just about take all the unrelenting abuse and outstandingly cruel discipline that Isabella seemed to want to inflict on her all the time. If that was what it took to remain her house-slave, then so be it. A shorter, more practical hairstyle, she could live with that, no problem. But, damn it all, to tell her to cut off *all* her beautiful tresses, that was just too much to demand.

The day was already warm when Isabella woke up. Getting out of bed, she pulled the bedroom curtains and transparent light shone brightly through the window. It had been raining for most of the last week, sheeting it down constantly, but the rain had stopped at last. Isabella called out for Jacqui but there was no response. She looked for her all over the house but she was nowhere to be seen, and nor were her few belongings. It seemed that she had gone, sneaked off, stolen away like a thief into the night.

'Good riddance to bad rubbish,' Isabella said out loud to herself with deep disdain. She knew that this time she'd driven Jacqui off for good. 'Now, I wonder how much further I need to push that disobedient, deceitful cunt David before he gives up the ghost too.'

Isabella was looking forward to finding that out as much as she was looking forward to being reunited with her husband, an event which was now imminent. Alan was in the process of flying back from the United States and would be home today. It

235

was true that he had scheduled in only the briefest of visits before returning to the States to carry on building the *La Fetishista* business over there – so brief a visit, in fact, that he wasn't even bothering to bring the kinky twins with him – but his visit would be very welcome, nonetheless.

Latterly their marriage had developed into such a long distance affair that it was barely a marriage at all, Isabella had rather sadly conceded. But their shared passion for sadism left them with a powerful bond she was confident would never be broken, no matter how far apart they drifted. So, watch out David, watch the fuck out.

Chapter Forty-two

Alan Stern's deep-set eyes traversed the dungeon Isabella had created in his absence. It really was most impressive, he considered. For one thing, the lighting she'd had put in created just the right ambience: eerie and dim and subtly focussed on the dungeon equipment. For another thing all that equipment came from *La Fetishista* – but, of course! – and was therefore of the very highest quality. For another, nearly all of it was encased in soft black leather.

Nearly all of the people who were currently in the dungeon were also encased in soft black leather, himself included. He, Isabella, Caroline and Kate were all wearing skin-tight body suits and knee-length boots. David, by contrast was wearing nothing at all, not even the chastity device he'd had to wear ever since his incarceration. Isabella had very recently removed that item from his genitalia, not before time. But she'd done this only so that his genitals could be, as she'd gleefully informed him, "properly tortured".

No wonder David was shaking like a leaf as he cowered before them all. No wonder his face was deathly-pale and his head bowed, his eyes never leaving the floor. No wonder there were dark smudges under those eyes. No wonder that he kept wetting his lips uneasily and that his hands were sweating. This was clearly an extremely frightened slave, a petrified slave. And he had every reason to be petrified. Alan Stern knew that for an absolute certainty because he knew what was about to happen to him.

Isabella went to stand beside her disgraced slave before turning to face the others. 'Can I have your attention please,' she said and it suddenly became so silent in the dungeon you could have heard a pin drop. 'First of all I would like to thank Alan for making the time during this flying visit of his to help me to organise this evening's little entertainment.'

'You're welcome,' her husband replied with a mock-formal tilt of the head, his dark eyes glinting.

'The reason we are here,' Isabella continued, 'is to discipline my slave, David, and you all know why. In brief, it's because he's a disobedient, lying motherfucker.' She eyed him with the utmost contempt.

'Could you remind us again of the rules of your entertainment?' Caroline said, not that she or Kate or Alan needed reminding in the slightest. This was for David's benefit, to rub proverbial salt into his soon-to-be anything but proverbial wounds.

'By all means,' Isabella replied. 'I would like each of you in turn to discipline David. Don't hold back. Be as cruel as you like, I mean *really* cruel. The only thing I would ask is that you make his punishment apt.'

'Make the punishment fit the crime,' Kate offered.

'Exactly,' Isabella confirmed. 'Now, who wants to be the first to discipline him? How about you, Caroline?'

'Sure,' the flame haired dominatrix replied, picking up a black leather hold-all, walking forward a few steps towards David and putting the bag on the floor by her side. She turned to look at Isabella. 'May I start?'

'Yes, please do,' Isabella said.

'Let me tell you the way I see things here,' Caroline said, addressing her attentive leather-clad audience after directing a brief scowl at David. 'First, this sorry excuse for a slave here must be a blind fool to have disobeyed his Mistress and done what he did with Jacqui. Hence this.' She took a black leather blindfold from out of her bag and put it over David's eyes, buckling it tightly into place behind his head. 'Yes, a blind fool,' she repeated. 'And a treacherous cocksucker too in the attempt he made, pathetic though it was, to deceive his Mistress.' Caroline delved into her bag again and took hold of an inflatable dildo-gag, which was also black. She instructed David to open his mouth and placed the rubber dildo inside.

238

'Yes, a treacherous, deceitful cocksucker. Close your mouth, slave,' she added and there was a hiss as she worked a hand operated air pump to make the rubber in his mouth inflate. It grew ever larger, forcing his mouth apart unmercifully until it was crammed full, the cock-shaped gag wedging behind his teeth.

She went on to secure David's wrists to the steel manacles at either end of a nearby spreader bar, which was attached to ceiling chains. She secured his ankles to a similar spreader bar with manacle attachments that was on the dungeon floor immediately beneath it.

'He has been exposed as a treacherous, deceitful cocksucker and that puts him in something of a predicament,' Caroline continued, warming further to her theme. 'He needs to fully consider the *weight* of that predicament.' Chuckling mirthlessly, she reached once more into her bag and this time brought out three heavily weighted clamps. She attached one each to both of his nipples and, taking hold of a fold of skin below his balls, attached another to his scrotum. The pain was more intense than David could have imagined, like a fire on his flesh, and he bucked desperately against his bonds – which just made the pain even more agonizing.

Caroline then dipped again into her bag, this time picking out a retractable riding crop and lengthening it. She stood behind David and beat his backside savagely with the crop, causing jolts of pain right through his body. She then moved to his front and flicked the leather tip of the crop over the weighted clamps attached to his nipples and scrotum. Withering pain was now coursing through David's body like dark electricity.

'Miserable, blind, treacherous, deceitful, cocksucker,' Caroline said, spitting out each of the words. 'You really are up shit creek, aren't you? But don't worry, I've got the paddle.' She delved into her hold-all again and pulled out a heavily studded leather paddle with which she began beating David's backside furiously. 'I'll teach you to disobey your Mistress and then try to deceive her about it, you worthless piece of shit,' she rasped, beating him mercilessly until his flesh burned with agony. Then Caroline stopped abruptly. 'I'm done here,' she said.

'Splendid – most impressive,' Isabella said, her eyes shining. 'Now, how about you to go next, Alan?'

He nodded his agreement.

'I trust you intend to be suitably excessive,' Isabella said.

'I certainly do,' her husband replied, striding forward. 'And may I say how impressed I was also with Caroline's contribution. It was very creative, I thought. I did think these were a particularly inspired touch.' He pointed to the weighted clamps, and then removed them from David's skin, anything but gently, causing a pain like liquid fire to burn into his flesh as he gasped and choked into his dildo gag.

'Let me tell you how I view this regrettable matter,' Alan Stern went on in measured tones. 'First, I think it is important that David see, and I do mean *see*, the error of his ways. So, we will take this off.' He reached behind David's head and unbuckled the tight blindfold. 'Also, you must bear with me. I do have certain peccadilloes, shall we say. One of them is that I simply *love* to hear a slave scream in agony.' He unbuckled David's dildo-gag and let the air out of the rubber dildo. With a hiss of escaping air the dildo went soft and he pulled it from David's mouth.

He then released him from the spreader bars and clamped a hand on his hair. 'Come this way, you pitiful fucking loser,' he said and pulled him by the hair over to the leather-covered bondage table. He told him to lie on the table on his back and then strapped his wrists and ankles to its four corners. David's body was trembling uncontrollably in its bondage and his eyes were moist with terror.

'I have nothing but contempt for this worthless slave,' Alan went on. 'He clearly can't hold a candle to his Mistress. But I can hold a candle to him.' He lit a large red candle and began drizzling hot wax on David's chest, genitals and the soles of his feet, causing him to gasp and cry out.

'By trying to deceive Isabella with this thoroughly troublesome Jacqui bitch I've been hearing about he was clearly playing with fire,' Alan continued, glaring at him angrily. 'He was just asking to get burned, as I am about to demonstrate.' He waved the candle over David's chest and torso again, dripping more burning hot wax onto his body. Then he set fire to a swirl of his body hair, just above his pubic area. David screamed in terror.

'That's what I like to hear,' Alan said with a sadistic smile, before casually flicking out the flame.

He then released David from the bondage table, led him to the whipping bench and positioned him over it, his severely punished backside in the air.

He said, 'Here's an old saying for you, 'You can't flog a dead horse'. I prefer my version, though, 'You *can* flog a live whore-son.' And that's what I'm going to do – and with the most vicious flogger I can lay my hands on, as well.'

He grasped a braided black leather whip, raised his hand high and brought the flogger down as hard as he could again and again until David was in agony, his backside patterned a deep, painful red. On and on he whipped him, laying into his backside with relentless savagery.

'How dare you cheat on your Mistress and lie to her, you worthless son of a whore,' Alan Stern shouted, his saturnine features turning puce with rage. 'How dare you! How dare you!' He whipped David with unrelenting viciousness until, racked with coruscating pain, he began screaming a terrible piercing scream that rose higher and higher. His voice full of ever-increasing agony, he screamed and screamed.

Chapter Forty-three

Alan Stern let his victim's screaming run its course and then stopped torturing him. David was still in such pain that it was fogging his eyes. He was also shivering without control, his limbs jerking and trembling with the aftershock. Alan told him to stand up next to the whipping bench over which he'd just disciplined him with such savagery and to face his "audience".

Alan's place was then taken by Kate. It rapidly became clear that the ash-blonde dominatrix was eager to at least match if not exceed his vicious efforts. Unerringly loyal as always to her former Mistress, Kate was absolutely furious with David. It radiated from her like a force field. David had broken the most cardinal rule as far as she was concerned. In her book, trust wasn't just the name of the game in BDSM. It was a holy writ. A slave should never try to deceive their Mistress, *never*. If they did they deserved every damn thing they got.

Wearing an expression like thunder, anger firing her violet eyes, she immediately launched in. 'When Isabella told me what David had done with that treacherous little slut, Jacqui,' she said as she strode purposefully over to the still-trembling slave, 'it really needled me.' She looked with scorn at David and then placed an open box of large sterilized needles on top of the whipping bench. 'Yes, I was really needled,' Kate repeated. 'Then, I thought, why should I be needled? It should be this sad fuck.' She took a large needle from the box and plunged it through David's left nipple. His nerves screamed at the needle as it scratched and dragged his skin with sharp cold agony. And David screamed too, a high, inhuman sound.

'A prick for a prick,' she added, putting another large needle through his right nipple. He screamed again, that same inhuman noise, as the bright flash of agony shot through him. Both nipples were now raging.

'He's been exposed as a prick, certainly,' Kate went on when his screaming had tapered off. 'But, more than that, he's been exposed as a snake. What would be appropriate to beat this snake with? Ah yes, my snake whip.' Behind and above the hand now holding the whip, Kate's eyes remained as angry as ever. She went on, 'All right, turn round, snake – prepare to be skinned.'

Kate dragged the thongs of the whip back and forth across David's backside for a few seconds and then made her first strike. The whip sang through the air and when it landed instantly inflamed his backside and the back of his thighs as it bit into his flesh. Again and again the snake whip seared his body and he squirmed and cringed.

Soon David was lost to the world, writhing in a dance of agony to the music of the whip on his flesh and his own agonized cries. And while he was in this trance-like state of agony something else happened, something that hadn't happened for weeks and weeks, something he really didn't want to be happening now…

Kate stopped whipping David. 'Turn back round,' she ordered and when he did, his cock waved in the air in front of him, huge and taut and aching. Fresh agony burned sharply through his tender nipples as she pulled out first one, then the other large needle, causing on both occasions an elaborate burst of precome to spray from his cock.

'As I say, he's just a prick,' Kate concluded. 'I rest my case.'

Last but – God knows – by no means least, it was Isabella's turn. David looked up, his eyes wide with terror as he watched her approach. It was like watching a dark and terrible storm move in across a valley.

Isabella came to a halt before David and half turned. There followed a tense hush, every ear in the dungeon directed to her. Then she broke the silence. 'I'll be very brief,' the dominatrix said, gazing directly at her cowering slave and giving him the most pitiless of looks, her eyes cold and hard. 'I'm dumping you, David. End of story.'

David felt as if he was half floating out of his body, that it was going to die on him. He let out a strangled cry of anguish. 'No, Mistress, please,' he pleaded, the expression on his face desperate, his eyes wild. His very worst fear, his worst nightmare, had been that she would do this.

'I've said all I have to say,' Isabella replied, her features now cast in stone.

'Can I say something?' David begged. 'Please, Mistress, please?'

'Go on,' she said with evident reluctance, still stony-faced.

'Everything I've been accused of being here this evening is true, every last word of it – I've been a prick, a snake …'

Isabella gave a snort of derision. 'Tell me something I don't already know.'

'I deeply regret what I did, Mistress. I'd give anything to turn back the clock, anything.'

'You can't though, can you?' she said, giving him another cold hard stare.

Struggling desperately under that pitiless stare, David replied, 'No, Mistress, but I swear I'll never let anything like that happen again, swear on my life.'

'Irrelevant, slave,' Isabella responded brusquely. 'Like I said, I'm ditching you. And I'm doing it as of right now.'

'Mistress, Mistress, please, oh, please?' David was utterly distraught now. 'I'm begging you not to dump me. Torture me like you've never tortured me before, flay me alive, do anything you like to me. But please don't desert me. You're my whole world. I worship you. I was a complete fucking idiot to do what I did with Jacqui.'

'You were indeed.'

'I didn't let my head do the thinking, but my cock.'

'You said it,' she agreed, eyeing his groin; he looked down too. 'So, what's new?' David was clearly in a state of the most chronic distress imaginable yet his cock was still ragingly hard, it was mortifying.

'I'll change, Mistress. I will. I will,' he cried.

'I'm not sure I want you to change,' Isabella said, toying

244

with him now.

'Uh?'

'There's definitely something to be said for a man who thinks with his cock. That amazing libido of yours was one of the reasons I chose you as my house-slave in the first place, you must have realised that.' She continued, 'now, what was that you were saying about wanting me to torture and flay you like I've never done before? You *did* say that, didn't you?'

'Yes, Mistress, but ...'

'But me no buts, slave – it's way too late for that,' she said as she picked up a rattan cane. 'Turn round and reach towards your toes.'

Once David was in position, he gritted his teeth and waited. Isabella brought the cane down extremely hard, its impact a pure scarlet spear of pain that caused him to let out a loud shriek. She went on to beat him over and over in rapid fire motions. Isabella brought the cane down hard in criss-cross stripes across his hips and backside, relishing the sadistic pleasure of striking his already severely punished rear with the thin, cutting instrument and listening to his shrieks of pain.

Next Isabella led David over to the horizontal torture chair that on this occasion had in place a mechanical dildo attachment, which she lubricated before she strapped him into the chair. She buckled his wrists so that they were held behind his head and his legs so that his knees were held up and wide apart. David concentrated on relaxing his sphincter muscles as best he could in order to accommodate the giant rubber phallus that she now pushed against his anal hole. The head of the dildo popped through his sphincter immediately and he absorbed it with a cry of pain. At the same time his cock hardened still further and let out a spurt of precome that splattered back down onto his torso.

Isabella started the machine and the dildo began to push all the way in and all the way out of David's anus. It picked up speed too and he cried out as it jerked in and out of him. There was only intense pain at first but eventually this turned into hot, exquisite pleasure from each energetic thrust of the mechanical dildo as his internal muscles contracted and released around it.

Pure pain had become pure pleasure – which Isabella was definitely *not* prepared to allow, and which was why she turned the machine off.

Once she had brought the mechanical dildo to a stop she pulled it from David's anus and he felt lubricant trickle from his hole. Isabella released him from the horizontal torture chair and led him across to the horse, strapping him across it on his front. She picked up a heavy leather flogger and began whipping his rear. Isabella used the flogger to sear David's uplifted backside over and over, making him jump and strain against his bonds. His rear now burned like a raging inferno and the resounding crack of each blow mingled with his tortured cries of pain.

Next Isabella released David from the horse and told him to lie flat on his back on the dungeon floor. She took hold of a genital lead made of chain and leather and, kneeling down briefly, buckled it tightly into place round the base of his achingly erect cock and the top of his scrotum. Isabella then stood up, told David to get on to all fours, and yanked at the lead so that his genitals were pulled back hard between his thighs. Still grasping the genital lead, she took hold of a cat o'nine tails and rained it down onto David's backside, taking care to catch his cock and balls with it as frequently as possible. The pain was excruciating and David sobbed and whimpered at the agony of trying to bear it, tears cascading down his face and onto the dungeon floor in a constant stream.

Isabella then unbuckled and removed the genital lead and led David over to the vertical torture chair. She strapped him to it on his back, and attached clamps to his nipples and genitals. Isabella kept adding magnetic metal weights to these, each one causing fresh agony to burn through his body. It was like nothing less than Hell on earth for David. His eyes bugged, his face went red, the veins popped on his neck.

Finally the agony was too much for him and he was overpowered by it completely, reaching the absolute end of his tether. His whole world suddenly exploded into crimson agony and, screaming for mercy, he climaxed in great bursting spasms. The orgasm Isabella had ripped from David seemed to go on for ever as he screamed and screamed maniacally, spraying out an endless load of come.

Chapter Forty-four

After experiencing an ordeal as harrowing as that there was a bit of sorely-needed good news for David the next day. There was however some bad, some *lousy* news for him as well. The good news was this: Isabella told David that as soon as she'd seen her husband off at Gatwick airport and returned to Brighton she was going to release him from the dungeon. She was as good as her word and did this straight away upon her return. Also she did not kick David out of the house and out of her life, which had been – and continued to be – his worst fear of all.

The bad news was that, on letting David out of the dungeon, Isabella made it crystal clear to him that he remained as much as ever *persona non grata* with her. And that coloured everything as far as David was concerned. Knowing that he was still in complete disgrace with his Mistress meant that he continued to dwell as much as ever under a black cloud of mortification and abject fear about his future. Nothing had fundamentally changed at all.

'I'm going out presently, slave,' Isabella informed David one evening, several days after she'd released him from his incarceration in the dungeon.

'Yes, Mistress,' he replied meekly.

'Remind me where I'm going.'

'To an orgy at Mistress Kate's house, Mistress.'

'Mistress Caroline will be bringing your friend Matthew to the orgy,' she said tauntingly. 'I *did* tell you that, didn't I?'

'Yes, Mistress.'

'Remind me why I'm not bringing you, slave.'

'As a further punishment, Mistress.'

'What for?' she asked.

'For my disobedience and deceitfulness, Mistress.'

'Correct. And what do I require you to do in my absence?'

'Kneel in the corner of the room with my face to the wall and reflect on my shortcomings, Mistress,' David replied.

'That's right,' Isabella said. 'Do that now. Get into position.'

'Yes, Mistress.' David immediately did as he'd been told and at the same time Isabella strode towards the living room door. Just before leaving the room she turned and said, 'Goodbye, slave. I'm going off to the orgy now.'

'Goodbye, Mistress,' he replied. 'I'm most desperately sorry for what I did. I'd do anything to make things right. I'd …' It was too late. She'd already gone. It was funny, though, he hadn't heard the front door shut. Isabella poked her head round the living room door. 'OK, you can come with me to the orgy.'

He turned to look at her. 'Mistress?'

'I said you can come with me.'

'Why the change of heart, Mistress?'

'I've decided to forgive you.'

David could hardly believe his ears. 'Why, Mistress?'

'I think you've suffered enough.'

Isabella parked her car just past the entrance gate to Kate's house, a double-fronted property close to the seafront in Hove. The last slither of the sun was sinking into the sea and a warm orange light suffused the air around Isabella and David as they walked up the front path. The door opened a crack soon after Isabella had rung the bell and it was a stark naked Kate who let them in and ushered them into the living room. It was not only Kate that was nude, as quickly became apparent. Tony, Caroline and Matthew were all also stripped for action. And very soon Isabella and David were as well.

It was only then that David realised that Isabella had duped him. He realised it for the simple reason that she told him so. And precisely what it was that Isabella told David sent waves of sickness coursing through his brain. Suddenly Isabella seemed to be addressing both David and the other naked occupants of the room at the same time. 'All right, slave, here's the deal with this orgy,' she announced. 'You will be required to pleasure everyone here, bring each of us in turn to a climax. We, on our part will do our best to bring you to orgasm, which you must resist at all costs. If you are successful you get to go home with me tonight.'

'And if I fail, Mistress?' David had suddenly gone a sickly shade of pale.

'You'll go back to your own home alone, I'll go back to my home – and I'll shut you out of my life for good. I'll have nothing further to do with you for as long as you live.'

David's face became even paler, as white as a sheet, and his head began to swim. He stammered, 'Y ... you c ... can't be serious about this, Mistress.'

'Never more so,' Isabella replied and David could see from the look on her face now that this was indeed the case. She was positively glowing with malice. 'If you blow this, David,' she went on, a mocking light in her eyes, 'you'll be completely fucked, and not in a nice way!'

'So, when you said you'd forgiven me, Mistress ...' The sickness was mounting even more, making him dizzier. He felt as if the ground underneath him was no longer stable but tilting, this way and that.

'That's right. I lied,' Isabella said, smiling thinly. 'But, of course, you know all about lying, don't you?'

'Yes, Mistress.' David closed his eyes for a second, trembling, trying to force down the ever rising tide of panic. This couldn't be happening, it couldn't. Isabella had said she'd forgiven him, that he'd suffered enough.

Isabella looked away from David and then right through him. 'Now, speaking for myself, I feel incredibly horny,' she said. 'So let's have no more crap from you, David. Make a start – get on with pleasuring me.'

'Yes, Mistress,' David replied shakily although he felt himself starting – just starting – to rally. It was true that he was still in an advanced state of shock but it was beginning to disintegrate, still in him but spread through his body, less and less a centralised force. And mixing with it, adulterating it, was a real feeling of resolve. It was already beginning to harden ... and so was his cock; it was stiffening more by the moment.

David was determined to succeed against all the odds in what would undoubtedly be by far the most difficult challenge of any of those that Isabella had set him since he'd first fallen under her hypnotic spell. In a perverse way, the fact that what was being required of him was so incredibly difficult and that there was so much – everything – at stake, turned him on inordinately. The colour had begun to come back into David's cheeks, his mouth had gone dry with sexual anticipation and his blood was now rushing through his veins, making his shaft rigidly erect now. He mustn't fail this time, it was vital; he wouldn't fail.

Isabella told David to kneel in front of her as she lay back on the sumptuous black leather couch that graced Kate's elegant living room. 'Masturbate me,' she said, spreading her legs wide apart. David plunged two fingers of one hand into her pussy, which was drenched: all ripe and ready for him. He also began to tease her shiny clitoris with the middle finger of his other hand.

'Get to work with your tongue now, slave,' Isabella ordered him next and he pressed his lips to her sex, pushing his tongue in and licking her labia and clit.

'Lie on your back on the floor,' was her next instruction to David and when he did his hard cock stood up like a flagpole. Isabella climbed off the couch swung her hips over his face so that he could continue to eat her pussy. He sucked at her clitoris with his mouth, his tongue both tender and rough, while she pulled up and down on his aching shaft with an insistent rhythm.

'Fuck me now and fuck me hard,' Isabella ordered as she climbed off him, her breasts jiggling, thighs quivering. 'Take me from behind.' She got on to all fours and David positioned himself behind her and thrust his cock deep into her pussy, which was now even more slick and oozing and wet for him. He went on to fuck her with strong, fast thrusts, pumping into her more and more until she climaxed powerfully.

'That's one down,' Isabella said after she'd allowed her orgasm to fade. 'And an easy one too – I've never allowed you to ejaculate inside me, and you never have. It was frankly unthinkable that you would have broken that particular rule on this of all occasions. So, as I say, that's one easy one down. Four more to go, though. *Four*. Get flat on your back again, slave. Kate, straddle his face and blow him please.'

The ash-blonde domme immediately did Isabella's bidding. She squatted over David's face, pushing her sex onto his mouth, and he stuck out his tongue to lick her juices. At the same time she leant forward and fastened her own bright lips tight on his cock, which was moist at its tip. She sucked that moistness away, prompting an agonized whimper from David. He had to bring Kate to climax as soon as possible or he'd be finished, he realised, and he began to move his tongue very quickly over the lips of her sex. He licked and licked at her, slurping and swallowing, but that only made her redouble her efforts as she sucked even more violently on his stiff cock. And then she abruptly stopped ... but only to change positions.

Kate lay flat on her stomach before David, stretched her lips and wrapped them purposefully around his cock again. He balanced himself on his elbows and she looked into his eyes, a wicked glint in her own. David could feel his pleasure rising dangerously as she took his shaft deep into her throat. She pulled it out again slowly, accentuating the pressure of her lips, aware that his breathing was getting faster, and then plunged it deep in her throat again. And so she continued. If she carries on much longer like this, David said to himself fearfully, I'll be completely done for.

But she didn't. Kate stopped blowing him, sat on the floor with her legs parted and demanded that he pleasure her with his fingers and then his tongue. David lay on his front between her thighs and tried very hard to calm down as he fingered her pussy and played with her clit. She arched upwards, her knees up and legs spread wide as he went on to expertly tongue her sex, licking deep inside her.

'Get on to your back again,' Kate said next and when David

did she sat on his aching erection and began riding him. He moaned with her movements as she slid up and down on his shaft, her pussy tight and moist. Then, groaning deeply, she climaxed while David held himself back from the brink with an absolutely monumental effort of will.

'That's two down,' Kate said as she climbed from his shaking body.

'You're doing OK so far, David,' Isabella said. 'But let's not forget that you still have three more people to bring to orgasm. Now you, Tony.'

Tony came forward, his cock full and stiff, and David immediately got on to his knees and began working on his shaft energetically with his mouth. With a bit of luck he didn't think it would take him long to make Tony come if he kept working at it hard. This time he'd suck *him* dry, and he'd be damn quick about it. But all too soon Kate got back into the act again. 'Get on to your hands and knees, David,' she told him, and he did this while continuing to suck Tony's cock as vigorously as he could. Kate knelt behind David and pressed her lips to his anus, hot and tight. His anal muscles pulsed around her slippery tongue as it wiggled and wiggled. It made David burn with a pleasure that he so did not want to be experiencing.

'I've just been getting you ready for a good butt fucking,' Kate explained after a while, gesturing to Tony to get into position to do the deed. Tony then replaced Kate in kneeling behind him and prised the cheeks of his backside apart. David felt the head of Tony's cock, wet with precome mingled with his own saliva, rub gently against the ring of muscles at the entrance to his anus. Tony pushed inside skilfully, going deep into his rear, sending tremors of anguished delight through his body.

Tony entered and re-entered David, thrusting faster all the time. He soon climaxed, which was a great relief to David. Even so, the sensation of his fellow slave's hot come gushing up his anus very nearly pushed him over the edge. But it didn't. He held himself rigidly in check, all too aware that if he didn't he would lose for ever the most important person in his life, the person who gave him his very reason for living.

'Three down,' Isabella said, grasping David firmly by the hair and pulling him to his feet. 'Now let's join Mistress Caroline and Matthew.'

Chapter Forty-five

While David had been busy pleasuring for all he was worth first Isabella, then Kate and finally Tony, Caroline had been busy as well, employing her rope bondage skills on Matthew. When Isabella dragged David over to her she was standing above Matthew who was kneeling upright on the shiny wooden floor, his body expertly tied with black bondage rope at the torso, upper arms, wrists and thighs. His shaft was as hard as a rock.

'May we?' Isabella said to Caroline, pointing towards the tumescent slave in his rope bondage.

'You certainly may.'

'Two to go,' Isabella said, her eyes gleaming. She let go of David's hair and pushed him forward roughly. She looked at his erection, which was now positively bloated, seemingly ready to erupt at any second. She ordered him to put it into Matthew's mouth, telling Matthew to suck him off, and he obeyed with all diligence – or *appeared* to. David needed all the help he could get at this critical point and his old friend Matthew, who had never once let him down for as long as they'd known one another, didn't let him down now.

Matthew's tongue worked on David's shaft and licked its thickness, yes, but not anything like as vigorously as he appeared to be doing. He was careful to hold back too, always stopping when he felt David's pleasure mounting perilously close to the point of no return. And because he did, David was able to as well – just. He did not climax but he did eject a stream of precome into his friend's mouth. And this triggered – Matthew *made* it trigger – Matthew's own climax. With a series of intense moans, he climaxed, the hot flesh of his cock spilling its fiery load onto the shiny floor beneath him.

Matthew then immediately widened his lips, extracted David's cock from his mouth and bent forward as quickly as his rope bonds would allow in order to lick up his own ejaculate. In so doing he was anticipating the almost inevitable instruction from his Mistress to perform that very act and – the true reason for his action – giving David a desperately needed breather.

'Four down, David,' Isabella said, her voice rasping. 'Only one left. Caroline, over to you.'

The flame haired dominatrix started by kissing David's mouth aggressively hard, her tongue slipping and sliding ardently over his. Next she moved her lips down his neck to his chest and then to his nipples. She first kissed and then bit them, causing David to moan in pleasure and pain. His heart was hammering with excitement, his shaft throbbing.

Next Caroline ordered David to kneel down and she did the same. She knelt to one side of him and then brought her head down so that she could blow him. His heart rate increased even further; his shaft throbbed harder still. While Caroline licked and sucked his cock he began to masturbate her, first grinding his fingers against her stiff clit and then working inside the wetness of her pussy. David twisted three of his fingers deep inside Caroline and plunged them in hard over and over again.

This robust finger-fucking was not, as it turned out, a good idea at this perilous stage in the proceedings as it made Caroline markedly increase her attentions to David's cock. She began to suck his shaft with all the enthusiasm that Matthew had feigned, making him tremble with a desire so incredibly strong that it threatened to overwhelm him at any moment. David could feel lust rushing through him now, tight and urgent, and he felt desperate beyond measure for release.

Mercifully Caroline stopped all of a sudden. She lay on her back with her thighs wide apart and David crawled down so that he could lick her clit while working his fingers in and out of her sodden pussy. He was so close to climaxing now it was almost unendurable. His lust had swilled right up to bursting point. Even the pressure of the floor on his shaft could easily have brought him to an orgasm and he did his best to lift himself away from it. He just *had* to make Caroline come soon before it was too late.

David worked his fingers feverishly in and out of her pussy and kissed and licked her clitoris as if his life depended on bringing her to an urgent climax. And in a very real sense it did depend on it. Isabella *was* his life. Without her he would cease to exist. Christ, what on earth had he been thinking to have put everything he held most dear at such severe risk in the way that he had? And for what, for God's sake? For a quick blow job from that manipulative screw-up, Jacqui, that was all. He must have been stark staring mad to have allowed that to happen, certifiably insane.

Finally, David's frantic finger-fucking of Caroline and the equally frantic cunnilingus he was performing on her brought the dominatrix to a peak. She began to tremble without control and then came to a noisy, shuddering climax. 'Five down. None to go,' she said with a gasp, still revelling in the last quivers of her orgasm.

David let out a sigh of relief. He had won through, only barely and with more than a little help from his old friend, Matthew – considerably more than a little help, truth be told. The important thing, though, was that he had won through. But had he? He couldn't be absolutely certain. Only Isabella could say for sure. She was the ultimate arbiter of his fate.

David lifted himself to his knees and gazed up beseechingly at her, his face wet with Caroline's juices, his erection still pounding from the orgasm he'd just about managed to avert. He bit his lip and waited.

Isabella took her own good time. She gazed back at David, her eyes as black as night, her expression unreadable. After an endless, agonizing silence she spoke. 'If I agree to reinstate you as my house-slave, David, do I have your word that you will always comply with your slave agreement and never disobey me again?'

'Absolutely, Mistress,' he said, trembling with emotion.

'Will you ever try to deceive me again?' she asked, holding him with her eyes.

'Never, Mistress.' He could feel his heart pumping wildly away, his erection throbbing wildly away too. Say it, Mistress, say it.

Silence.

The pounding of David's heart – and of his cock – grew wilder and wilder.

Silence, unbearable silence.

'OK, I'll reinstate you,' Isabella said finally. 'But this is absolutely your last chance.'

David's pounding heart leapt violently. His pounding cock leapt violently too. 'Thank you, thank you, Mistress,' he blurted out in delight, his whole body shaking. 'Thank yo … oh … oh …' he added incoherently, as he began a long drawn-out moan, pulsing uncontrollably with the climax he simply could not restrain a single moment longer. David was overtaken by an orgasm of the most incredible intensity he had ever experienced; the muscular spasms ripped through him like a tsunami.

Spurt after spurt of hot come shot out of his cock and into the air, raining in profusion onto the shiny wooden floor beneath him.

David did not need to be told what to do when that mind-blowing orgasm was finally over and he had spurted at last to a stop. He brought his lips to the come-bespattered floor and started to lick and swallow, working away with his mouth and throat.

His mind was working away too. Isabella had – joy of joys – decided not to cast him out of her life for ever but to reinstate him as her house-slave instead. But she'd made it clear that she would give him no more second chances. It was absolutely essential that he get it right this time and there was only one way to do that, wasn't there.

He'd have to make certain, come what may, that he was always a "good boy" from now on. There really was no other alternative. And that was just fine by David. It was more than that, so much more: it was perfect – because this time he wouldn't be living a lie. This time he'd be being true to himself. This time he wouldn't lose *Her*, the only woman in the world. He felt it in his bones that this was so. He felt it for sure, knew it for certain, and it was all he needed to know.

David lifted his face and looked up with eyes shining with devotion at his cruel Mistress. He was ready and willing to do whatever she told him to do next, ready to do that for the rest of his life.

His sense of elation was total, his delight complete. David felt that at last, broken though he was, he was also whole, that finally it all made sense.

Mistress of Torment
Alex Jordaine

When dark fantasy turns to darkest reality…

Self-bondage addict Paul is submissive to the core but
craves constant hard discipline. A chance meeting with an
old friend brings him within the thrilling orbit of top
professional dominatrix Mistress Nikki and the ultra-
sadistic Mistress Alicia.

ISBN 9781906373825, price £7.99

Naked for Mistress
Alex Jordaine

Peter has never been able to accept his deep need to be dominated. But that changes with a vengeance. By means of a cunning deception, his wife Christine hands him over to the formidable Mistress Claudia. Meanwhile she trains to be a dominatrix herself. Claudia turns Peter into her 'bitch', willing to take all the brutal punishment she can dish out.

Claudia returns Peter to be enslaved to 'Mistress Christine'. But Christine wants more – and finds it with the equally dominant Liz and the androgynous Sam. Becoming a sex-slave has made Peter a new man. But something perversely, *thrillingly* different will be required of Sam...

ISBN 9781907726569, price £7.99

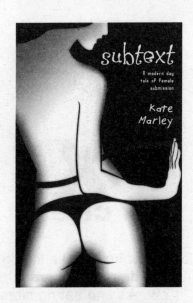

Subtext
Kate Marley

Kate is a submissive.
In this candid account she explains exactly what that means and what exactly an independent, 21st Century woman gets out of relinquishing her power and personal freedom to a dominant man for their mutual pleasure. From the endorphin rush of her first spanking right through to being collared, Kate explains in frank and explicit fashion the road she travels as she reconciles her sexual needs with the rest of her life. She'd call it her journey if, in the current climate, that didn't make her sound like a reality TV reject.

Daring, controversial, but always fun and astoundingly honest, *Subtext* will be a book no woman can put down.

ISBN 9781907016455   price £7.99

MISTRESS EXTREME

An erotic novel

ALEX JORDAINE

Published by Xcite Books Ltd – 2011
ISBN 9781908006929

Copyright © Alex Jordaine 2011

Printed and bound by CPI Group (UK) Ltd, Croydon, CR0 4YY

Cover design by Zipline Creative

To Mistress G, always and for ever

'The degradation which characterises the state into which you plunge him by punishing him pleases, arouses and delights him. Deep down he enjoys having gone so far as to deserve being treated in this way.'
Marquis de Sade